BEYOND SUNLIGHT
A PEBBLE DRAGON'S TALE
BOOK 1

NICK EVE

WITH ILLUSTRATIONS BY
TINA FRANCISCO

CAVE SHADOW PRESS

Copyright © 2023 by Nick Eve

All rights reserved.

No part of this publication may be reproduced, distributed, or transmitted in any form or by any means, including photocopying, recording, or other electronic or mechanical methods, without the prior written permission of the publisher, except as permitted by U.S. copyright law. For permission requests, contact Cave Shadow Press at permissions@caveshadowpress.com.

CAVE SHADOW PRESS

The story, all names, characters, and incidents portrayed in this production are fictitious. No identification with actual persons (living or deceased), places, buildings, and products is intended or should be inferred.

Book Cover by Nick Eve

Illustrations by Tina Francisco

First Edition 2023

For my family, my beloved companions on this wonderful adventure called life.

From <u>A Study of the Creatures of the Dark</u> by Winneus Hupplebum, Court Academician

Rocklings, affectionately called Pebble Dragons by researchers due to their species' belief in a Draconic heritage, are a relatively clever variety of lizard creature. Adults typically grow to between two and three feet in height. Rocklings live in semi-organized groups of up to several hundred individuals and are known to protect their warrens fiercely. They build their homes in caves deep underground, demonstrating exceptional skill at carving and manipulating stone. If left alone, these creatures present little threat to surrounding Human communities, and due to their lack of collective wealth, represent little excitement for the prospective adventurer. Isolated in their remote homes deep below the surface, the charming but harmless Pebble Dragons are unlikely to play a significant role in the course of Human history.

From <u>The Book of Nog</u> by Nog, Rockling Priest

What Humans don't understand would fill the oceans. But this never seems to stop them.

CHAPTER 1
OUT OF THE EGG

Neek, like all of his kind, began life by breaking from an egg.

The egg was about six inches tall. It had a black shiny shell that cracked with a low pop as the infant Rockling poked his tiny claws through it. As Neek worked off the top of the egg, he pushed his neck out into the darkness, revealing his reptilian, scaly skin, and the beginnings of little horns on either side of his reddish-brown head.

Neek sniffed the air. It took a few moments for the nostrils on the front of his snout to clear, and then, for the first time, he smelled the world outside his egg. He had no words yet to describe the sensations he was feeling. The overwhelming intrusion of the musty vapors filling his underground world thrilled him though, so much so that he worked up the energy to slowly open his eyes.

Neek's huge eyes glowed bright red in the darkness of his nursery, as his brain worked to understand the first glimmers of the world around him. Even in this pitch-black cave, Neek could make out in shades of delicate grey the shapes of the other eggs around him, the ornamented basin the eggs were sitting in, the carved walls of the cave, and the pictures lining the walls of this sacred birthing place. He sat there for a while, marveling in the wonder of this new reality, enjoying the warm comfort of his sticky egg, scanning the walls with his infant eyes, as a larger shape moved toward him, reached out, and lifted him up.

The woman holding Neek had horns like his, over which she wore an elaborate headdress. Later in life, he would understand this to be a Priestess, in particular a Dragon-Mother, among the most revered in Rockling society. But for now, she was just a strange bundle of unknown forms, grabbing him and removing him from the safety of his warm, gooey shell. She held him aloft, looking up and down his scaly body, and over the length of his long, pointed tail. She carried him closer to one of the carved walls where she lit a tall red beetle-wax candle using a tiny fire emanating from her finger.

Glints of many different colors sparkled in the candlelight, shining like tiny firecrackers in the darkness over Neek's skin. The Dragon-Mother's eyes were wide and her brow was raised. Someday, Neek would understand that this facial expression was demonstrating surprise, but not yet versed in such things, the little Rockling was worried she was going to eat him. Neek began to sputter and cry as the Priestess quickly hugged him to her bosom in response and spoke softly to him.

"Have no fear, little one," she said in a comforting voice, bouncing Neek up and down gently in her arms. "I didn't mean to scare you. We've just never seen a treasure quite like you."

The Dragon-Mother carried Neek to a table nearby and wrapped him in a fuzzy blanket before lifting him again and snuggling him softly in her arms. She began to sing a gentle lullaby. The words meant nothing to Neek of course, but the deep, low reverberations in her chest relaxed him, and the warmth of her body made him feel just as calm and comfortable as he had been in his egg. Neek closed his tiny red eyes and slept.

∼

It was not a good time. Dragon-Mother Malika knew that. Goblins had been encountered in the east. New veins of ore had been discovered in the south. The Tunnel Wardens and Trap Layers were working triple shifts, and everyone seemed frantically busy these days. But the birth of an All-Shade was an extraordinary and serendipitous event, the stuff of legend, and even during such a difficult time, Malika knew she must tell the Chief immediately. Leaving the infant dozing comfortably in the warm creche burrow behind her, Malika walked off quickly, eager to share her news with the tribe.

The path from the nursery, where the eggs were hatched and the infants were cared for, to the main gathering hall, where the Chief spent most of her time, was long and convoluted by design. In the world of the Rocklings, there is no more precious treasure than their young, kept safe and hidden away behind a maze of tunnels and secret passages, all protected with layer after layer of deadly traps and obstacles to prevent marauders from ever reaching them. You had to be smart to be a Priestess, and smarter still a Dragon-Mother, to remember all the twists and turns, the secrets and tricks, to safely traverse this path quickly, day after day in the dark. Malika had actually designed several of these obstacles for her warren, and she walked with tremendous grace, even for a woman of her age, moving rapidly through the hazardous corridor toward the commotion of the main chamber beyond.

As she waited for the last layer of moving stone to slide aside, opening the final door in her journey, Malika could hear many raised voices. Clearly it was an even worse time than she had anticipated.

Two voices were raised in heated argument, a rarity in a race and a tribe that prided itself on cohesion and group coordination. Bartok, one of the highest-ranking Warriors, was shouting the loudest.

"The Goblins must be handled now," Bartok argued, "before they put down roots in the caves nearby. You know that Goblins are cowards when they first enter a place, but they will be emboldened if we give them time to learn the ins and out of our tunnels. They will eventually find clever places to hide and make our lives intolerable with their wicked mischief. We chased off a party of ten the other day. This isn't just a few Scouts idly wandering. They intend to make a home here."

As Bartok spoke in booming tones, the necklace of teeth, horns, and scales he wore proudly around his neck shook and rattled. Rocklings of Neek's tribe carried their lost scales, horns, and even teeth on bands around their neck, showing their status by the number and quality of the relics hanging there. Bartok's teeth were large and wickedly hooked, his horns were long, black, and sharp as knives, and his scales were thick and dark as pitch, so even a few would look imposing, and he wore a great many, having lived more than forty years so far. Bartok, despite his short stature of three feet, was large for a Rockling, and his wide, muscled frame was uniquely well-developed. It bothered Malika to see him so agitated.

The other voice in the argument was firm, but not as sharp, coming from a smaller Rockling with many more relics on his necklace but all of a smoother, brighter hue, with a less jagged cut. This was Beemo, one of the oldest and wisest Tunnel Wardens of the tribe.

"We can always scare Goblins away," Beemo protested, "but if we have Dwarves, or even worse, Humans down here, we'll be doomed for sure. The silver vein we found is massive, one of the biggest ever discovered in these caves, and it is far too close to the open dark to go unnoticed for long. If we don't hide this trove quickly, we'll have a mine on our doorstep, and you know that will mark the end of us, at least in this place."

Malika saw clear logic in both of their arguments. A troop of Goblins could be a real nuisance, and a danger, especially if they were allied with other intelligent beasts. However, if a mine was established nearby, undoubtedly the tribe would need to relocate, yet again. It had been a few years now since their last migration, but Malika, having lived through a half dozen moves already, knew that peace rarely lasted.

Despite the lavish attention that Rocklings spend on digging and refining their tunnel warrens, carefully concealing them from surrounding caves, and protecting them with elaborate devices and tricks to keep out unwanted visitors, outsiders always seemed to find them eventually. And if those outsiders were Humans or Dwarves, so arrogant in their self-entitled ownership of all the gifts of the world, they would root out the Rocklings without mercy, eliminating them like ants or some other unwanted pest. It had always been thus, Malika thought to herself, since the birth of the original dragon, the First-Mother, and would always remain this way, until the Rocklings were able to develop into the Dragon Lords they were someday destined to become. The Dragon-Mother had helped with relocations before, and every one of them had been terrible, full of danger and distress, as her people, seemingly hated and unwanted by the whole world, desperately sought out a new refuge far below the earth.

Chief MakMak looked flustered. Her typically stoic face showed signs of exhaustion. This argument had clearly been going on for a long while, and from the number of frustrated looking Rocklings filling the main chamber, it was apparent there were many other problems to be decided on as well. These two venerated leaders were just the loudest and most insistent in getting the tribe's attention.

"I hear. I understand," MakMak answered, "but unless we have time to think, and the peace in which to do that, a decision cannot be made. These problems are not the only ones we face. We have hatchlings about to pop. We need to expand our food stores. There are rumors of deadly adventurers in nearby lands. The Orcs are on the move. We have worries aplenty, as you've heard from your kin," MakMak said, gesturing to the other presenters scattered around the hall.

Rockling society's strength generally came from its social cohesion. Alone, they might be relatively weak creatures, short in stature compared to a Human or a cave bear, but together, they were powerful, and could accomplish great things. This tribe, the Hardhands, were well adapted to communal success, especially under the past few years of Chief MakMak's leadership. The great hall was a gathering place where concerns were shared, and decisions made by the tribe, with MakMak acting more as a conductor than a ruler, helping to craft a group choice rather than determining on her own what should be done. There was much wisdom in this, Malika thought, as every Rockling seemed to have their own gifts, and this kind of cooperative decision-making let everyone contribute. At times though, especially during dangerous, complicated periods like this one, this dynamic could be tricky, with long hours wasted in argument and dispute, yielding no clear victor among the contrasting suggested paths forward.

Out of respect to Chief MakMak, the two bickering Rockling elders quieted in response to her plea, though many others around the chamber continued chattering. Malika took this opportunity to quietly signal Eekee, MakMak's personal Guard and assistant. Even amidst the commotion of the chaotic meeting, Eekee instantly recognized Malika's gesture.

Eekee was one of the fiercest Warriors in the tribe, though her tall, thin frame may not have rendered that fact obvious to the casual observer. What truly made Eekee such a fine Guard however, and so valuable to her Chief, was her exceptional perceptive abilities. Eekee could see a tiny bug making its way across the other side of a large chamber, even in the dark, and her ears were so keen she might even hear its footsteps.

Eekee was quick to react to Malika's signal. The Dragon-Mother very rarely brought business before the great chamber, so when she did, like now, she was well-respected, due in part to the Rocklings' reverence for their young and the ones that protect them. Eekee spoke quietly in MakMak's ear and motioned Malika over.

"We will take a break now," Chief MakMak announced to the hall, "and will make some decisions shortly. Come back in two meal lengths and we will try to finish this discussion."

MakMak walked with Eekee across the chamber, meeting Malika in a small room off to the side of the main hall where they would have some privacy. Matters involving the young were usually handled more discretely than other issues, so as not to panic the general community.

"How can we help you, respected Dragon-Mother?" MakMak asked, concern clearly showing in the corners of her eyes.

Malika's anxiety intensified. Were things really that bad? Chief MakMak never looked this worried. Malika smiled in response to the Chief's question, thankful she had good news to share. She noticed MakMak's face ease in response.

"Has the Hatching begun?" MakMak asked.

"Yes, my Chief. Several eggs opened up today. The Hatching is going well. But I interrupt you now because one of them," Malika explained, pausing briefly, "one of them is an All-Shade."

"An All-Shade?" MakMak gasped, her eyes suddenly flush with excitement. Could it really be, the Chief wondered, suddenly swept away in her thoughts from the pressing matters and loud arguments of the hall. "Are you sure? It has been many generations since we had a youngling with even three colors, much less all of them."

"Yes, my Chief. He shares the many colors of the First-Mother. Every one of them. Please come and see for yourself," Malika urged, motioning toward the nursery.

Chief MakMak followed the Dragon-Mother back to the Rockling creche, a look of eager anticipation on her face. Imagine that, Chief MakMak thought to herself, an All-Shade, at this difficult time in the tribe's history.

Neek was still sleeping when they entered the chamber. He was snoring softly and dreaming deeply as the Dragon-Mother lit numerous candles around the room. Malika then carefully lifted Neek up and out of his blanket to show off his scales, glistening in all their different shades, like a rainbow in the candlelight.

"The hues are all here, my Chief, see for yourself," Malika gestured, pointing to various patches around Neek's slumbering body. He giggled and snuffled in his sleep as she gently poked his belly.

"And the eyes?" MakMak asked.

"Wake up, dear one," Malika gently spoke into Neek's ear, stroking the scales of his back until he woke from his reverie.

As Neek opened his eyes, Chief MakMak stared deeply into them. She gasped. She could see tiny twinkles of color flowing and sparkling through the pools of red, flashing one color and now another, through all the hues shown on his scales. There was no doubt, this boy truly was an All-Shade, from tip to tail.

Anyone viewing the clear delight on Chief MakMak's face would have thought her a leader without a care in the world. And at least, for a moment, that was exactly what she was. The youngling was an All-Shade. What a glorious gift. What wonderful surprises must be in store for my tribe, she thought, to have the First-Mother bless us so?

"Let him sleep, and after he wakes and eats, bring him to the great chamber," she told Malika. "The tribe must be told. An All-Shade has been born to the Hardhands. This is truly a glorious day."

Like most creatures, a Rockling cannot remember the things that happen to it during the very beginning of its life. How unfair it was then that Neek would never recall his part in one of the tribe's most historic celebrations. He slumbered peacefully for hours, and awoke to a wonderful meal of warm milk. Snugly wrapped in a blanket, his belly full, Neek was happily looking around the lit nursery, enjoying all the new sights and sounds, as Malika raised him up and carried him toward the great chamber.

This was the first time he had ever been through a tunnel, those spindly pathways through the rocks he would likely spend his life digging, carving, and traversing day to day. Neek's sparkling eyes, even more powerful than a typical Rockling's, could pick out every nook and cranny, every tiny lizard running along a rock, every bit of moss pushing into the dim wisps of air pulsing through this passage so far underground. After a few short minutes, he saw a wall move aside, and then, hundreds of faces, tons of candles and lights of different colors, and even a wave of wonderful sounds that he would later understand to be music, greeted his arrival.

The entire tribe, hundreds of Rocklings, filled the chamber, all staring with fixed intent at the tiny bundle in the Dragon-Mother's arms. Malika carried Neek toward Chief MakMak, who sat on a simple throne, now wearing the jewels and adornments that formally identified her as the tribe's leader. Two Rockling Musicians, Gronk and Slooboo, played stringed instruments to give the occasion a festive air. Neek enjoyed their tune, tapping his tiny claws against his chest as he was brought forward. He examined all the unfamiliar faces, all the red eyes looking back at him, and felt both excited and terrified. Who were these strange beings? Just as Malika reached MakMak's throne, the Chief stood up and raised a short scepter with a softly pulsing light at its top, addressing the crowd as the music stopped.

"As our kind have since the beginning of time, we now face many challenges," MakMak began. "Enemies are at our gates, and dangerous treasures to lure even more. Lately, the caves have not provided as plentifully as they once did. Fear not though, my friends, as the First-Mother is with us. Behold, she has delivered us an All-Shade!"

Chief MakMak took Neek from Malika's arms and lifted him up and out of the comfy blanket, high into the air, exposing his multicolored scales to the fascinated crowd who cheered loudly. The roar of the audience was deafening, and being removed from his warm blanket didn't agree with Neek, who was tempted to cry, but all the faces around him were smiling such wide smiles that he smiled instead, prompting the tribe to howl with even greater fervor.

"Tomorrow we will face our problems, but tonight we celebrate," MakMak continued, giving the babe back to Malika and clapping her hands together. "Bring in the food."

Numerous Rockling Cooks entered with trays of fish, snails, cave moss, and various other delicacies to wild applause as the Musicians again began to play. Malika tickled Neek's chin and wrapped him back up in the blanket as the tribe swarmed around her, trying to get a peek at the promised child and his magical eyes.

Neek looked out at his fellow Rocklings with wonder. The exotic smells from the food they were eating made his belly gurgle. The dance of the strange music in Neek's ears made him want to wiggle his tiny feet to its rhythms. The glorious sight of so many living creatures filling the hall made his heart race with excitement. There were hordes of them, in all shapes and sizes. Each one struck him as amazing, and he wasn't quite sure why they were so interested in him when there were so many other marvels all around them. What was this mysterious world he had arrived in? Maybe leaving his egg wouldn't be so bad after all.

Neek snuggled into the blanket, nestled safely in Malika's arms, and greeted all who came before him with a surprising calmness for such a tiny newborn. Malika, who had been nervous that Neek might be upset by the crowd around him, was impressed by his composure. She had raised many children before him, and she knew that very rarely were they able to handle so much social activity so quickly. He loves people, she thought. That is good, given his gift, and the responsibilities that must surely come with it.

To understand the tribe's excitement, it is important to know some of the things all Rockling children are taught early in their lives. Rocklings, as a rule, worship a god named the First-Mother. The First-Mother was the world's first dragon. She created the world beyond sunlight, the underground tunnels the Rocklings call home, and gave birth to all the other dragons, including the Rockling race, smallest of the dragon children. While modern dragons come in many shapes, sizes, and colors, surviving in diverse environments ranging from the scalding heat of lava-filled volcanoes to the icy depths of frozen waters, the First-Mother, mother of all dragons, contained all of their variations within herself. Her skin displayed all their different shades, and she could change her form and color at will. She could conjure fire, cold, or whatever else she desired from her grand mouth as she used her gifts to shape and build the world. Her eyes sparkled with all of the colors of her skin, and were said to be able to see through not just the light and dark, but through solid matter, past the stars, and even through time itself.

Most Rocklings take after one or sometimes two different dragon lineages, their scales matching known dragon colors and exhibiting some level of hardiness against their associated elements. Malika, for example, who had traces of gold around her eyes and neck, could produce fire from her hands, and was not bothered by the heat. If you looked closely, you could see golden flecks in her red, glowing eyes, clearly marking her as Golden-Born, comfortable in the hottest regions of the world. Neek though, like the First-Mother, showed traces of all the shades, both on his scaly skin and in his eyes, a marvelously rare phenomenon indeed, hardly ever seen in a Rockling child. The birth of one such as Neek was an omen that the First-Mother again walks the earth, taking particular interest in the affairs of the tribe blessed with her gift.

If only more Rockling children paid better attention to the other stories the Priests told them, they might understand that things were not always so simple. Yes, the First-Mother was many-colored and powerful, but so also was she cursed and hated by the other gods, who feared the dragons and sought to limit their power. Despite blessing the world with the caves and other wonders she created, the First-Mother was ultimately betrayed and jailed by the other gods, jealous of her gifts. Trapped deep inside the earth, she struggles still to escape and roam the world again. In her imprisoned state, the First-Mother is weakened, and so the Rocklings are weakened, only to be made powerful again when she is finally freed.

Biding her time, the First-Mother lives beneath the earth, birthing eggs and giving life to all the dragons you find roaming the world. The increasing number of dragons to be seen these days is a sign to most Rocklings that she inches closer every day to the release all Rocklings so desperately hope for. Powerful, yes. Generous, yes. But jailed, and despised by non-dragons, such is her lot. And so, her touch, so rare and special, is not so easily understood. But that is how skeptical Priests see the world, not excited children, who wait expectantly for their wings to sprout and to fly through the air.

The crowd celebrating Neek's birth was full of these hopeful feelings, a sureness that this special child promised a bright future for their tribe. Neek continued smiling, just to hear these funny people cheer, and was thrilled when someone put a tiny piece of delicious fish in his eager mouth. Like those around him, Neek felt excited and happy. Today was wonderful, this special day he would quickly forget.

CHAPTER 2
THE CAVE IN

Rocklings develop quickly, able to walk and even climb in just a few short weeks. Neek was no exception. He was soon hopping about and enjoying life in the youngling playroom, a large chamber adjacent to the main nursery. This cavern was adorned with pillars to clamber up, boxes to hide in, and other toys to entertain the children. Neek was born during a particularly plentiful clutch, so he had many brothers and sisters to frolic with.

Normally the young were allowed to romp about independently for much of the day, with the Dragon-Mothers coming in for only a few hours to feed, clean, and set up challenges for them. Rockling life is treacherous, and the hatchlings had to learn rapidly to face the dangers that infested their underground world. Even during the earliest days of life, the Dragon-Mothers were already encouraging the younglings, giving them tightropes to walk, puzzle boxes to unlock, and elaborately carved structures to climb and swing from. Outside these short periods of supervision, the young were mostly left alone with their toys and their compatriots, needing to comprehend quickly how to get along with their kin and solve problems together.

Though young Rocklings are seemingly independent, and Dragon-Mothers are in fact loathe to interfere in their playtime, other than to deal with truly dire situations, the little ones are already being watched and judged during these early days. Rockling society is broken up into castes defined primarily by the tasks performed for the tribe. Some Rocklings are good at making traps, or digging tunnels, or fighting, or any of the other skills needed by their community, and the elders work diligently to ensure all Rocklings' skills are recognized and used for the good of the group. Dragon-Mothers play a hugely important role in this process, observing the young and looking for possible proclivities and failings, strengths and weaknesses.

Due to Neek's multicolored skin, and the special promise it suggested, Malika was studying him, and his peers, even more closely than she would normally follow a clutch. An All-Shade was legendarily rare, and Rockling tales generally cast them as leaders, or inventors, or heroic Warriors, liberating caves from the monstrosities of the darkness. Would Neek follow one of these roads, Malika wondered, as she watched him leap from a large box and land on the shoulders of one of his older brothers. So far, from what she had seen, he was clever and quick to be sure. He was light on his feet, and he had tons of energy. But honestly, beyond all these worthy traits, Neek seemed to be an unusually affable and loving youngling. He was constantly laughing with and hugging his brothers and sisters, and seemed to spend a lot of time helping or encouraging them.

Neek will perhaps be a leader, Malika thought. He wasn't bossy though. Some younglings came out clearly desiring to tell others what to do, insisting their games be the focus of everyone's attention. Barnag, one of Neek's older brothers, was certainly like that. He would hoot and stomp his feet to get the others to play throwing games, his seeming favorite, even though Barnag himself wasn't much good at hitting targets. That one will likely be a frontline Warrior, Malika thought, bossing around a group of lesser-skilled Warriors, doomed to fall in some skirmish with another tribe, a sacrifice for the survival of the community. Neek never seemed to push others to play his games, watching and intervening playfully instead in whatever his siblings were doing.

If anything, he would just inspire them to keep trying until they succeeded. Perhaps he'll be a great Priest, Malika thought. It was too early to tell.

After many months of this free play and observation, the Dragon-Mother and the Priests began to take a more active role in the younglings' lives, with the beginning of formal lessons in the different skills of the tribe. Those perceived to show some talent for one area or another would be given additional instructions and tests to see if that might be a good path for them.

Someone from the appropriate caste, such as a Cook for example, might come in and make a stew with a few of the young, seeing whether they could follow the recipe and discern whether the spices and other ingredients were being mixed in the right amounts. Potential Warriors would play games with sticks and balls to test their reflexes and their toughness. Potential Carvers would be given stone and the tools to work it, being led by experienced masons through simple exercises such as crafting a statue of a bat or making a perfectly straight line in a column of rock.

Young Rocklings would be exposed to and tested in a variety of areas, often multiple times, to truly understand where they would best fit in the society as a whole. While his siblings seemed to attend only a few of these lessons, Neek appeared to take part in nearly every one. His free playtime was severely limited these days, much to his frustration. Like Malika, the Priests and the caste leaders seemed unusually curious about what such a special boy might achieve. And so, for hour after hour, Neek cooked, and carved, and fought with sticks, and readied traps, and little by little experienced every aspect of organized Rockling life.

Outside of these focused lessons, all the young were given general lessons in underground survival. How to walk quietly. How to recognize noises and understand what they meant. How to climb. To hide. To trick someone as to your location. Neek loved these lessons the most, as they were generally open-ended and playful in nature. By far, his favorite survival activity was

Secret Treasure, a Rockling variation of the Hide-and-Seek game familiar to most people.

In Secret Treasure, an object was typically designated as the Treasure, and then hidden somewhere in a huge maze of tunnels, with a sensory clue being given as to its location. The object might be a bit of food, doused with a particularly strong scent, that Neek would have to sniff his way toward. Or the teacher might leave a jug of water slowly dripping in a hollow recess in one of the cave walls, requiring Neek to listen carefully and find the hidden cache. In Neek's favorite version of the game, a youngling would be designated as the Treasure, and the other Rocklings would have to find them. This challenged the whole group, as the Treasure tried to pick a good spot and hide quietly, while the others used their senses as well as they could to find them. Whenever Neek took part in survival exercises, he always requested this game from his teachers, and today was no different.

"Secret Treasure, let's play Secret Treasure," Neek pleaded.

Tunnel Warden Torgal, who was leading the lessons today, was happy to grant Neek's wish. Letting the young run around this elaborate system of twisting caves and passages would help him to assess the security on this side of the Hardhands' warren. If there was a collapsed tunnel, or something shiny, or something living where it shouldn't be, the young would soon find it with their keen, healthy eyes, making his job of tracking the state of this complex much simpler.

Teachers always brought a few Warriors with the group, to keep the young safe, and today Torgal had about twice what one would normally bring, due to heightened concerns about the recent conflicts with the Goblins. Bartok, the Warrior captain, had been correct, the Goblins had indeed made a claim in the east, and there had been several fights in recent weeks, with losses on both sides. Goblins and Rocklings, despite the hostilities, would normally not do anything to the children of the other group, except in the direst times of famine, so conflict was unlikely, but with an All-Shade in the group, the tribe wasn't taking any chances.

"You go last, Neek," Torgal insisted, and while Neek's face registered disappointment, it mainly seemed to be for show.

He always had to go last, due to his seemingly uncanny ability to stay hidden. While most of his siblings could hide successfully for a few minutes at most, Neek could obscure himself from the group for ages. He had once remained unfound an entire hour, even with the Warriors looking for him, only appearing after being threatened to be banned from the game in the future.

The truth was that hiding had become so simple for Neek, he usually wasn't found unless he wanted to be. He would grow bored after about twenty minutes, and having proven himself sufficiently in his mind, he would let himself be discovered, trying to trick one of the seekers by, for example, sitting down behind them as if to suggest he was in an obvious place they should have easily spotted earlier. While Neek would snicker and smile at his frustrated finder, he was never nasty about it, and always made it seem in the end that they really had done a good job in flushing him out.

Today, Neek was more excited than usual, as he had never been in this part of the warren. This was a deep set of tunnels, seldom used by the tribe other than as a hiding place during dangerous times. Even Torgal had to think a while before he could remember canvassing this area. With all the recent excitement, the Tunnel Wardens just didn't have as much time as they'd like to walk all the nooks and crannies on the periphery like this.

Neek relished new adventures, and this tunnel complex had numerous passages going up and down, providing lots of climbing opportunities which he loved. Neek's trick to being so good at hiding, as least as far as he understood it, was his willingness to climb up to high alcoves, or to slither down into deep wells. While most of his siblings would look right and left, seeking the cover of twists and turns to hide themselves, Neek always looked high and low, knowing that climbing was harder work than walking, and that this would not be his siblings' impulse. So, for a few hours, Neek joined his brothers and sisters, rabbiting through the warren to find them wherever they hid. Finally, with the end of the lesson approaching, it was Neek's turn.

"Not too long now, Neek," Torgal reminded him, "or you'll be in trouble. The Cooks always need help cleaning up fish guts, and you'll be working with them all week if you're hidden more than a meal time."

Neek nodded in agreement and headed out. He had seen a particularly appealing slide downward in the middle of one of the chambers he had passed earlier. You could sometimes find shiny rocks or Glow-Slugs in the lower depths, and they were deeper here than he was used to. Climbing down of course is very dangerous, as all Rocklings are taught very early on. A tunnel might turn and plummet fifty feet, and if not careful, a young Rockling might fall to their doom.

Neek had a knack for understanding what unseen passages would do. For some reason, he felt like he could almost see through the stone to the tunnels beyond. So even in a new place, Neek was rarely surprised, and almost never stumbled or fell. Today, he sensed that the narrow hole ahead of him would open and slide smoothly downward, which it did, for almost sixty feet, before turning for twenty feet or so and opening at the end to a few branching veins.

He closed his eyes and listened. He could hear something. Was that water? Yes, he could hear a few soft splashes from down below where it sounded like a slow drip was falling into the edge of a pool. A water source was always of great use to the tribe, and Neek became excited. This game might end with the retrieval of a true treasure for a change. He made his way toward the sound, a broad smile on his face. If only his young nose was better developed, Neek might have sensed he wasn't the only one approaching the pool.

THE CAVE IN   23

∾

Barnag wasn't happy today. Truth be told, Barnag wasn't happy most days, but today in particular he was in a foul mood. He had been hidden mere moments before Neek had found him earlier in the lesson. He hated Neek. Neek with his special scales. Neek who was always hugging and laughing with the other Rocklings. Neek who hid so well he had to be threatened by the teachers to give himself up, who was always trying to teach Barnag how to do things right.

Not today, Barnag thought. Today, I will be the teacher.

Barnag had cheated, and followed Neek as soon as Neek headed out, not closing his eyes or giving Neek the customary time to go and find a hiding spot before seeking him. Barnag, while not a genius in any sense, was clever, especially when he was angry, and he had hidden himself away from the rest of the group precisely so he could follow Neek in this way without being detected.

Barnag watched Neek disappear into the tunnel, biding his time before following him and watching him descend down into the depths. Barnag knew that climbing down was dangerous for many reasons. Sure, you could slip and fall, every Rockling knew that. But Barnag also knew that going down was dangerous because there wasn't always another way back up. Vertical connections between different cave levels were rare. So, if the tunnel caved in, it might be a while before you found an alternate route out. Maybe quite a while if you were unlucky. And today wasn't going to be Neek's lucky day if Barnag had anything to say about it.

Barnag looked at the downward slope, and sure enough, like most tunnels, there were a few places of potential weakness. Neek had been clever, Barnag was sure, not to pull on certain stones or put his weight on certain areas of the wall that would be better avoided. But Barnag wasn't looking to descend carefully. No, he was looking to teach Neek a lesson.

He reached out and pulled on a few of the obviously precarious stones. There were some trickles of dirt but the wall held. He pulled more stones, and still it didn't budge. Finally, seeing weakness in the lining of the wall, Barnag kicked out firmly with both of his feet in frustration. He kicked once, twice, and then a third time, until finally, there was a rumbling sound, and in a cloud of confusion and an explosion of noise, the tunnel wall gave way.

Neek had just begun to head down the passage toward the dripping sound when the soft plopping noise of the falling water was drowned out by the roar of a mountain of rock, rumbling and moving in the bowels of the earth. Young as he was, Neek had never heard the sound of a cave in before. Yet, despite his lack of experience, Neek could instinctually feel the danger in his belly. This was bad.

A cave in meant the rocks' form had changed, which invited all kinds of potential problems. He could always come back with his teachers to find the water, Neek decided. For now, he had to return to his siblings. As he made his way back up toward the tunnel though, he could see this would not be possible. Rocks had tumbled in as far down as the turn in the slope, meaning there was at least sixty feet of stone between him and the tribe above. The cave in was clearly a bad one, with hundreds of tons of material filling the tube he had slid down to hide here. He wouldn't be able to clear that. He would have to find another way up.

Normally quite jovial and easy-going, Neek was truly afraid for the first time since the Dragon-Mother had lifted him up out of his egg. Even if he could find another way up, it would probably be a slow endeavor, involving the exploration of lots of unfamiliar territory, perhaps through areas unknown even to his tribe above.

Young as he was, Neek already knew the dangers of the underground, the perils that walked its halls.

Even if I'm not eaten, Neek worried, they'll surely never let me be the Treasure again. Perhaps that is what Neek was scared of most of all. A dragon doesn't panic though, Neek told himself. A dragon breathes. And so Neek, tiniest of the tiny dragons, inhaled long breaths, slowly in and out, as he wracked his brain for a clue as to what he should do next.

The joy Barnag briefly felt when the wall he was kicking gave way quickly turned to terror as the stones below him fell away and he found himself pitching down through the floor to the bottom of a deep cavern below. In the dark caves of the earth, a fall is seldom pleasant. You don't land on soft straw or thick grass, or merciful, forgiving ground. No, if you are exceptionally lucky you land in water, or perhaps mud, or a patch of dry earth away from any stones. Most of the time though you land on rock. Painful, backbreaking rock. If you land on a sharp edge, you might never get up again.

All things considered, Barnag was actually pretty lucky, especially given his awful decision to cause a cave in inside a tunnel he himself was occupying. Though he had fallen about twenty feet straight down, his body had landed mostly on large mushrooms. His chest, his neck, and his head were all mercifully cushioned by a layer of thick cave fungi lining the ground of this cave.

His right leg, however, was not so lucky. His leg had crashed onto hard flat stone, and large rocks had tumbled down upon it. And even though, thankfully, there was nothing pinning him to the ground, Barnag could feel that his leg was broken, and his left hip screamed with pain. The young Rockling cried out, calling for his brothers, his sisters, and his teachers, but there was no way they would hear him through the thick layers of stone above.

After a while, he stopped yelling, and began examining the chamber around him. It was fairly open, with a tall ceiling. Mushrooms and moss lined the walls. Barnag could not see any holes or openings through the cave roof above. Even if there was a hole up there, how could he climb with only one good leg? Barnag tried to stand, and then quickly fell back to the ground, screaming in pain. His leg wouldn't hold him. He would have to crawl his way out of here, across the mushroom floor.

The room smelled awful. Like some of the places his tribe used as toilets. Were the mushrooms making this terrible smell? He sniffed them closely but didn't recognize the scent there.

As Barnag peered at one of the particularly large mushrooms in front of him on the floor, he noticed for the first time it had some bite marks on one side. Extremely large bite marks.

THE CAVE IN

~

In the quiet of his thoughtful meditation, Neek still heard the dripping noise coming from a chamber somewhere below. Much as he tried to ignore it, the sound intruded upon his concentration with its incessant drip, drip, drip. When lost, map all available pathways. Yes, that's what he would do. Drip. Drip. Drip. But wouldn't that increase his chances of encountering something dangerous? Perhaps he could make noise and his siblings or his tribe would find him. Drip. Drip. Drip. But no, the noise would just draw dangers toward him even faster. He must be quiet and stealthy, not loud and obvious. Drip. Drip. Drip. His mind spun as he continued his deep breathing, his entire consciousness being overwhelmed by the never-ending dripping noise he couldn't block out. Finally, he looked past his anger and his fear, and something clicked.

"Water makes a way."

One of the teachers had told him this. Beemo, probably, during one of his highly abstract stories about how natural tunnels were born.

"Water cuts stone like a blade, splitting the earth. You can try to stop it, but water always makes a way."

Yes, it had been something like that. Perhaps the key to finding a way back up was to track down the water he was hearing. Perhaps, wherever it was dripping from, was a conduit large enough to take him back to his warren and his brothers and sisters. At the very least, it might provide him with something to drink and possibly some fish to eat.

He thanked the First-Mother for her wisdom. Malika had told him to listen to the earth, hadn't she? She'd explained that the First-Mother speaks to us through the caves. The First-Mother was guiding him there, he was sure of it. He begged forgiveness for being annoyed with her soft watery song, and headed off slowly, quietly, and cautiously down the tunnel, toward the noise. Drip. Drip. Drip.

Though his leg was broken, his arms were mercifully unharmed, so Barnag dragged himself as quickly and quietly as he could toward the opposite side of the cavern he had landed in. As far as Barnag could tell, there was only one way out, and nowhere to hide. If he met whatever had recently been eating the mushrooms here, that would be the end of his story, he was sure. With each pull of his body, his hip sang out in agony, but his desire to live pushed him through the pain, and he slowly made his way across the floor.

As he approached the mouth of the cavern, Barnag's right hand poked something sharp, and looking down he saw his palm was on the rib cage of a large rat skeleton. He recognized the bad smell was stronger here, and looking around saw several more skeletons littering this side of the cave. Was something living here?

Barnag crawled faster, his heart racing.

Torgal, the Tunnel Warden, was feeling quite upset with himself. He was a revered and wise member of the tribe. Rocklings looked up to him. He could walk most of the tunnels of the warren almost by memory with his eyes closed. He should have known better.

It had been a decent enough plan, he thought. Let the younglings play and explore while he mapped out some of the lesser known areas on this edge of the warren. He had scouted it briefly some days before and saw no obvious signs of danger. He should have known better, Torgal told himself, as soon as he heard the tell-tale signs of a cave in. How many younglings might they have lost, he wondered? How could he forgive himself for allowing this to happen?

Torgal immediately called over the Guards and had them round up everyone they could find. He was relieved to see so many of the young ones there, unscathed. The cave in had clearly been in a deeper tunnel. After a few minutes though, he noticed that they were still missing Barnag and Neek, precious Neek, the All-Shade that the whole tribe was so excited about. The miracle child that bore witness to their tribe's power and the blessing of the First-Mother was missing. He should have known better.

Torgal's expert ears had pinpointed the spot quickly, and as he surveyed it and the collapse that had occurred there, he was dismayed. A filled downslope is terribly dangerous. If either of the young ones were in there when it fell in, they were likely severely injured or even dead. Even if they were alive, Torgal would need to find another way down to reach them.

He was embarrassed to admit he hadn't even noticed this downspout in his earlier scouting sessions. How had the younglings found it, he wondered? It was almost completely concealed by an overlap of rock. That Neek truly is gifted, he thought. But then, how had Barnag found it as well, he pondered? That one was not so talented.

Torgal sent some of the Warriors back to the central warren with the younglings, and they returned shortly with the best Scouts in the tribe. The search party would need to find a way down, and quickly, if they were to retrieve the two missing children. Torgal showed the Scouts the cave in and explained the task at hand. They spread out, searching for ways around the obstacle.

After what felt like an eternity, one of the Scouts came back to report he had found a new fissure opening off of the tribe's central cooking well which was flowing downward nearby. They hadn't found a wide vein yet, by there must be one. Water finds a way.

Many meal times passed until one of the Scouts joyously reported he had indeed found a passable route. Torgal, two

Warriors, and the group of Scouts all headed out, hoping the tunnels would lead them to their missing young.

Following a sound in a cave can be quite challenging, even for creatures who have spent their whole life exploring the underneath. Sounds bounce and wind along in tricky pathways around walls and down tunnels, misleading even the best trained ear. But, thankfully, here the pattern of tunnels was mercifully simple. Even young Neek was able to follow it without issue, reaching a cave opening after about ten minutes where he was sure he would locate the pool he was tracking.

Neek stopped abruptly, dead in his tracks, and flattened himself against the cave wall. He had noticed another noise as well. Something was drinking in loud, long slurps. From the sound of it, something much larger than he was.

He had just slipped through a narrow passageway a few minutes earlier, so Neek was confident that if pressed, he could run back there and hide on the other side of it. He doubted the creature he was hearing would be able to fit through it as easily as he had with his tiny frame.

"Use the stone as your shield."

One of the Warriors had taught him this, Neek remembered. It was a simple technique the Rocklings had used to their benefit for thousands of years.

Neek should have expected that he might not be alone. Any source of water in the underneath is a precious resource, and all manner of beasts which wandered below would be thrilled to find it. The danger of these pools was such that the young were never sent to gather water unaccompanied. Neek had not yet learned to be as cautious as most older Rocklings would have been. Water is a wonder, but a dangerous wonder best approached with caution.

Since he had the narrow tunnel behind him as an escape route, and no other clear path home, Neek decided he would at least hazard a look at the dripping sound ahead that had tempted him to follow it. He would poke his head carefully around the corner and see what he could see. If the First-Mother had led him here, she must have had some kind of plan for keeping him safe. He had better have a look and figure out what that might be. After a few long breaths, Neek slid his body slowly toward the tunnel opening and peered around the corner.

∼

Barnag had made it out of what was clearly some large beast's lair, and was crawling through a long tunnel lined with glow moss. While there are a few beautiful underground mosses that shine in bright shades of pink and blue, most varieties are in truth quite dull. To those that need light to see of course, any glow is welcome, even the sickly green haze given off by these common Pickle-Moss plants.

To a Rockling however, who sees well enough in pure darkness, glow moss just spells danger, and the chance that you'll be spotted by regular-sighted creatures. Barnag was dismayed as he made it around the corner only to find another long hallway full of these plants ahead. He had no choice though, and kept propelling himself forward slowly along the floor, plagued all the while by the awful pain of his busted leg and hip.

Barnag tried to be quiet, but this was nearly impossible as he was dragging his entire body across a floor of sand, gravel, and tiny rocks. Try as he might, he was at best as quiet as a large box being pulled along a road.

After the effort of sliding himself along, and enduring so much pain, Barnag's arms and body were tiring, and there was still no end in sight to the trail of glow moss he was crawling over. Barnag dropped to the ground and wept, as quietly as he could, and lay in the dirt and the moss for a while thinking that surely he would be spending eternity in the cave he had just left, keeping the rat skeletons company in that smelly room filled with mushrooms.

As Barnag's tears ceased, more from exhaustion than any kind of calm or comfort, he heard something in the distance. Thankfully it wasn't the sound of footsteps, or a roar, but a soft repeating splash. Drip. Drip. Drip.

Neek poked his head around the corner and was relieved to find himself overlooking a chamber with no clear walking path downward. No easy path down meant no easy path up. Whatever might be waiting on the cavern floor ahead would have to climb to get to him, and Neek knew that very few things could do so quickly.

He had emerged from a hole twenty or so feet up on the side of a large cavern. He noticed the edge of a pool of water on the ground below that seemed to extend to the opposite wall. The dripping noise was much louder here, as was the slurping sound, which continued. Neek could not see a beast, nor any kind of downspout or drip, as beyond the opening he was looking out of was a rocky ledge with a few large boulders to one side of it. This ledge blocked most of his view of the cavern and pool below, and whatever was thirstily gulping down such huge slurps of water.

Taking one last deep breath so that he could proceed forward silently, Neek inched his body out across the ledge to examine the rest of the chamber and whatever creature was drinking there. As his nose extended over the edge of the rock outcropping, and his eyes were finally rewarded with a clear view, Neek's stomach sank, and his heart raced in his chest. What was the First-Mother thinking sending me here, Neek thought to himself? He fought valiantly against his Rockling survival instincts which were all screaming at him to turn around and run at top speed toward the narrow tunnel he had seen above.

~

The Rock Boar was happy today. He had been happy most days since he had set up camp a few weeks ago near this clear, refreshing pool of water with its seemingly endless supply of delicious mushrooms. Eating the mushrooms seemed to relax the beast, and kept its belly full between the occasional meals of rats, carrion, Goblins, and whatever other meat it could find in this bleak landscape. When it ate the mushrooms, it could swear it heard the funny green mossy plants make noises, almost as if they were singing to him. All in all, it was one of the most pleasant periods in his long and mostly dull life.

The giant beast, with the head of a pig, and the body of a bear, covered in a solid, beetle-like carapace, had spent most of the day just wandering about listening to the moss sing to him. He had gone for a swim earlier in the pool, and had taken a long nap at the water's edge, his head softly cushioned by the sweetly singing magical moss.

Something loud had woken him. Not that he truly thought much about it. He had been asleep, then a long, loud rumbling sound had rattled the earth, and he had been awake again, thirsty and hungry for more mushrooms.

The Boar went to his beloved pool, drank long deep draughts of the refreshing water, and thought to himself how lucky he was to finally find such a wonderful home. His head, slightly clearer than normal after his long nap and momentary break from the mushrooms' power, listened to his nose rather than his ears for a change, and between gulps he sniffed something in the air. Was that another rat? He had captured a giant, plump one just days ago. Perhaps one of his brothers, the Rock Boar thought. And he turned his giant frame back toward the tunnel leading to his lair, that glorious hallway full of singing green moss that greeted him every morning and night. His eyes were a bit fuzzy from the nap, but he could swear the rat was right there, not more than twenty feet from him. And my goodness, it was a big one.

The Rock Boar's day was made only moderately worse when the giant rat began to scream and throw rocks at him. Hmm. This was not like the rats he was used to. No, not at all. How curious.

Rocklings, like most industrious races, try to teach their young from a very early age that hard work will be rewarded. Rockling life, like most lives, is full of work after all. Tunnels to dig. Fish to catch. Dangers to avoid. And so Barnag had, like all Rockling children, been told many times in his short life about the stories of the journeys of the First-Mother, and the gifts she received after completing her seemingly impossible labors. How she had received the gift of fiery breath after cooling the volcano Ozamir at the center of the universe. How she had earned her legendary claws by digging rivers in the earth. Work hard, and you will be rewarded was the lesson of most of the tales told to the children, and even someone as distracted as Barnag had clearly gotten the message.

Thinking back though, Barnag had a hard time remembering any day where he had worked as hard as he had today. For what felt like hours, he had been dragging his broken body across the mossy earth, searching for an escape from what was clearly an inhabited lair. He had made it through long, seemingly endless tunnels, and now, was finally at the edge of an open cavern. His reward for this hard work though looked to be death, as he faced a massive creature, a giant, muscular beetle with the head of a pig and the teeth of, well, to be honest, Barnag had never seen teeth as large as these before. This must be the beast he had been working so hard to avoid.

None of the usual Rockling tools were available to him. He couldn't run, his leg was broken. He couldn't hide, the beast was looking right at him. Thankfully, the monster looked as if it must be sick or something, as it stared at Barnag with a dazed look and hadn't chomped him immediately upon being spotted. Barnag had nothing at his disposal except this cursed green moss, a few mushrooms, and the rocky floor of the cave. The rocks, yes, that's it, he thought. Perhaps this beast was dumb enough that Barnag could hit it with a rock and scare it off. Perhaps in its sickened state it would be too weak to want a fight and would just scamper away. Perhaps deception rather than hard work might be the answer here. Perhaps.

And so, in what he assumed would be his last action in this life, Barnag picked up the largest stone he could find and flung it at the beast's head, yelling at the top of his lungs, screaming in his native dragon tongue the foulest words and darkest threats he could summon for one so young.

Neek was quite clever, and despite his young age, he rarely felt confused. Today had been different in so many ways though. He didn't understand why the tunnel he had climbed down had collapsed. It had seemed strong enough to him as he as journeyed through it earlier. He didn't recognize the strange creature he had seen slurping water at the pool's edge. This particular monstrosity had not been in any of the stories his teachers had shared with him. Most of all though, he was shocked when he saw a rock hit the beast and heard Barnag's voice thundering from a tunnel below. How had his brother found him all the way down here? And why in the name of the First-Mother was he attacking this huge monster? Barnag liked to fight, he knew that, but this seemed incredibly bold and foolish, even for him.

Perhaps Neek's confusion had come from the whirlwind of emotions he had felt in the past few moments. Fear, at first, upon seeing this terrifying creature so close to him. Then, some sense of relief in realizing that the beast could not climb up to get him, high as he was on the side of the cavern wall. Even a sense of hope had washed over him briefly as the monster finally finished its long drink and had turned to seemingly wander off to some

THE CAVE IN 37

other part of the underground. The terror was back now though, in full force, as Neek heard his brother's voice, saw the creature growl, and watched it advance, curiously slowly toward a large tunnel opening in the cave below. Neek had to act quickly or his brother would be eaten. Barnag might not be his favorite sibling, but Neek knew, like all Rocklings should, that you need your brothers and sisters, and you protect them, no matter how different or annoying they might sometimes seem.

Neek looked around for anything he could use as a weapon. There were no long thin stones he could use as a club. No sharp bits of metal he could flick as darts at the creature. There were a few large boulders at the edge of the ledge he was on, but they appeared far too heavy and securely based to be pushed down onto the beast below. Perhaps, as she had done in so many stories of her trickery, Neek could follow the First-Mother's example and just distract it long enough for Barnag to run away.

Neek summoned his courage, walked to the edge of rock shelf before him, and started shouting at the Boar. The beast looked up at him, staring blearily with its dazed, groggy eyes. It studied Neek briefly before turning back toward Barnag, clearly choosing the simple meal over the pie in the sky. Neek started jumping up and down, dancing about, smacking the boulders next to him. He picked up the little stones on the ground around him and chucked them down on the beast. Neek did everything he could think of to try to distract the monster and save his brother. "Run, Barnag. Run and hide!" he yelled, over and over.

The Boar started wondering if perhaps he was still asleep and dreaming all of this. There was now not just one, but two giant rats, screaming strange sounds at him and throwing pebbles. No, the one high up in the cavern couldn't be a rat as it was standing on its hind legs. Goblins maybe? But this one had bumpy horns on its head. Some new delicacy, the Boar hoped, licking his lips.

He turned back to the creature throwing rocks from the floor before him. He would eat this rat first, and then think about how to get the thing up above. Wait, no, this couldn't be a rat either, he realized. Rats don't throw rocks. As he turned, the Boar heard new noises coming from the ledge above. The one up there was dancing now and jumping about. The movements synched nicely with the soft bits of music the Boar could still hear coming from the moss around him. Yes, surely, he must be dreaming. Oh well, he thought, things still taste good in dreams, perhaps even better than normal.

∽

Barnag concluded he must already be dead. He had fallen through the tunnel and been crushed, he decided, and was now trapped in some kind of tortuous afterlife. Surely there was no way he could endure such pain, spend such long hours dragging himself through this awful cave, and bravely face a hideous monster, only to hear his hated rival Neek screaming at him to run. He was being punished by the gods for trying to trap his brother, surely that was it.

Well, if he was going to be tormented, he wasn't going to go along with it quietly. "I can't run, you Goblin-kisser!" he yelled up to what he assumed was an illusionary Neek. "My leg is broken. My hip is shattered. I can barely crawl. You'd be better off asking me to fly," he joked, "that would be just as likely to come true."

∽

Despite the many relics on his necklace, Torgal was still a spry Rockling. He was angry with himself for his poor scouting of the caves where the young were playing, and this anger spurred him on. He insisted on leading the search party downward into the unexplored caves where he hoped they might find the missing children. He was frustrated with the tunnel he was following that crept along so slowly. If they didn't find the young soon, they would be doomed. There were dark things in the unexplored regions below. Dark, dangerous things.

"Come on, make haste," Torgal barked at his companions, trotting nimbly forward as fast as his old legs would take him.

Neek leaned over the edge of the ridge before him. He could see Barnag there on the ground. So, Barnag was hurt. Now things made sense. The terrible beast was only a few meager yards from his brother and was no longer interested in Neek's dancing. If Neek was going to help, he had to act now. Neek pushed against one of the large boulders in front of him. He saw no other option. If Neek could somehow move this huge stone and drop it on the beast, surely that would hurt it enough to stop its advances, or scare it away. He pushed with all his might, but it felt hopeless. The boulder was huge. It was solidly fixed to the ledge floor and wouldn't budge even an inch. If he had some tools, he could chip away at the base, but there was no time for that and he had no such tools.

Neek could hear his brother screaming, and he felt true rage for the first time in his short life. The anger washed over him, filling his senses, and as Neek looked down at his tiny Rockling hands, he noticed his scales were shimmering with a red glow, much brighter than their normal reddish-brown hue. If his brother was going to die, Neek vowed, it wouldn't be while he wept about it, and Neek renewed his efforts, pushing frantically against the boulder in front of him, using all the force he could muster against the thousands of pounds of stone in his way. Neek strained until every muscle on his tiny frame seemed about to burst, and his vision went red and hazy. I must have broken something in my brain, he thought, as he heard loud cracking sounds. As the cracking and popping intensified, he felt his hands lurching forward. The boulder was moving!

Barnag was impressed with the lengths to which the gods were going to toy with him using this illusion they had created. It really did sound like Neek's voice. He even saw a head like Neek's poke over the ledge, and a body like Neek's dancing around up there. He saw through their trickery though, as the fake Neek's body started to glow a bright red before pushing a gigantic boulder over the side of the ledge he was dancing on. Neek was a tiny thing, and not particularly strong, even for a Rockling. Barnag knew he could never push a huge rock like that. As he watched the boulder fall down on the giant beetle beast in front of him though, Barnag began to question why the gods would scare him so only to save him seconds before he was to be eaten? Barnag was too sore and exhausted to wonder much more. He collapsed on the ground and closed his eyes. Let the gods play their games, he was going to sleep.

Down the boulder fell, smashing onto the upper shell and head of the Boar which stopped moving immediately. Neek watched and waited a moment to see if it would get back up, but it seemed to be still. Had he killed it? He wasn't sure. He saw Barnag wasn't moving either. Had the stone hit his brother too? His love for his brother overwhelmed his fear of the monster and Neek clambered down the rocks to the cavern floor, rushing over to Barnag's body.

"Barnag, Barnag, wake up, we must go," Neek urged him, shaking his brother's body gently.

Barnag was slow to rouse himself, clearly wiped out from the pain of his injuries.

"Gods, quit your illusion and leave me alone, I need to rest," Barnag replied.

Perhaps the stone had hit him after all, Neek thought, not comprehending what Barnag was babbling about. Despite his brother's objections, Neek pulled him up onto Barnag's one good leg and helped him hobble to the side of the nearby pond. Neek scooped water from the pool to wash the dirt off of Barnag's wounded leg, clearing the debris it had gathered as Barnag dragged himself down those long, littered tunnels.

As he cleaned his brother's wounds, Neek scanned the tunnel roof where the water was dripping down. Sure enough, there was an opening about fifteen feet up. It was small, but so were they, and Neek figured they could likely make it through. If he could just get Barnag up there, they would probably find a tunnel up to the level above where their siblings must be missing them.

It had been several meal times since he had gone to hide, and Neek imagined he would be in deep trouble when he returned home. Better off in trouble than in that monster's belly, Neek thought, turning back to glance at the Rock Boar. Now, how am I going to get my brother up to that hole, Neek wondered? He looked around for some way to climb to where the water ran slowly into the pool in front of them. Drip. Drip. Drip.

∽

As opposed to earlier, when the Boar had wrongly thought himself to be dreaming, he was now well and truly asleep. It had been a disappointing dream, the earlier one he had imagined, ending with a terrible heavy weight dropping on him, leaving him with bumps and bruises all over his shell and head that would probably bother him for weeks to come.

This current dream was far better. His beloved green moss had grown legs, many pairs of legs, as an army of long, lithe bodies stood up all along his favorite passage and walked toward him. They caressed his sore head and spoke softly to him.

"Oh, big and beautiful Boar," the moss creatures said softly, "we are sorry about the pain you are feeling. The rats are too loud and bothersome here. Follow us and we will find you a much better home." They motioned him forward, their faces full of smiles as they began to sing again their heavenly music.

He would follow them, he decided. He would have followed his beloved moss anywhere. And he would take a big bunch of the mushrooms with him. Yes, as soon as this dream was over, that's what he would do. He snorted in his sleep, imagining the wonders the mosslings might have to share with him, and looking forward to exploring his new home.

As he was scanning the cave side, planning his ascent to the narrow waterspout above, Neek considered several routes. He would have to lift Barnag from ledge to ledge until he could reach the opening and push him through. It would be tough. Barnag was larger than he was by several inches, with a much broader build. But if he could move that giant boulder, Neek decided, he must be able to carry his brother as well. What choice did he have? He wasn't sure if the beast behind him was still alive, or whether it would be waking up soon.

As if on cue, the Boar snorted, and Neek made up his mind, they had to get moving. Turning to make sure the beast was not yet coming at them, Neek began prodding Barnag to try to wake him.

"Come on, brother. We must climb now or we'll be eaten," he begged.

Barnag was delirious, tired from the exertion, all the pain and the fear he had gone through over the past hours. He could barely focus his eyes, much less reach his feet. Neek pulled and pulled at his brother's shoulders, finally wrenching him into a sitting position.

"Come on, Barnag, wake up," he urged, but the injured Rockling was still too weak to help.

The Boar snuffled a few more times. One of its legs stirred.

Once again, Neek felt his scales grow warm, and they began to

THE CAVE IN   45

pulse with the red glow from earlier. Neek found the strength to lift his brother to a ledge about a foot off the ground. He could hear the beast behind them stirring, its legs clattering to find its feet, but Neek didn't even turn to look at it. There was no time. He hoisted his brother up with frantic abandon to the next ledge, and then the next, over and over again, until Neek was finally placing his brother into the small opening where the droplets were flowing from the cavern wall. Only after he had shoved Barnag in and followed behind him did Neek venture to look back out to the cavern floor below.

The Boar was gazing up at them. His monstrous eyes seemed even cloudier than before. Neek was convinced though that the many vicious teeth in the beast's mouth had formed into a smile. After a moment, the Boar turned away, and wandered off down another large tunnel, heading out of the cave in the opposite direction from its lair.

The Boar woke up to the sounds of scuffling. Turning, he saw a red glowing creature, carrying the rat he had planned to eat, climbing up along one of the cave walls. The curious red beast shoved the rat into a small hole high up on the wall and followed him in. On any other day, the Boar might have been angry to have his lunch stolen from him in this way, but his head hurt, and his shell ached, and he was much more focused on the green mosslings leading him toward a passage in the north.

"This way. Come this way," they sang in their alluring voices, moving their bodies in wonderful swaying patterns as they walked along.

They danced, and he followed. Where would they lead him, the Boar wondered? Would his new home be as soft as this one? Would it have a pool as cool and clear? The Boar smiled as he thought about what amazing things awaited him down the road. He was so entranced, he forgot to even take any of his treasured mushrooms with him as he ambled forward, up and out of the cavern.

∼

The tunnel opened up after a short distance, making it easier for Neek to coax and drag Barnag sluggishly forward. The delicate trickle of water over his skin from the floor below seemed to be doing Barnag some good, and he was slowly coming to his senses.

"Come on, brother, I cannot carry you like this forever," Neek implored.

Barnag tried his best to help, pushing against the tunnel walls with his arms and using his one good leg to amble slowly forward while Neek supported him. Inch by inch they moved along. Foot by gradual foot.

The tunnel had no branches, but it did meander somewhat, left and right, like a slithering snake, as they made their way along it. Thankfully, no branches meant no confusion. No difficult decisions about which way to turn. But it also meant nowhere to hide. If anything came upon them here, they would have no choice but to run back to the cavern where that awful beast was, surely not in a good mood after having a giant rock dropped upon it. Who was he kidding, Neek wondered, they couldn't run anyway. If anything found them here, given Barnag's current state, they would be doomed. End of story.

Just as he had these thoughts, Neek heard the soft scuffling of footsteps. Wet footsteps. Quite a few of them. Someone or something was coming their way. The footsteps were close now. Judging by their number, it must be some kind of large centipede, Neek guessed.

Neek covered his brother's body as well as he could, sticking to the side of the tunnel wall and hoping that whatever was about to eat them would do so quickly.

∼

THE CAVE IN 47

Torgal was just about to give up, when he turned yet another corner in this infernal, unending tunnel, and lo and behold, there before him he saw a young Rockling lying against the wall. It was Barnag!

"Barnag!" he yelled, running toward the boy who was obviously hurt.

Where was Neek though, precious young Neek, the hope of the tribe? Within seconds, his question was answered as Neek seem to appear next to Barnag out of thin air. How could he have missed him, Torgal wondered? There were no alcoves here, nowhere to hide. He had missed the downspout earlier, and now missed spotting Neek. Perhaps he needed to talk to one of the tribe artisans about making him some new glasses, as his eyes were clearly deteriorating. No matter, the younglings had been found. They were alive. The tribe would be overjoyed to see the disaster averted.

Torgal's old Rockling arms lifted up both the boys and he carried them, with the help of the Warriors, back up to the warren, back to warmth and food and friends, and away from this channel of damp darkness.

CHAPTER 3
STONE SHAPER

Neek enjoyed retelling the story of his adventure in the cave with the Rock Boar the first ten or so times through. He had recounted all the details to Chief MakMak, Dragon-Mother Malika, Torgal, and nearly every other elder in the tribe. On multiple occasions. Now, repeating the tale again for what must have been the hundredth time, Neek was exhausted by it.

"And you carried Barnag all the way up the wall?" Gremble, one of Neek's younger sisters, asked. "That's amazing," she continued, looking at him with wide-eyed wonder.

"I don't really know how I was able to do it. The excitement must have given me strength," Neek replied sheepishly, trying to think up some excuse to get away from the group of younglings that were gathered around him hoping to hear the story of the cave in and his escape yet again.

Neek was overwhelmed by all the attention. It was not new of course. His whole life so far, short as it had been, Neek was always a focus of the tribe's interest due to his unique, colorful scales, that celebrated sign of the First-Mother's blessing he could never hide. The other Rocklings often stared at Neek when he entered a room. Since the episode with the Rock Boar, things were worse than ever. Rocklings watched him all the time now. The youngest ones followed him around. The older tribe members would smile and wave whenever he passed them. It seemed to Neek that, to many of the tribe, his story somehow validated the promises made by his skin. A sign of great things to come.

Neek didn't like the weight of those eyes, and the expectation they held. To his mind, there had been many heroes in the cave that day. Despite his injuries, Barnag had dragged himself out of the beast's den. Wise old Torgal had found a way down to locate them. And most importantly, the First-Mother had somehow blessed Neek with the strength to push over that boulder and carry Barnag up the cavern wall to safety.

The new attention wasn't all completely positive either. Malika had been extremely cross with Neek for climbing so far away from the group during their game of Secret Treasure. She and Chief MakMak had decided that from now on the children's games would be played in safer, more well-known caverns, and the number of Guards accompanying the younglings would be increased dramatically. All in all, Neek was left with little privacy, and found most of his favorite activities curtailed. Not much of a reward for supposedly heroic behavior, he thought.

The only truly wonderful change that had happened since Neek's return was the discovery of the new swimming ponds. The water system giving rise to the pool Neek and Barnag had found was mapped out extensively by the tribe in the days following the boys' rescue. The Tunnel Wardens had identified a new cavern nearby, with several large ponds and a stream, all of which had been fairly easy to protect by collapsing a few unfamiliar exits. The water was a great boon to the tribe, for drinking, washing, preparing food, and other vital day-to-day tasks. There were even fish in some of the rivulets that flowed through rock openings the Rockling hunters could reach with their fishing lines. Most importantly of all though, from Neek's point of view, there were a number of wide, flat, fairly shallow pools that were safe enough for the young Rocklings to swim and play in, provided of course they had an armed escort.

Due to the lack of pools like these in most underground

ecosystems, a great many Rocklings live their entire life without ever having a swim. The Rockling form, slim and devoid of body fat, was not very well-adapted to the water. Rocklings just don't float well. However, Neek's tribe lived fairly close to a number of underground lakes where the older, trained Rocklings would go and fish in small boats to gather food for the tribe. While normally only the trained fishers of his tribe would learn to swim, the discovery of these new pools meant that all the young could learn this rare skill, a decision Chief MakMak had made, typical of her leadership style.

"The more we know, the stronger we are," MakMak announced to the tribe. "The young will learn to swim, and we will all be better at fishing, better at exploring, and better at protecting watery passages. The First-Mother gives us a gift and we must use it."

The pools provided many new opportunities for play that delighted Neek. His favorite involved bounding over the wide basins of water. Jumping is a crucial survival skill that all Rocklings are expected to master. Many a Rockling Explorer would follow a novel tunnel only to encounter a vast chasm blocking their way. And if they were being chased by something dangerous, Rocklings needed to be able to cross such gaps quickly. Many of the most common Rockling traps involved hidden pits with spikes or sharp rocks at their bottom that would send an unsuspecting enemy plummeting to their end below. So, it was considered essential to jump well. It was also great fun. Neek especially enjoyed falling purposefully into the center of a pond with a great splash. He loved the feeling of the liquid rushing over his scales, and the sensations his tail felt as he thrashed through the water.

∽

Neek hadn't been the only one telling stories for the past few days. Torgal, the Tunnel Warden, had been speaking with many of the other elders. Torgal recounted with great excitement the size of the huge boulder Neek had been able to push over, the difficulty of the climb Neek had accomplished while carrying his brother, and the shocking way in which Neek had appeared out of thin air. Torgal was a practical and somewhat skeptical Rockling, so while he respected and honored the First-Mother, he felt that wherever she was, it was certainly a long way off. The Rocklings had to solve their own problems, he believed. However, the remarkable feats Neek had performed were causing Torgal to question his convictions. Perhaps the hands of fate were guiding this young boy. Perhaps the First-Mother was closer than Torgal initially imagined.

The head Priestess of the Hardhands tribe, Loodnar, had been pestering Chief MakMak daily, requesting that the Chief rethink her earlier reluctance to bring in outside help to assess Neek's magical potential. Loodnar shared many tales with her Chief from the Rockling histories about youngling mages who had disrupted tribal life when their mystical powers erupted prematurely and disastrously due to inadequate training. MakMak finally relented, permitting an emissary to be sent to the Kindlehoof clan, renowned for their arcane prowess, requesting their guidance and their help in understanding the boy and his special talents.

Barnag's tongue had also not stopped wagging since his return to the warren. With his injured leg and his shattered hip, there was little Barnag could do at first other than sit around and talk. Even after the Priests had healed his wounds though, Barnag didn't grow tired of telling the tale, and would regale anyone who would listen with his own account of personal bravery, whether they wanted to hear it or not.

One could listen to Barnag recite his story over and over again, and never grow bored, as the details seemed to change with each telling. Each time through, Barnag's description of how he heroically pulled himself out of the den of the beast, fighting off rats, and throwing stones into the mouth of the roaring Boar, became longer and more elaborate. And each time, Neek's role in the story seem to shrink. On occasion, Barnag seemed to suggest that perhaps Neek hadn't even pushed the boulder down on the Boar, but that the stone had fallen by accident, as part of the cave in, or due to Barnag hitting the wall underneath it with rocks. In the young Rockling's account, when it came to the topic of the climb, Neek had only nudged him a bit. Barnag had bravely hauled himself up the wall, in his version, despite his awful injuries. And of course, the story always began with a description of the obviously dangerous state of the tunnel Neek had climbed down, and how negligent it was that Neek had put his siblings in danger by hiding in such a precarious place.

Most Rocklings didn't take Barnag very seriously. They humored the boy, who had been hurt they knew, and who must have been scared out of his mind, almost being eaten by a Rock Boar. Some of the older, wiser Rocklings could discern that Barnag was lying about some of the details, but they didn't intervene. The other younglings must learn to see through such deception. Having the ability to distill what was true or useful or important about the stories they were told was a skill all Rocklings were expected to develop. Learning to read between the lines was part of growing up, part of learning about the other members of your tribe. Whenever Malika heard Barnag tell his unlikely version of the story, she thought to herself that the young one must be repeating these untruths in the hope that one day he might finally come to believe them.

Barnag's jealous feeling toward Neek were also rare in the tribe, but there were some younglings who shared Barnag's resentment about the attention given to Neek and his special skin. Following Barnag's lead, these few treated the disparaging stories he told about Neek as if they were absolute truth. Top among these believers was Whizzle, a young cluttermouth.

Whizzle had been born with teeth that were too large for his jaw, and new ones grew in faster than the old ones fell out. This resulted in him having far too many, all crowding and jostling for space, with sharp barbs sticking out in all directions. Rocklings called this somewhat uncommon malady cluttermouth.

Whizzle and Barnag were good friends and frequent sparring partners, banging dull play swords together in the dark for fun, both dreaming of one day being Warriors. Whizzle had been deeply distressed when Barnag went missing, and blamed Neek for almost losing his friend.

I'll return the favor one day, Whizzle thought, watching Neek splash around in the swimming pond. One day soon.

In addition to the lavish attention he was getting from the whole tribe, and the extra Guards that always seem to surround him now, Neek noticed that his training schedule was changing as well. Malika would pull him away frequently from group survival activities such as Secret Treasure to have him sit down with seasoned craftspeople from the various castes. These survival games were Neek's favorite lessons, and he felt frustrated to have his fun time taken away. Instead of climbing and hiding, or walking over traps without setting them off, he'd be stuck in a cave with an older Rockling trying to cook an elaborate dish, or hook up a convoluted spring mechanism, or sometimes, as he was today, carving a piece of rock.

Carving is a highly revered activity in Rockling life. Stone must be shaped to adjust tunnels, to make caverns habitable, and to transform barren hunks of rock into useful tools. There are many stories of the First-Mother and her magical claws, able to shape stone as easily as clay. Rockling legends told of how the First-Mother had used her talons at the beginning of time to carve out the elaborate crisscrossing world of underground tunnels the tribe now called home.

Carving tools were similarly revered. Young Rocklings would purposefully be given crude, dull tools, and then assigned impossibly difficult tasks to complete with them. Only once they had successfully demonstrated their talents would the younglings be allowed to move on to more precious instruments. This was done in part to discover what potential talent the young ones might have. As the saying goes, only a truly fine Carver can succeed with a rough chisel. As importantly however, this challenge was also given to prospective stone shapers to test their ability to manage frustration. Between cave ins, stone crumble, and a variety of other disappointments plaguing the efforts of even the most experienced artisans, carving could be a terribly difficult task. Patience and resilience, almost as much as touch or creativity, were critical to the job.

Neek's task today sounded simple enough at first, but it was proving to be much harder than he had initially imagined.

"Show me what the Rock Boar looked like," Altak, the carving teacher, told him. "Show me its body shape, the patterns on its shell, the curve of its snout, the hollow of its eyes, whatever you can recall."

Neek remembered every detail of the Rock Boar clearly. He could see its huge tusks. He could smell the sweat of its body. He could hear it snuffle and its legs kicking against the earth as it started to wake from its dream. He could see its wide, bleary eyes looking up at them as he pulled his brother to safety.

Looking down at the rock he was working though, Neek saw none of this. He saw a rounded lump with a bulbous protrusion on one end. It looks like a turtle's shadow, he thought, or a badly made club. In his mind, Neek envisioned many captivating ways to transform the stone, but his hands didn't seem to be playing along, and he felt disappointed in his effort. If he was honest, his heart wasn't in the task. He enjoyed carving, but he didn't really want to see the Rock Boar ever again. He didn't want to relive those feelings of fear and panic.

Altak was playing a double-sided trick on Neek today. Not

only had he given Neek the dullest chisel in the studio, and a hammer with a weak grip, but he had also given Neek a very difficult type of stone named Puzzlax to work on. Puzzlax is incredibly hard, so you must use strength to cut it. Even worse though, Puzzlax naturally has many tiny fault lines in it that run in seemingly random directions. If you weren't careful, the straight line you had spent hours trying to carve might fall away at an angle, ruining your piece. Altak was in part testing Neek's patience, and his sensitivity to what the stone might do, but mostly the carving master just wanted to spend a good block of time with the promising young boy. Nothing goes quickly when working in Puzzlax.

Neek, despite the limited progress he was making with his sculpture, was enjoying his time with Altak. The carving teacher seemed interested in many aspects of Neek's life that the other elders never asked about, and he entertained Neek in turn with colorful tales about the exotic creatures the teacher had encountered in the travels of his youth. Carvers are often good storytellers. Given stone's all too frequent resistance, their trade required them to sit still and concentrate for long periods of time, providing ample hours for chatting, and Altak was a true master at all aspects of his craft. Altak shared many silly jokes, which Neek loved, and so, even as he sat there with his awful mess of a carving, Neek was smiling.

Neek was growing impatient though, not with his abilities or his tools, but because he didn't want to miss out on swim time. There were only a few opportunities left this week when the young could go to the pools. Guards were needed elsewhere. Conflicts with the Goblins were escalating, and there was less and less time for them to accompany the younglings to the ponds. Neek knew his sculpture looked nothing like the Boar he could see in his mind, and he had already spent several hours just to reach this point. How much longer would it take him to finish?

If he could just get the head to be the right shape, Neek thought, he could then move on to some of the other details, which Neek hoped might make the carving look less like an overfilled water sack and more like the powerful creature which had nearly eaten him. If he didn't finish soon, he would completely miss his chance to swim today, and it would be a few days, if not another week entirely, before he got to go back to his beloved pools. Lost in thought, Neek's hand slipped, and his chisel hit the neck of the sculpture too forcefully, causing the head to break off in his hand. Looking down at the crude shape in front of him, Neek realized there was no way he would complete the carving in time. His heart sank.

Altak saw the error. He had been expecting it. He had worked Puzzlax before, and made many such mistakes in his youth. He could see the emotions on Neek's face, but to his credit, the boy didn't complain, just stopping for a moment to look with despair at his broken statue before reaching for a new stone to begin the sculpture of a Boar a second time.

"Don't despair Neek," Altak told the boy. "This is difficult stone, and a mistake sometimes makes our work more interesting. The stone is a test of your mind as much as your hands. You know the statue of the crouching Warrior near the main hall?"

Neek nodded. It was one of his favorites.

"I carved that one years ago. He was initially going to be standing proud. That is, until his head broke off," Altak explained, with a slight smile. "I had to change my design to accommodate the flaw, and the work was better for it. The stone sometimes has a story it wants to tell, and we just need to have the ears to listen." He paused to let the words sink in. "I'm going to grab us something to drink and some snacks," Altak explained, standing up. The carving teacher then headed off toward the kitchens to give the boy a moment to compose himself and his thoughts.

How long will he last, Altak wondered, already impressed by how patiently the boy had labored at so difficult a task.

After Altak left, Neek put down the chisel. He hated this dull thing he had been holding for the past few hours. How could anyone use such a tool? It barely had a sharp edge at all. You needed to use the corner of it to get any kind of impression in the stone, and hammering it flat would just break the rock. And this black material he was trying to carve, what was it? He had never seen dark stone like this with such jagged fissures in it. He noticed fine lines running below the surface of the rock and traced them with the edge of his claws, marveling at their meandering patterns. It reminded him of the pools, his watery playscape, and the stream running along the far end of that cavern. Neek imagined his finger was his body, tossing to and fro in the waves of the pond, jumping from a great distance and landing with a splash.

Bright as he was, and destined for whatever glory the tribe might hope for from him, Neek was still just a young boy. He wasn't even a yearling yet, and hadn't yet taken his Trials. And so, it would have surprised no one in the tribe that might have been watching to see Neek playing with his broken statue like a toy. Neek used two of his fingers as legs, the tips of his claws their feet. They ran across the table, jumping into the air, and crashing down repeatedly onto the hard ball of rock. For hours now, Neek had been concentrating solemnly on the stone while his elder Altak monitored his every move. With Altak gone, Neek was relishing the chance to play and relax before the work began again. Surely there was no way he'd be able to swim today. He'd be here all night probably unless Altak took mercy on him and let him stop carving.

How high would he be able to jump when he was fully grown, Neek wondered? He lifted his fingers, higher and higher each time, imagining himself flying through the air, a mighty dragon with wings, before splashing down with a great crash into the pool below. He smiled. It was a pleasant daydream. Neek's smile quickly faded though as he attempted to pull his fingers back to make them run again. His hand wouldn't budge. He looked down and saw his claws had cut deep into the rock! His fingers were embedded nearly an inch inside the body of his headless sculpture.

∼

Altak was hungry, and a bit bored. The kitchens were busy working on dinner for the tribe and Altak was having to wait longer than he had hoped for the food he so desperately wanted. While he waited, his thoughts returned to Neek. The boy was gentle, and kind, and clever enough. The youngling made a few jokes of his own that made Altak laugh. Yes, he was a good soul, but Altak didn't see in Neek all the magic that everyone else was going on about. Surely, the boy's scales were lovely with their multiple hues, and he had survived a cave in. There was nothing so unusual about that though. Altak remembered with pride and sadness all the difficult challenges his tribe had survived over the years. Yes, Neek will probably grow up to be a useful member of the tribe, Altak presumed, and that was a wonderful thing, but we should stop treating the boy differently than our other children. They are all gifts. Well, most of them anyway.

Though the boy would likely grow up to be a good Rockling, Altak wasn't so sure he'd grow up to be a good stone shaper. Neek had the temperament, yes, and he seemed patient enough, but the crude bag shape Neek had carved wasn't particularly impressive, even for a young one working in such a difficult stone. It is just as well, Altak thought, as the tribe would never let him be a Carver anyway, not with that special skin and that promised destiny. Altak's food finally arrived, and he gathered up the bowls of stew, along with a jug of water and two glasses, and headed back toward the room where Neek had been working on the stone. I should let him go and play, Altak decided. He has struggled long enough.

∼

Neek's fingers were wedged more than an inch down into the unforgiving black stone. He had no idea how they had gotten there. Surprisingly, they slid out quite easily. Had the rock cracked, he wondered? But no, there were no fault lines or jagged edges where his claws had been, just two smooth indentations matching the width of his fingers.

Neek gazed long and hard at the stone, and then back at his hand. He noticed there were bits of rock dust under the tips of his claws. The dust resembled the residue on the end of the chisel he had been using. He was confused. Did I really just do that, Neek wondered? He tried pressing the tips of his claws against another area of the stone. At first, Neek's fingers just tapped the rock and did nothing. But then, emboldened by what he had seen earlier, Neek concentrated and pushed forcefully, and after a moment, his claws began to glow a bright green color and sank slowly into the stone. With a few more experimental touches, Neek discovered that when he focused his thoughts in a certain way, giving all his attention to the tips of his claws, he could activate that strange green light, and that when he pressed that light to the stone, it cut the rock with very little effort. Unlike during his earlier efforts, where the stone seemed to be brittle, and fall apart along its strange, jagged seams, Neek found he could now draw clean lines that seemed to ignore the stone's imperfections. He also noticed the rock was warm to the touch where his green claws carved it.

Perhaps I'll have the chance to swim after all, Neek thought. He focused intensely on his glowing claws, tracing quickly and easily the shape of the Rock Boar he held in his mind. The stone fell away with uncanny precision. Neek smiled and continued carving, thinking fondly of the pond diving he would soon be doing.

As Altak approached the cave entrance where Neek was working, he was disheartened to see the chisel on the table next to the boy.

He's given up. How disappointing, Altak thought. He approached Neek from the back, wondering what he was doing if he wasn't carving. Playing probably, he supposed. Well, he was a young Rockling after all.

As he rounded the table, putting down the food and the drinks to share, Altak saw that he had guessed correctly. The boy was playing. What Neek was playing with though gave Altak a shock. Rather than the crude, semi-rounded turtle shape Neek had produced earlier, the youngling now held a finely carved Rock Boar statue, one that Altak himself would have been proud to make. And out of Puzzlax no less. How in the world did he do that, Altak wondered, revisiting his earlier thoughts about the boy's specialness and realizing he might be wrong after all.

"Where did you get that?" Altak asked, pointing to the Boar sculpture Neek was making walk about the table. To be honest, Altak felt silly asking the question. He couldn't think of anyone in the warren who would have a Rock Boar sculpture in the first place. They weren't common beasts, nor beloved to Rocklings by any means.

"I carved it," Neek replied.

"But how?" Altak wondered, looking at the seemingly unused chisel sitting on the table with its dull, rounded edges. There was no way Altak himself could use that crude tool to make such a detailed sculpture. Altak would have to apply his finest blades to achieve that kind of result.

Neek paused briefly as Altak stared at him in amazement. The young Rockling wasn't sure he wanted to show his teacher what his glowing claws could do. Neek knew it would probably mean even more attention, more stories to tell, more questions to answer, and perhaps worst of all, no swimming today. What choice did he have though? Neek couldn't lie to the wise old man, and not answering would be disrespectful.

"I don't really understand why," Neek answered honestly, "but, if I concentrate in a certain way, I can do this."

Neek reached for a bit of the rubbish stone he had cast aside.

He activated his claws and cut the rock in half in a straight line. Altak's mouth hung open in shock. The Carver stood there, motionless, for a few moments, in that pose of disbelief, and Neek began to wonder if his teacher was feeling alright.

"Please, wise Altak, I'm very sorry to ask, but may I leave now and go swimming? This is the last time this week that soldiers can go with us, and I really don't want to miss out," Neek explained. Altak nodded and waved the boy on his way, not taking his eyes off of the exceptional statue and the remarkable piece of Puzzlax stone, cut perfectly straight as if by a sword blade. Neek dashed off, a broad smile on his face.

Altak remained for a while with his thoughts. No Rockling in recorded memory had ever cut hard stone with their claws. That was the kind of story Altak hadn't heard since he was a boy, when the Priests spoke of the First-Mother carving the earth. He sat down, still staring at that impossibly well-crafted statue, wondering how many things he had been wrong about in his life. The boy was clearly special after all. I must tell the Chief, he thought.

Altak's stew sat on the table, growing cold. The Carver had forgotten his hunger completely.

CHAPTER 4
SWEPT AWAY

Neek raced to the swimming chamber as quickly as he could. Despite the long hours he had spent with Altak carving, Neek hoped he would still have some time to splash around if he hurried. Sure enough, when he arrived, his siblings were still happily swimming about, and their Guards looked relaxed, with no indication they were preparing to leave. Neek whipped off his relic necklace, hanging it next to those of his siblings on a row of small stalagmites to one side of the cave, and dove in.

The water was warm today. Dragon-Mother Malika would come down sometimes and use her fire magic to heat the pond for them. Neek felt wonderful as he slipped his whole body into the pool, his tail sinking below the surface before he came back up. He liked the sensation of the water dripping off his tiny horns and running down between his shoulder blades.

Most of the other young Rocklings were playing Flip Fish, a game where they'd pass a small fish back and forth. One of the younglings would toss the fish between two of the other swimmers who would race to be the first to catch it. There were many small fish and other creatures here, transferred to these little ponds by the tribe's fishers who used them as makeshift farms. Capturing them as you swam around was a challenge the young Rocklings enjoyed, much as a Human child might dive down to retrieve something off the bottom of a pool. These were tiny fish, much too small for eating, and the Rocklings played gently with them so the fish would live on to grow large and become a meal for the tribe in the future. Fish were a cherished staple of the Rockling diet and revered creatures in Rockling culture. The First-Mother herself had even changed into a fish once to swim to the bottom of the great ocean that covered the world at the beginning of time.

Margle, a young sister of Neek's, had found a Flash Frog, a translucent red and white creature with bright red glowing veins that shone in the darkness like burning flames. Frogs like these were a sign that the water was clean and the fish were healthy here. These pools would likely serve the tribe for many years. Margle was lifting the frog up, placing it on larger and larger rocks away from the water, and watching it jump back down, splashing into the pond below.

Neek's love of the pools came in part from the creatures like this that you could find within them. Just last week, one of his brothers had found a two-headed salamander. All the young ones were fascinated by it, offering the salamander small bits of food and seeing which head would lunge for the snack first. Neek often stared at the few large holes in the floor of the cave system that had rivers you could hear running deep into the darkness beneath them, wondering what other forms of life must lurk there.

Underground streams were extremely dangerous. Rocklings falling into them often went missing for good. If you weren't lost beyond finding, you could easily drown in a passage full of water with no air. And so, the younglings, and most grown-ups, weren't allowed in or even near the holes with the powerful rivulets running underneath them. Only experienced fishers of the tribe were allowed to use these streams, casting their hooks into the holes from above, never venturing into the water below.

Not all of Neek's siblings shared his enthusiasm for the mysteries of this aquatic world. Whizzle disliked sitting around in the wet doing nothing. He and Barnag usually spent their time here splashing one another, or more frequently, pestering their brothers and sisters to join in some kind of competition. Somehow, those two could turn everything into a fight or a contest, regardless of what they were supposed to be doing. Barnag was loudly challenging everyone to play Great Leap, a game where the younglings tried to jump over one of the ponds. Neek enjoyed this game, and would normally join in. Today however, tired from the long hours of carving, and deep in thought about his recent discovery of what he could do with his glowing claws, Neek was worn out and he just wanted to rest in the warmth of the water.

Some of the other Rocklings were more receptive to Barnag's goading, and so a game of Great Leap ensued. The young Rocklings took turns leaping over one of the medium-sized pools off to Neek's left. The contest was building in intensity, with lots of splashing and laughter, as the young ones pressed their muscles to the limit.

Whizzle and Barnag never intentionally fell in the water, as Neek and many of the others did. To the two brothers, jumping the farthest was a sign of status, and they longed to demonstrate their superiority. They were a bit older, and slightly more physically developed than most of their siblings, something the two boys lorded over the rest of them. The smaller ones were catching up though, and almost everyone, even the youngest of those playing, was successfully leaping over the pool they were using today. Barnag seemed frustrated.

Neek noticed that Whizzle also appeared to be grumpy. Whizzle kept peering over at where Neek was lounging in the water, giving him long, stern looks. He must still be angry with me about Barnag's accident, the young Rockling thought.

Despite saving Barnag's life, Neek felt guilty about what had happened with the cave in. Neek blamed himself for picking a dangerous tunnel. Barnag's treachery was something Neek hadn't recognized. More than that, it would never have occurred to Neek that such behavior was possible from Barnag or any of his siblings. Rocklings worked together. That was the key to their success in a dangerous world.

The Rocklings might compete in games like Great Leap in order to practice their skills, but there was no sense that one of them was better than the others, even if they could jump the farthest. Each had their own gifts, talents bestowed on them by the First-Mother. Their abilities enabled the Rocklings to help one another and to protect the group from the dangers they faced. These blessings were supposed to be a source of responsibility and connection, not pride.

Neek was also sorry to have been an unintentional witness to Barnag's weakness and fear when the two of them had been together in the caves below. Barnag was a proud and competitive youngling, and Neek knew his brother was likely frustrated to have needed the help Neek gave him. Rather than the shared dangers they had faced bringing them closer, Neek felt a strange distance from his brother since the incident, and he blamed himself for this loss. I will try to make it up to him somehow, Neek thought, as he dove beneath the water, swimming to and fro in his small pool, quite separate from the rest of his siblings.

When Neek surfaced again a few moments later, he noticed that the group playing Great Leap had moved. They were standing on a far end of the chamber, dangerously close to one of the large river openings. The tone of their voices had changed somehow, and when Whizzle or Barnag laughed, the sound echoed uncomfortably around the room. The Guards were currently eating, and they hadn't seem to notice that the young Rocklings had ventured into a forbidden area. Anxious about his brothers and sisters, Neek hopped out of the pool to investigate what they were doing.

"I can make it over," Barnag was claiming. "Easy."

"Me too," boasted Whizzle. "No problem."

His brothers' words were meant to signal confidence, but Neek could sense fear underneath their bravado. Peering nervously toward the edge of the hole the two were discussing, Neek heard a powerful stream raging from somewhere below the opening. The gap over it was a long one. Neek had seen his brothers jump before, and Barnag and Whizzle were probably right, they likely could hurdle it. But if they slipped, or made any other slight mistake, they would plummet into a whirlwind of water, probably never to be seen again. It was a foolish, unnecessary risk, especially if the brothers managed to convince any of the younger ones in the group to try.

"It's not worth it," Neek said, starting to walk toward the group. He would have shouted more forcefully about the risks they were taking, but Neek didn't want to startle any of the younger ones who were standing near the edge. "Who really cares if you can cross a gap like that or not?" he continued. "Distance isn't everything. How fast can you go? How high? You can test all that out over here. Come on, I'll join you." Neek motioned toward the pool they had been leaping over before.

"That's too easy," protested Barnag. "You just don't want to try here because you know you can't do it, Neek. You may have pretty scales, but you don't have wings, and you aren't strong enough to make it. You're scared." The group seemed to be forming into a line to determine who would get the first chance to make the treacherous leap.

Neek paused, panicking. He wasn't certain he could reach the group before somebody jumped. He had to try something else to keep them out of danger.

"You're right," Neek responded loudly, now hoping to draw the attention of the Guards who were still finishing their food. "I might not make it. And I certainly won't risk hurting myself trying. Come on, let's have fun instead." And with that, Neek ran near to where the Guards were sitting and dove into the closest pool, splashing them as he crashed in.

Both of the Guards yelped in protest as the water pelted them and their lunches. As Neek had hoped though, this drew the chaperones' attention to the group standing near the stream opening. "Come away from there, younglings, now!" one of the

Guards stood and shouted. The other Warrior ran over to the group and began shepherding them away from the ledge.

"This area is not for playing," the second Guard admonished. "You know that. Get back to the other pools." He stepped between the youngest ones and the ledge, nudging Whizzle, Barnag, and the rest back toward the safer ponds they had been jumping over earlier.

Neek jumped back into the warm pool he had been playing in before, relieved that his plan had worked. He started up a game of Tail Circle with his siblings. The younglings held each other's tails as a group and swam around in a ring. This created a whirling torrent of water that continued to spin them all around even after they let go. The little fish seemed annoyed by this game as the swirling waves buffeted them about the pond. The children were laughing though, and enjoying themselves again in safety.

For a brief moment, Neek wasn't thinking about his glowing claws, or the incident in the tunnel with Barnag, or any of the other worries and mysteries of life he had been encountering lately. Neek was just another member of the group now, spinning about and laughing as the water splashed the cavern floor around them. He wasn't worried about being different, or special, or some kind of sign from the First-Mother, and nothing was expected of him. It was glorious.

Just then, there was a noise that made Neek shiver, despite the warm water he was sheltered in. It was the blast of a signal horn, several of them in fact, sounding from somewhere far above. Every young Rockling learns this sound in their early lessons, but few hear it outside their studies. These signal horns were blown only when there was a serious danger to life inside the warren itself, in inhabited parts of the Rockling caverns. Neek could hear voices shouting something about Goblins. Goblins had made their way into the tribe's home!

One of the reasons Rocklings pride themselves on their stone working is because it plays such a pivotal role in their survival. During emergencies, Rocklings would trigger hidden mechanisms in their tunnels to close them up, dropping walls of rock down to block off areas they wished to protect. When the danger had passed, these walls would be winched up again, restoring the Rocklings' home.

Unfortunately, the pools where the young were swimming were a relatively new part of the warren, and this area had not yet been equipped with these protective mechanisms. The closest closing barrier was hundreds of yards down the passage ahead. Luckily, that wall was a strong one, so the group would probably be safe down here. The Guards told the young Rocklings to hide, and took up defensive positions in the tunnels above.

"Don't worry, we will be fine," Inko, the tallest and oldest of the two Guards told them. "They are likely just a few Goblin raiders looking to steal food, I'm sure. Gather your things and hide. We will come back for you shortly when the danger has passed."

The youngsters dried themselves off and quickly gathered up whatever toys or bits of clothing they had brought with them. When Neek went to look for his necklace though, it was gone. Had one of his siblings taken it by mistake in the confusion? He looked around but no one seemed to have it. Neek was worried. Even though he had only lost a few of his baby teeth so far, three in fact, and no scales or horns yet, and his necklace was still fairly empty, these were still his first relics and he would be sad to lose them.

Unlike Humans, who might offer their teeth up to fairies, or even throw away the teeth they lost, Rocklings held onto their teeth, horns, and scales throughout their lives on a length of braided rope they wore around their neck. In part, these necklaces were a sign of status, showing your age by the number of items that hung there, or your power by their sharpness or thickness. They were also a keepsake though, a reminder of the life you had lived.

A Rockling's teeth and horns change throughout their lives. Their youngest growths are smooth and rounded, replaced later in life by increasingly sharp and jagged ones. When a Rockling loses a tooth or sheds a horn, they add it to the others on their necklace, thinking about their former lives and all that has happened to them since their last relic fell. You can usually tell when a Rockling is dwelling on a fond memory, as you will see them rubbing a tooth or horn on their necklace associated with that time, often unconsciously.

To Neek, who already felt so different from his siblings, and whose early days had been so dramatic and confusing, losing his first few relics felt like a disaster. He searched desperately around the stalagmite where he had hung his necklace, guessing that perhaps it been knocked to the ground or fallen behind a rock somewhere. But despite his efforts, Neek found nothing.

"Come on Neek, come hide," Neek's sister Margle called to him urgently from behind a boulder in the corner. He didn't want to give up, but Neek knew she was right. He would have to find the necklace later. Neek ran over and hid next to his little sister, putting his arm around her shivering form.

Even though she had watched him come and sit beside her, and even though she could feel his hand holding her own, when Margle looked over at where Neek should have been, right next to her, she couldn't see him. Despite what her eyes were telling her, the warmth from Neek's hand and the sound of his breath signaled to Margle that she wasn't alone.

So there they sat and waited. Two young Rocklings hiding in the dark. Both scared. Both unsure of what to expect next, or what the Goblins were doing in the tunnels above.

∼

Bartok, the tribe's leading Warrior, was confused. This wasn't typical of the Goblins at all. Like most Rocklings, Bartok despised Goblins, thinking them to be mostly dim-witted and cowardly creatures. He had encountered Goblins often enough to understand that whatever might be said of their kind, there was a logic to how they conducted their battles. Goblins were usually very cautious, hiding out and picking off their opponents carefully until the odds were in their favor. They were not reckless like the Orcs, rushing in with their chests puffed to confront the enemies directly. No, Goblins would only attack head-on when their forces greatly outnumbered their opponents. So, why in the world would the Goblins send such a small raiding party to attack the Rocklings' central warren like this? It made no sense.

The raiding party consisted of just eight Warriors, armed with spears and slings, and carrying a few large sacks between them. What had they been hoping to steal? The Goblins had been defeated quite near the tribe's central storage area. Were they here looking for treasure? The Rocklings were careful not to collect too much of anything that others might covet. Gold and other valuables, even in small amounts, were tempting to outsiders. No point in making yourself a target. Had they been looking for food maybe? These particular Goblins did look quite scrawny. But there were certainly safer ways to feed themselves. The streams were all rich with fish, and those streams must run through the Goblin caves as surely as they run through ours, Bartok thought.

It didn't make much sense. But that was the Goblin way, wasn't it? Chaos and confusion. The Rocklings would just have to be more vigilant, Bartok decided. We must send out more patrols. Collapse some of the unnecessary tunnels. Clearly something was wrong with these Goblins, and the tribe would have to be more careful in the months ahead.

The defeated Goblins' bodies were gathered up and discarded in one of the caverns far from the main warren. Groups of

Rockling soldiers accompanied by Tunnel Warden guides worked their way through the tribe's home and all nearby tunnels to ensure that there were no more Goblins about. When Chief MakMak felt confident that the tribe's safety was assured, the signal horns were blown again, in short bursts of three puffs, letting the Rocklings know that all was safe again. The walls that had been dropped were raised. Life began to return to normal.

Perhaps if Rocklings had a different attitude toward treasure, they would have more carefully searched and looted the bodies of the invading Goblin party. If they had been lucky, they might even have found the hidden piece of parchment with a drawing on it inside the Goblin leader's belt. The drawing showed a headdress that looked very similar to the one Dragon-Mother Malika wore day in and day out. This simple illustration was to have grave consequence, not just for the future of the Rocklings, but for all who lived in these caves, and even those on the surface world above. But alas, that drawing remained undiscovered. It lies with the bodies of those Goblins in a dark cavern, deep below the surface of the world, likely never to be seen again.

It felt to Neek like the younglings had been hiding for hours before the all-clear signal was finally sounded and the Guards came to retrieve them.

"All is well. You are safe," Inko the Guard explained reassuringly. "Come, let us get some food into you," he continued, ushering the young ones up toward the main warren above.

Neek was relieved. And hungry. He had run off to swim before he even had a bite of the stew Altak the Carver had grabbed for him earlier, and between the lessons and the swimming and the fear he felt during their long session of hiding, Neek was famished. He was so ravenous in fact, that Neek walked quite a distance from the cavern of pools before he remembered his lost necklace.

"Inko, please, I must go back and find it," Neek pleaded. "I'll be up with the rest of you in just a few minutes, I promise."

"Ok, but be quick about it," Inko insisted. "I'll give you five minutes and no more. If you aren't back by then, there'll be no swimming for you next week," he warned.

Neek was off in a flash, saying a quick "Thank you," as he dashed down the tunnel to find his lost treasure.

Whizzle spoke up as well, "I'll go help him," he offered, not waiting for Inko's permission before heading in the same direction Neek had taken. "It will be faster this way," Whizzle suggested, though something in his face didn't match the friendly tone in his voice. Whizzle ran down the tunnel with a strange glint in his eye, Neek's necklace carefully balled up and hidden in the palm of his right hand.

Few things are as terrifying as time can be. The very old know this. People who are late for something important know this. And today, Neek knew it as well. He had but a few short minutes to find his missing necklace or he would be banned from swimming. With the Goblin mess, who knew when they might be coming back to this chamber? This would likely be his only chance for ages to find his relics. Neek searched frantically around the chamber, scanning every rock, every nook, every cranny, for any sign of his missing keepsake. He was working as quickly as he could, but the faster he raced to find the necklace, the less confident Neek was that he would actually find it. Speed somehow wasn't useful in this situation.

The true danger of time is not that it passes. This cannot be stopped. It will march on, no matter how much we might wish otherwise. The true danger is that when we worry about time too much, we usually focus on just that one thing, to the detriment of everything else. Neek, usually so alert, would normally have noticed Whizzle enter the chamber. Neek typically would have seen him walk over to the edge of the ledge above the rushing stream, take ten paces backwards, and then run and vault over it. Neek certainly would have heard him land with a thud on the other side, standing on a ledge in the cavern face mere inches from the hole beside it.

But Neek noticed none of these things. Saw none of the movements. Heard none of the sounds. Neek was so busy scouring the floors of the cavern for his necklace that he never noticed Whizzle at all, until finally Whizzle spoke.

"Are you looking for something, little Neek?" Whizzle asked wickedly. Whizzle altered the tone of his raspy voice as he said Neek's' name, making it sound like something awful in his mouth, something no mother would rightfully name their child.

Neek looked up and saw Whizzle standing on a ledge on the other side of a great hole over a rushing river. This was the same dangerous opening Whizzle had been discussing with Barnag earlier.

"Whizzle, be careful," Neek warned, thinking first of the peril his brother faced if he dropped into the stream below. It took Neek a moment to notice that Whizzle was holding Neek's missing necklace between his fingers, the thin, braided rope dangling precariously over the dark torrent of raging water below.

"I'm not afraid," Whizzle replied with a smile, waving the necklace back and forth a few times over the abyss, enjoying the worry he could see in his hated brother's eyes. Then Whizzle twisted his body in a circle before jumping, only barely, back beyond the stream opening to where Neek was standing. "I thought you could use the help," Whizzle continued, dramatically rolling his eyes toward the ledge where he had previously been standing.

Neek looked and saw his relic necklace lying on the ledge Whizzle had just jumped from. Neek felt confused. Wasn't Whizzle just holding it? And where did Whizzle find it in the first place? Looking at Whizzle's wicked grin though, Neek began to understand the nasty trick his brother was pulling on him.

"Barnag almost died because of you, Neek," Whizzle said with a scowl. "You led him to that dangerous cave where he broke his leg and was almost eaten. And still, everyone treats you like a hero. Well, if you're such a hero, Neek, go grab your necklace. It shouldn't be a problem for an All-Shade like you." Whizzle smiled, turning back toward the tunnel where the others Rocklings were waiting above. "See you later hero," Whizzle joked, taunting Neek as he left.

And so, there it was again, time. His great enemy. Neek could run up to the Guards and explain everything, but surely Whizzle would lie, and who knows how they would react. With the Goblin scare from earlier, he was doubtful the Guards would help him, and if Neek didn't get the necklace now, the splashing water from the stream might wash it down into the hole. Whizzle had left it precariously near the edge. A rat or some other such creature might come along and knock it down or run off with it. It was now or never. Neek had to act.

Time is especially dangerous because when you feel its crushing weight upon you, you often make bad decisions. Risky choices you would never select if you could leisurely think things through seem somehow appealing instead. Taking a few steps back, Neek make such a decision, running and leaping over the gap to where his necklace lay. The roar of the stream below filled Neek's ears as he soared over it. Neek stumbled a bit upon landing, and felt like he might fall backwards, but he managed to grab the side of the cave and steady himself. Whew, I did it, Neek thought to himself, his heart racing. Neek reached down and grabbed his necklace, securing it carefully around his neck.

Turning back to the gap behind him though, time finally caught up with Neek. He realized the difficult situation his decision had landed him in. There was no room to back up here. No way to get a running start. Yet the distance he had to cross, the jump he had only barely accomplished, lay in front of him still, just as broad and treacherous as it had been before. Despite his feelings of anger and frustration toward his brother, Neek had to admit there was something impressive in Whizzle's ability to leap over this gap from a standing position. Whizzle was certainly a strong-legged Rockling. Could Neek match his strength? He wasn't so sure.

But what choice did he have? Neek could scream for help, but then he would surely be in big trouble for hopping to the ledge and getting himself into this mess in the first place. Altak would lecture him about his impulsive decision to give in to Whizzle's goading. Neek might be banned from swimming for good, or worse, banned from the playtime activities altogether. If Whizzle can do it, so can I, Neek decided. The young Rockling took a few deep breaths, coiled his legs, and sprang.

To his credit, Neek came quite close. He was only a few inches short. Unfortunately, a few inches short is a few inches too many when it comes to jumping a hole over a raging river of death. You either make it or you don't. Close just isn't good enough.

Sometimes our worst enemies become our best friends. So too, time can switch sides in our struggles. Yes, time marches on, and no, you can't avoid it, but time will mercifully slow down for you during a moment of pure terror. Perhaps it is not time itself that slows, but rather the mind which speeds up to such a degree that even time cannot keep pace. Certainly, as he was falling into the hole, Neek's mind raced at a million miles per hour. Somehow during his dizzying descent, in the few milliseconds Neek had before he would hit the water, his mind managed to communicate something important to his otherwise frozen body. "Your claws!" it screamed out to him. "Use your claws."

As fast as lightning, Neek grasped not just the idea, but also the edge of the rocky ledge in front of him. His hands lit up and he snatched frantically forward, sinking his claws into the stone and holding himself up, inches above the torrent below. Neek strained to lift himself, climbing slowly and painfully, using his claws to create handholds in the vertical wall of rock. Neek's feet were useless here, finding no purchase on the slippery, wet stone, soaked by the raging river below. His arms and shoulders ached as Neek pulled himself up, inch by agonizing inch, until he finally reached the top of the shaft. Neek wrenched himself over the edge and out of the hole. He curled up on the floor, panting heavily, his heart racing, his ears still full of the roar of the stream below.

Neek's body began to calm as it finally understood that the danger had passed. He had made it. He had survived. Neek felt for the necklace around his neck. It was still there. First-Mother, how can I ever repay you for these gifts, Neek thought? He gathered himself, took a few deep breaths, and stood up.

As Neek turned around, he was surprised to find that Whizzle hadn't left after all. His brother was standing right in front of him, only a foot or so from where Neek was just getting to his feet. "Nice jump," Whizzle said, as he pushed Neek hard in the chest, sending the helpless young Rockling through the opening and down into the rushing water below.

"Nice fall too," Whizzle added with a chuckle, as he watched Neek being swept away by the wall of water thrashing through the pit. Whizzle smiled a wide smile, his jagged cluttermouth teeth pointing wildly in every direction. He then turned and ran up the tunnel toward the others.

"Come quick, come quick!" Whizzle yelled, his voice changing tone yet again. "There has been a terrible accident."

CHAPTER 5
SILVER FISH

MakMak, the Rockling Chief, was outraged. "How could you let this happen?" she yelled at Inko and Urbar, the two Guards who were supposed to be watching the younglings during their afternoon swim. "We successfully repel a Goblin attack, and you carelessly let our precious All-Shade fall in a river? You two will be cleaning out the tribal toilet caves until he returns. And if he doesn't return, you'll be working in there for good!" she screamed.

Dragon-Mother Malika, who was in charge of caring for the young, felt as angry as Chief MakMak sounded. Her many years of dealing with children had taught Malika the patience to control her anger though, and she just sat watching silently. Truthfully, her feelings of heartache were too strong for her anger to move her to action in any case. How cursed this beautiful child seemed to be. First, he had been trapped in a cave in and almost eaten by a Rock Boar, and now he was lost, somewhere in the watery tunnels underground. She knew few Rocklings ever returned from such falls. I shall never see Neek again, she thought. And she held a tooth on her necklace, one that looked slightly out of place compared to its siblings, for a good long time, rubbing it mournfully as small tears made their way down her cheek.

Malika wasn't so sure about the story Whizzle was giving

them. "He was looking for his relic necklace," the boy with the wickedly full mouth of mismatched teeth had claimed, repeating his account yet again for the tribal leaders. "He must have been distracted because he got too close to the stream opening and tripped and fell in. I tried to grab him, but the river washed him away."

No, Malika didn't trust this story at all. Neek was many things, but careless and clumsy he was not. Even a groggy Rockling would be hard pressed to miss the sound of a raging underground stream and just accidentally fall in a giant gaping hole like that. If her people were that slow-witted, Rocklings would have died out centuries ago, she thought. That's the kind of thing a Goblin might do on a bad day perhaps, but not a clever young Rockling like Neek. What's more, if Whizzle's story was true, if he had tried to fish Neek out, why wasn't Whizzle wet? Why wasn't there dirt or gravel on his knees or elbows? Malika's instinct for the truth was well-honed. After so many years of working with younglings, who often tried to disguise their failings with fibs, she knew the dimensions of an honest face. This boy, even disregarding his off-putting jaw, didn't have an ounce of honesty in his eyes whatsoever.

"Well dear, you've had a tough day," Malika said to Whizzle reassuringly. "I'm sure the Goblin raid frightened you, and the loss of your brother must be very difficult for you as well. Why don't you go and get some food and some rest?" She noticed far too much relief wash over the boy's face as Whizzle thanked her and the Chief before running off toward the kitchens.

"I don't trust that boy one bit," Malika said to Chief MakMak. "I would have him watched, from the shadows. He may be a clan cleaver. I fear this is a truly tragic day for our tribe."

Chief MakMak's eyes widened. It was rare to hear Malika, well known for her calm temperament and careful words, say something so harsh about anyone, much less a young member of the tribe. "A clan cleaver? Are you sure, Dragon-Mother?" MakMak asked.

"His story is a lie. That much I can tell you," Malika replied. "Neek did end up down in that hole. That I believe. But from a clumsy fall? No. The boy's tale is a partial truth at best."

MakMak considered Malika's words. In Rockling society, since social cooperation was so vital to day-to-day survival, it was rare for members of the tribe to purposefully try to hurt each other. Fights broke out sometimes, of course. Members of the tribe might quarrel. But someone purposefully trying to kill one of their own siblings? That could not be tolerated. Such social deviants were called clan cleavers, and represented a fundamental threat to the tribe's survival. Behavior like that ripped at the fabric of the tribe, and so such individuals were exiled, branded with a mark, and forced out into the darkness alone. Could Whizzle truly be so depraved a creature at such a young age? MakMak wasn't sure she could believe it.

What might the boy be hiding, the Chief wondered, her eyes turning to the other problems in the room. "It's your lucky day," MakMak told Inko and Urbar, the two Guards she had been berating a moment earlier. "Toilet duty will have to wait. I want you to watch the boy, from a distance, silent as shadows. See if he tells those who are close to him a different tale when he doesn't know adults are watching."

"Anything you wish, my Chief," Inko responded. "But you should know I am not the best at hiding. I did poorly in that part of my Trials, and I've never had the knack. Urbar, on the other hand, he is quiet as the grave. Perhaps he would be better off doing this alone. And if I may speak honestly my Chief, I was hoping I might be allowed to join the expedition being sent to try to find the boy. I am good with unknown tunnels, and nearly joined the Explorers instead of the Tribal Guard."

"If only you had," MakMak replied angrily, "perhaps some other Rockling would have been a more diligent and our child would not now be lost." Inko's face fell in disgrace, clearly hurt by her words. "Still, you do speak some wisdom. Urbar, you go and watch the toothy one. Let me know what you find." Urbar nodded and left. "And you," she said to Inko, fiercely poking him in the chest with her longest finger, "you go and join the searchers, and be sure you bring Neek back." Inko nodded and left as well.

A Goblin attack, the blessed child lost, and now possibly a young killer in their ranks? MakMak closed her eyes, put her hand to her head, and worried for the future of her tribe.

∽

So startled was he by the actions of his brother, that it took Neek a moment to fully process that he was falling. Even after hitting the icy cold water, his first impulse was to look up at that awful toothy grin and wonder why. Why had Whizzle done this to him?

The rushing waters gave the young Rockling precious little time to think though. Neek was being swept along at a faster pace than he could ever remember moving in his entire life. The stream was mercifully deep, so Neek managed to avoid banging into any jagged rocks on the bottom of the tunnel, but he was overwhelmed by the bitter chill of the water around him. This was not the warm, egg-like comfort he was used to in his pools above, so carefully heated by his beloved Dragon-Mother. No, this was, from the feel of it, freshly melted runoff from high up on the mountain somewhere, cold as death, and angry. The current buffeted him to and fro within the tunnel chamber. The water lurched rapidly left then right, falling downward sometimes in miniature spurts that flung him head over heels. Though he hadn't hit any sharp rocks yet, the moving water banged him against the sides of the chamber a great many times, and Neek was sore all over. Sore, confused, cold, and dizzy from the rapid movement forward, as on and on the water roared.

Cold-blooded by birth, Rocklings generally try to avoid the cold as much as possible. Though they don't need the light to see, Rockling warrens are full of great fires so their occupants can enjoy the warmth the flames bring to what can be otherwise a wet and chilly life under the earth. Those Rocklings who live in frostier environments have generally evolved a different, thicker type of scale, to better protect themselves against the cold of the ice. Neek unfortunately was no Snow Rockling. His warren was nestled beneath a warm valley, green, and full of sunshine. Their caves were cool, but never freezing. The same could not be said of the waters that surrounded him now. This was a frigid river of ice, and Neek began to lose feeling in his hands and feet. He wasn't sure how much longer he could endure it.

Just as Neek was starting to feel his vision fade, the tunnel turned, dumping him into a massive, roundish chamber where the water rose all the way to the ceiling. There was no pocket of space where the young Rockling could poke his head up for air. Neek was running out of breath. So much for the cold, he had bigger worries now.

As Inko entered the Tunnel Wardens' main chamber, he saw there were about ten Rocklings inside already. They were huddled around a number of maps sketched out on large pieces of parchment covering a grand table in the center of the room. There were a few Warriors Inko recognized, including Erratoog, second in command in the warren's military behind Bartok. Senior Wardens, Explorers, and the clan's Head Tunnel Carver were all in attendance. It was clear MakMak had made this rescue mission a priority.

"We know quite little about these streams," Torgal was explaining to the group. "We know where the water comes from, as it links to some of the main flows we've used for years now. Where this water goes to though, that is largely a mystery. If we are lucky," he said, motioning to parts of the maps where a great many twisting, intertwined tunnels were drawn, "it turns north, where we are well-versed. If it turns south, or goes straight, however, we have much exploration to do. We know almost nothing of the paths of the water in those directions."

"We can send pots of colored dye down the stream," Pripo, one of the younger Wardens suggested. "If we position people at the pools we do know, we can send the pots down and see if we notice them, or any of their colors flowing through the pools farther along. That might give us a sense of the direction the water would have taken him."

"That's a fine idea, Pripo," Torgal responded, impressed with the youngster for coming up with a strategy so quickly. "While we do the research, which will take time, some of us can go out and search in groups. Search parties can test some of the most promising veins and hope to get lucky. Time is not our friend here," he warned. Neek was clever, but very young. And water was always a danger. Torgal knew this.

"We should send three groups of four members each," Aloo suggested. He was the tribe's oldest and wisest Explorer. "Two Warriors and two Explorers in each party will mean they can split up if needed, to follow the various branches they find."

While the Wardens are tasked in Rockling society with digging, shaping, archiving, and maintaining tunnels, it is the Explorers who go out and search the more peripheral places the tribe has never visited before. Explorers must be stealthy, clever, and brave. Their lives are often more dangerous than those of the Warriors, except of course during times of war. During those times, Explorers often act as Warriors, and are some of the most feared Rockling soldiers.

"How quickly can you leave?" asked Torgal.

"I already have supplies being prepared," responded Aloo. "It will be a matter of moments before we can go."

"Good. Go then, and may the First-Mother watch over you," Torgal directed them. "You may select the groups, Erratoog."

Erratoog identified teams of four, as Aloo has suggested, assigning Inko, the disgraced Guard, after Inko had begged him earnestly, to one of the three search parties. Rocklings from the kitchens arrived shortly with the provisions and other supplies the groups would need for their journey. May I live long enough to see my home again, Inko thought to himself as he exited the chamber with his team. I will not return until I have found the missing child, he promised the First-Mother silently, heading out resolutely into the dark.

Neek didn't understand how he was still alive. He didn't seem to be breathing, but he also didn't seem to need to breathe anymore. Was he dead, he wondered? Was he a ghost now, doomed to spend eternity in this watery sphere? He looked at his scales, and seeing that their color had changed, feared this must be the truth. His body was a light silver color, and his scales seemed somehow flatter than normal. There were lines running along his body, but the borders between his scales had disappeared, and a solidly connected silver shell now covered Neek's entire form.

Moments earlier, dropping down into the expanse of water he was now surrounded by, Neek had looked around frantically. He twisted and turned but there was nowhere Neek could find to poke his snout out of the water to breathe the air he so desperately needed. The cold was overwhelming to him, his skin in agony, singing for relief. And with each second, Neek's lungs had felt more and more sore, as he hopelessly hunted for oxygen. Finally, after several long minutes of struggle, his eyes had glazed over. Neek remembered it now. His vision turned everything silver, and his lungs had stopped hurting. Neek wasn't so cold after that. Yes, he must be a ghost.

Just as Neek realized he might be spending the rest of eternity haunting this underground prison, he felt a curious sensation in his stomach. It grumbled. He paused for a few moments, and then it grumbled again. Did ghosts get hungry, Neek wondered? He wasn't sure. He certainly was starving though. His stomach was becoming as demanding as his lungs had been only a few moments earlier. What did ghosts eat, he wondered? He had heard precious few stories about ghosts, and certainly didn't remember any that involved them sitting down for dinner. He reached out to touch the cavern wall. His hand bumped firmly against it. Weren't ghosts supposed to pass through walls, to make their own secret tunnels between places, even across time?

Well, whatever he was now, Neek knew that he was hungry. He would have to find some way out of the chamber he was trapped in to hunt down something to eat. Since air was no longer an issue for him, Neek started scanning the bottom and sides of the cave for holes, and saw, deep down on the cavern floor below, a number of openings in the rock. Some of them looked large enough for him to fit through. He flipped his silvery body around in the water and began to swim toward the bottom of the cave.

The Cave Eel was hungry. And bored. Less and less fish had been pouring in from the river above. Clearly someone else, perhaps another Eel, was poaching his fish upstream, leaving less for him. Still he shouldn't complain, he supposed. He had been living in this cave for months now, maybe longer, with lots of fish, bright beautiful fish, to eat and play with.

Cave Eels, despite their fearsome reputation, are generally quite lazy. They like to find a place to hide out, and pick off shiny little fish as they swim by. If they find a good spot, a Cave Eel will stay there as long as possible, their whole life even, rather than having to swim off and find a new place to hunt. This laziness is perhaps why Cave Eels will fight so ferociously to protect their temporary homes, the holes they inhabit. The Cave Eel's viciousness, combined with its notoriously large fangs, and its famously fatal poison, make it a creature the average cave dweller hopes never to run across during an afternoon swim.

This particular Eel was exceedingly lethargic and quite fat. The fish had been so plentiful previously that he had grown huge and happy in his quiet little corner in the rock. Over the past few weeks though, the fish supply was diminished, and as a result the Eel was losing the paunch he had so proudly developed in his middle.

The last thing he wanted was to go back to being long and thin like the other Eels he'd known, a shape the Eel had experienced previously during the more trying times in his life. So, the Eel was quite excited when he saw the gigantic meal that had dropped in almost on top of him from the hole up above. He had never seen a fish quite like this one. It was scaly, yes, but it had a tail and horns, and no obvious fins. Its scales, while colorful and pretty in places, were overall mostly brownish red. Despite the fish's grand size, the Eel was a tad disappointed. He loved shiny fish, and this one, barring its few flashes of color, was a bit dull.

After a few moments of watching the thing above thrashing about, it was clear it didn't move well enough in the water to be a fish. The Eel looked on eagerly as the beast's entire body began to change to a lovely, silvery color. Ooh, this would be tasty treat after all. The creature had even started swimming straight toward him. Goodness, was he dreaming, the Eel wondered? If he had hands, perhaps he would have pinched himself to make sure he was awake. What a day this was indeed! His belly would be massive again in no time.

∼

Whizzle was thrilled. He had done it. Neek was gone, and nobody blamed him. The Chief and the other elders had questioned him, sure, but at the end of it all, was he in trouble? Nope. They had sent him off to dinner with a break from evening lessons. And he had even been given triple portions. He was licking tasty little bits out of his mangled teeth as he excitedly finished yet another huge bowl of stew.

The only bad thing was everyone seemed so gloomy. His siblings in particular were really being a drag. Margle wouldn't stop going on and on about Neek. Crybaby. Maybe I'll push her down next, he thought, a smile appearing for a moment on the irritated Rockling's face.

Whizzle couldn't take the crying anymore and went to talk to Barnag. "Come on Barnag, let's go practice our sword fighting."

"Sure, sure, let's go," Barnag agreed.

Whizzle found Barnag almost as confusing as the rest of the Rocklings his age. He expected Barnag would be smiling and happy, like him, but instead Barnag seemed conflicted. He doesn't want anyone to know how he feels, Whizzle guessed. People would be angry if he was too happy about it. Well, some fighting should cheer him up, Whizzle figured, and some privacy might give them both a chance to be more honest. Regardless, with all his pent-up energy, Whizzle needed to hit something, and he know Barnag would be more than willing to oblige.

The two young boys left the children's room and headed out to the training area to spar with their heavy, dull swords.

At the edge of the darkness, a shadowy figure followed them.

As Neek descended toward the bottom of the pool, he started to realize that he must not be a ghost after all. This must be yet another one of the strange powers he seemed to be manifesting over the past few weeks. Somehow, back when he had confronted the Rock Boar, Neek had found the strength to push down that boulder. Earlier today, he had been able to cut stone with his claws. In both cases, his body had done something strange and unexpected. His scales glowed red when he was strong. His claws turned bright green when they sliced rock. This silver skin he now wore must be another effect, Neek decided.

His colored scales had always been a focus in his life of course. The whole tribe made a habit of watching him, and Dragon-Mother talked frequently with him about being an All-Shade and what his skin might mean. She had never mentioned anything resembling what was happening to him lately though. She had never suggested he would develop anything like these special abilities or powers. She spent most of her time talking about things like destiny and prophecy, things that sounded grand and important, but which you couldn't see or really get a handle on. She also told many fascinating stories about the First-Mother though, and some of the details from those tales seemed familiar. The First-Mother had shaped stone with her claws, hadn't she? She carved their world of caves with her magnificent hands. Neek didn't recall anything about her going red, but of course she was strong. The First-Mother could move mountains. Did she ever turn silver? Or live under the water? Neek couldn't recall. The young Rockling regretted not listening more closely to Malika's stories. If he ever returned home, he promised himself, he would listen carefully to everything she said about the First-Mother. And he would share with her all the things he had recently learned to do.

Neek was approaching the opening at the bottom of the cave now, and it appeared that there was a light coming from the chamber below. At least I'll get out of this watery prison, he thought, heading to the edge of the hole.

～

All animals have some kind of wisdom, some specialized intelligence we would be lucky to learn from. Cave Eels know a great many things, including how to pick a good hole to sleep in, safe from prying eyes. They know the patterns fish follow when they swim, and perhaps most importantly to their survival, Eels know how to ambush a fish without letting it escape. Young Eels make the common mistake of trying to reach a fish that is too far outside their hiding spot. The hunger gets to them, and eager to use their poisonous fangs, the impatient Eels leap out prematurely. Young Eels are very quick, so sometimes they get lucky in these situations, but more often they spring out only to have the little fish fly off in the other direction, never to be seen again.

The problem is that every creature, big or small, intelligent or dim, gets nervous when going through a doorway, or into a hole in the ground. There is something about crossing a boundary, leaving one space and entering another, that all creatures instinctively fear. Older Eels understand this, so they patiently wait until the fish is as close as possible before pouncing. Ideally, you wait for the fish to poke its head into your lair, looking for something to eat, and then bam, dinner is yours, with no hope of escape for the poor little swimmer.

Today was clearly one of those lucky days. Not only had the giant creature fallen into the Eel's cave, and turned his favorite shade of silver, but now it was swimming directly toward him. Its arms were already entering the tunnel where the hungry Eel lay in wait. A few more moments and he would bite the fish in its neck, ensuring not just that it wouldn't be able to escape, but that it wouldn't even put up a fight. If the Eel had hands, he would have been rubbing them together in glee. Just a few moments more.

～

Neek felt a bit nervous as he pushed into the hole at the bottom of the cave. If there wasn't an exit down here, he wasn't sure how he would be able to get out. The other holes he had seen were too small for him to fit through. So, if this one didn't work, what next? Neek wasn't sure. He tried using his nails to cut his way out of the cave, but as he had activated them, the silver skin had faded, and he had grown cold and gasped for air again. He couldn't use both gifts at the same time it seemed. Hopefully there would be an exit through this hole in the rocks leading out into an open cave system and a way home.

Neek had pulled about half of his body through the opening, moving into the chamber beyond, when he noticed a hint of green out of the corner of his eye. There was a long, thick, tubular creature headed straight toward him. It reached him so quickly that all Neek could see was its broad, wide mouth full of yellowed fangs. Neek tried to turn away as it wrapped its mouth around his neck and bit down. Hard.

∼

Whizzle started to feel nervous. They had been bashing each other for nearly half an hour now, and Barnag still hadn't pulled out of his sulk. Could it be that he was actually sad that Neek was gone? Whizzle had done what he had to protect his friend, to shield Barnag from the lies and the shame that settled around him after Neek had made up his terrible stories.

"Are you okay?" Whizzle finally asked, as they took a break from a particularly brisk series of sword strikes. "I thought with what Neek did to you in the cave, putting you in danger and all, that you'd be happy to be rid of him."

"Well, yes, I suppose we are better off without him," Barnag conceded. "I'll be happy not to hear his version of the Boar story again. You'd think he had done all the work himself from the way he tells it. I scared the beast off in the end, you know. Neek just danced around and was useless." If Malika had been watching, she would have noticed the signals in Barnag's eyes that he really didn't believe any of what he was saying.

"With Neek around, no one would have bothered to notice what fine Warriors we are becoming," Whizzle argued. "Look how good you are with a sword, how quickly you move from defense to attack. Does anyone ever talk about that? Or how you can hold your breath for longer than anyone else? No, nothing about us. It's always just Neek, Neek, Neek. That's all they talk about. Neek the freak. Do you think any of that would ever have changed?"

"You're right, I guess," Barnag mumbled. "It is good that he is gone. We would have always been in his shadow."

Whizzle saw the hint of something coming from his friend, the first suggestion of an honest smile he had noticed since Neek and Barnag had returned to the warren from their ordeal. Whizzle's fears eased a little.

"I'm kind of surprised he fell though," Barnag continued. "Neek was too scared to even try jumping over that hole, remember? Why was his necklace even over there?"

"Maybe someone else put it there," Whizzle suggested coyly.

"Maybe someone brave forced him to try it." Whizzle puffed out his chest with pride.

"What are you talking about?" Barnag asked. There was an uneasy turn in his stomach.

"You saw him," Whizzle continued, "he was a coward earlier, like always." His face had broken into a smile now, his clutter of teeth visible from ear to ear. "I just decided to give him a little motivation."

Barnag looked as if he was going to ask something but stopped. He seemed to be looking for something in Whizzle's face. They were both completely still.

"He made the jump there, you know," Whizzle confided, breaking the tense silence. "He made it back too. Just barely. Not like me. I jumped way over. Neek had to catch the edge and climb up. You should have seen the look on his face. He thought he was in the clear. I had to do it though. For you, Barnag. It didn't take much. Just a little push. "

Whizzle looked down now, making small, barely perceptible pushing motions with his arms, waiting for his friend to react. Barnag was looking down also. He had stopped breathing.

A second passed, and then another. It was as if neither boy was going to breathe or speak again unless the other gave in first. Whizzle looked for some kind of confirmation from his friend, and finding nothing, picked up the sword Barnag had let fall to the ground and handed it back to him.

"Come on," Whizzle insisted with a nervous laugh, "let's get back to the fun." Whizzle lifted his own sword in a playful challenge as if nothing significant had just passed between them. Whatever had been said would just as quickly be forgotten.

After a long look, Barnag reluctantly raised his sword and rejoined the fray. Their mock battle resumed and the boys sparred furiously, their blades banging loudly against one another, echoing against the cave walls. Whatever they hadn't the strength to say to one another in words was communicated through their spirited battle instead.

If his feet made any noise, the sword fight would have covered it. But they made none. No noise at all. And as the boys continued sparring, Urbar slipped out of his hiding spot and down into the tunnel's dark shadows. It wasn't far from here to the Chief's cave.

∼

The Eel's timing was perfect. The fish had poked its head past his hole, mere inches from where he lay waiting patiently. The Eel swam out in a flash and bit down on the creature's neck, a precise engulfing strike. After such a well-executed plan, the Eel was thoroughly shocked and bitterly disappointed to feel its teeth clang feebly against his victim's flesh. This strange fish was as hard as rock. The Eel's confidence was perhaps overdeveloped, and it took him a few moments to understand the hopelessness of its attack as it snapped a second time, and then a third. The Eel finally gave up, but too late, as in its final attack the Eel shattered its fangs on Neek's silvery skin.

Horrified, the Eel pulled away. Eels do sometimes break their fangs. Usually this is when they are very, very old and near to the end of life. Though a mature beast, this Eel had a long stretch of years ahead of him still, and living with broken fangs meant dining primarily on dead fish, algae, and whatever other substances could be gummed up off the rock side. It was terrible, one of the worst fates that could happen to an Eel. Fangs didn't grow back. Time didn't go backwards either.

And he had planned things so carefully, the Eel thought. He had been so patient. The wounded beast sank back sullenly into his hole, and if he could, he would have wept. But Cave Eels cannot cry, they can merely think long and hard about the occasional bad decisions that haunt every life.

∼

The creature had him. He was in its jaws and its teeth were around him. And then, well, then nothing really. He didn't even feel it bite down. There was a bit of blood, but that seemed to be coming from the green thing that had attacked him. Then the fanged menace had fled, slinking back into its hole.

There might be more creatures coming, Neek worried, so he wouldn't wait around. He fled quickly through the hole into the chamber beyond. After passing through a few more meandering passageways, and swimming for what felt like an eternity, Neek finally reached a cave where there was open air above. He hurried to the surface and pulled himself out of the water. Neek crawled a few feet from the pool's edge and looked back, half expecting a swarm of green things to leap out after him. But nothing came. The water's surface was a still black mirror. All Neek noticed was a hint of his own face where the bluish light from the growth on the walls cast his reflection in the pool.

Neek relaxed out of his silver form, transforming back to his normal color. He sat for a few minutes, enjoying the feel of air in his lungs again. He remembered the creature that had nearly eaten him and was grateful for the unexpected strength of his altered skin. When I am silver like that, my skin is somehow armored, Neek realized. That's why I couldn't feel the bite. First-Mother, thank you for your gifts, Neek prayed silently. And as he huddled there, looking around an unfamiliar chamber, far from home, Neek wished for her guidance. He was cold, hungry, soaked, and all alone, far below the earth, with no clue which direction he should head next.

Neek hung his head, and wept. He was thankful, but exhausted. Relieved, but terrified. He leaned up against the glowing cave moss that went dark at his touch, and closed his eyes. In a few moments, Neek was asleep.

CHAPTER 6
TINY FRIENDS

Without the rising and setting sun to guide you, it can be difficult to tell time underground. Those closer to the surface can sometimes tell by the slight variations in warmth and cool whether the sun is overhead, and thus by the variation in temperature can sense time passing. Those deeper down must depend upon artificial means, such as magical devices, or the regular rhythm of the rituals of daily life, meals, work, and so on, to get their bearings. All alone, very deep in the earth, without gadgets or magic or his tribe to help him, Neek had no idea how much time had gone by while he was asleep.

He would likely have slept longer, but he was disturbed, quite rudely, by the sensation of something biting his toe. He sprang awake then, kicking out at whatever had latched onto him, and saw with revulsion that it was a rat. It chirped at him, menacingly, though it was tiny in comparison to Neek's admittedly meager form. Cave rats are a great source of sustenance, and Neek, hungry as he was, would have been happy to see it, even though it had bitten him, except it did not appear to be alone. The rat was only the closest of a great many that seemed to be swarming into the chamber where he had been resting.

Neek thought initially to turn his scaly skin silver again and shield himself, but he was so hungry, and tired, and sore, it didn't seem to work. His scales flickered silver briefly, but then changed back again to their normal hue. Just as Rocklings, when working together, could defeat larger foes, so rats, in a swarm such as this, would likely make a meal of a Rockling. Neek knew he was in trouble, and he turned and dashed toward the tunnel at the other end of the chamber. After running a few hundred feet though, the tunnel ended abruptly, with no exit in sight.

Neek turned and saw the horde of rats advancing on him, hunger in their beady black eyes.

Pripo's plan had worked brilliantly. They caught a lucky break. The pots of colored dye the Wardens released into the river where Neek fell had delivered color through the water downstream, and traces of the distinctive, fluorescent green pigment were found by one of the lookouts at a known watering hole in a region to the north of their warren. Of all the directions Neek might have been carried by the stream, this was likely to be the most hospitable. Word was sent to the scouting parties who fanned out in all directions from where the dye had been spotted.

There was still hope.

Chief MakMak, despite the good news, was feeling dispirited and more than a little bit ill. Urbar's spying had succeeded in bringing her the ugly truth that Whizzle had pushed Neek into the river. Such an awful act demanded a swift and decisive response. To exile a young one, however, was unheard of. MakMak couldn't remember the last time such a thing had been done. The thought that something like this should happen in her tribe under her leadership made her anger shift for a moment from Whizzle onto herself. How had she let things in the warren get to such a sorry state?

MakMak knew that being a leader meant sometimes doing things that were unpleasant. Much as MakMak dreaded the confusion and sadness that the revelation of Whizzle's crimes and his exile would bring to the warren, the safety of the tribe came first. Not only had this foul boy tried to kill another Rockling, he had attacked the blessed child, the chosen one the tribe was so hopeful about. There was no choice. Whizzle had to go.

MakMak explained her orders carefully to Eekee, her Guard and assistant. "Bartok must handle this swiftly and quietly," she insisted. "Return and tell me when it is done." Eekee left, to carry out her request, and the Chief sat, hands on her head, wondering how many more things could go wrong on this awful day.

Normally, it is easy to deal with a single rat. You can hit it with a rock. Poke it with a stick. Honestly, if you are quick enough, you can just give it a quick kick, and it'll go, scurrying away, never to bother you again. A hundred rats though was a different story, and there might well be more than two hundred here, Neek thought, as he stared at the mass of approaching fur and glimmering eyes.

Neek could rely on his claws for some defense, but there were too many of them for him to handle on his own. He had his silver scale armor, but that wasn't working. There were a few rocks lying around, but he would only be able to take a few of them out before being overwhelmed. If it had been a tall chamber, he could perhaps have climbed up and out of the way, but the ceilings were short here, with no clear footholds in the walls to climb. He should have been more careful than to sleep in the open. A clever Rockling always made sure their temporary home was safe and they were out of sight. Such regrets were useless now though and wouldn't stop the horde of vermin that were just a few feet from reaching him.

Neek wracked his brain, but no useful plan came to mind. As the rats reached him, his thoughts were no longer of what he could do to escape, but of the Rocklings he loved, and the home he missed, and the crazy things he had experienced lately. Out of hope, and without a plan to act upon, Neek decided just to scream at the top of his lungs. It wouldn't scare them away, but it would make him feel better. It would be something to hold onto during his few remaining moments of life.

～

Whizzle lay on his mat in the younglings' sleeping area feeling fairly content. His belly was full. His body was comfortably tired after more than an hour of swordplay. Most importantly, Whizzle had shared his troubling secret with his best friend Barnag, and he seemed to approve of it.

Life was going to change around the warren. His brothers and sisters would see now that he, despite his funny teeth, was a fearsome Warrior. He and Barnag were both strong. They would protect the tribe.

No more would he have to hear about Neek and his silly scales. Now he and Barnag would be the talk of the warren.

Whizzle felt pretty good, right up until the moment when a pair of hands covered his eyes and his mouth, and another set of hands grabbed his body and picked him up out of bed. In a matter of seconds, he was bound, gagged, and whisked out of the sleeping chamber. It was done so quickly, so quietly, that not even little Margle batted an eye.

All the young Rocklings slept soundly, unaware of what transpired around them. They would wake up to find two newly empty beds the next morning.

～

So panicked was he in that final moment, as the rats were about to reach him, that one wonders what words would have erupted from Neek's mouth had he been able to scream. Would he have shouted curses at them? Would he have let out a heart-wrenching roar, perhaps filling them with fear? Would he have shared something profound in his last moments? Or would he have scrambled around for something simple like "No!" or "Go away!" in the hope his wishes would be granted by some mysterious force?

What might have been said, we'll never know, for when Neek opened his mouth, what erupted was not a scream, but instead a steady stream of fire, pouring out in the direction of his terror. The flames covered the chamber floor and walls, smothering entirely the hungry carpet of approaching rats. In a brief, bright flash, all those beady eyes went blank. Their fur went up in flames, and the swarm stopped its advance. After that single terrible moment, not another squeak was audible in the cave.

As the fearsome fire had done, all of Neek's remaining energy left his body at once. He felt faint, fell back against the cave wall, and everything went black. It was as if the whole world just disappeared.

Runners went back and forth constantly between the warren and the makeshift camp the search groups set up near where Pripo's dye had been spotted. They ferried food, supplies, and news between the tribe and the groups of Warriors and Explorers searching for the lost youngling.

Most of the runners were chosen for their speed and their sense of direction. There was no time to lose, and only the swiftest and those that would easily find their way without error were selected. The latest runner though had been chosen primarily for his physical strength. You had to be strong to run with two young Rocklings on your back.

Whizzle and Barnag were wrapped up tight in a bag, their mouths bound, headed to the edge of the known Rockling world. They were both wide awake as the runner ferried them through the meandering tunnels toward exile. They could see hints of what was around them through gaps in the bag, and looked out with horror as the passages they were being carried through become increasingly unfamiliar. The brothers wondered how they would possibly survive without the tribe as a part of their lives.

Chief MakMak's sentence had been clear and firm, delivered swiftly and without debate. The boys couldn't have protested even if they'd wanted to. They were bound and gagged. Others in attendance, clearly disgusted by what they saw in front of them, refused to acknowledge the young Rocklings.

"Whizzle, we know you pushed Neek in that river," she told them sternly. "He is likely dead. Even if he lives, what you did is unforgivable. Barnag, you didn't push Neek in, but Whizzle shared his crime with you, and you did not report it. That makes you as guilty as he is. You are both a threat to the tribe, and you will live with us no longer. You are exiled. You will be taken by Barg here to the edge of our known lands and released. Tunnels will be collapsed behind you. You are no longer welcome in this warren. If you return, you will be killed. Normally clan cleavers such as you are branded, to warn any tribe from taking them. Because you are so young, and I hope that you may perhaps someday learn how wrong you were in what you did, you will not be branded in this manner. If you can get another tribe to take you, they are welcome to you. This warren, however, is not now, and will never again be your home."

And with that, Whizzle and Barnag found themselves bundled into a sack, heading farther away from things they knew than they had gone even in their worst nightmares, far away into the deep darkness.

∼

Neek woke again to the sensation of something grabbing his foot. Rather than the sharp teeth that had seized him earlier, he felt warm, soothing tendrils covering the area where he had been bitten. The marks left by the rat's teeth were no longer painful, and when he sat up to have a look, Neek saw the tiny wounds themselves were almost completely healed.

The little white tendrils touching his foot were connected to what looked like a large white mushroom with red and gold spots on its cap. The mushroom seemed to move the tendrils about like arms, shifting purposefully over the young Rockling's skin.

Neek had seen a great many mushrooms in his short life. They littered the caverns and were a staple in the Rockling diet. That said, Neek had never come across one with arms like this. Seemingly finished with its work, the mushroom pulled its tendrils back into its body. It lifted its cap to look at him, and Neek caught a glimpse of two eyes and a thin mouth. The mushroom was smiling. It turned, lifted two tendril-like feet out of the ground, and walked toward the pile of burnt rats farther down the chamber.

Neek was truly astounded. He could understand how a mushroom might have reaching tendrils. They were probably useful for grabbing nearby food, and resembled the roots most plants possessed. But a mushroom that could walk? He had never imagined such a thing might exist. Certainly, none of the mushrooms he had ever been served in the Rockling dining hall had gotten up and walked off like that.

He watched, transfixed as the little white mushroom creature went over to the pile of rats and extended its tendrils once more. This time it clearly wasn't healing. The rats were beyond such help. Neek could see tiny globules of red and black slide along the tendril hands to the central stalk of the mushroom where they seemed to disappear. These are being ingested, Neek surmised. This must be how it eats. And as the tiny globules were consumed the gold and red spots on top of the mushroom grew brighter in color. Was this the mushroom signaling its satisfaction?

The mushroom's meal brought to mind Neek's own hunger. While many races won't touch a rat in the kitchen, to Rocklings it is a welcome source of protein. They are plentiful in the underneath, and in such a dark and desolate place, one cannot be so picky. The strange fire that had erupted from him had clearly cooked these creatures, so Neek sat next to his new mushroom friend and joined in the meal.

His fascination with the creature distracted Neek temporarily from his recent troubles. He was still lost. Still alone. Still very far from home with no notion of how to get back there. But none of that mattered to him just now. He was singularly focused on this strange and wonderful mushroom creature.

As they sat together eating, Neek noticed other, similar mushrooms make their way tentatively toward the feast. These new mushrooms moved much more slowly than the first. Their skins were darker, and their spots dimmer than the little one who had healed him.

Of all the strange things Neek had seen in his life, this was by far his favorite. He wanted more than anything to understand this creature, to get a sense of its life, its slow and slippery world. If only I could talk to you, he thought. Neek wanted to thank the little one. The mushroom had healed his foot, and in some unexplainable way was helping to heal his heart as well.

"You probably cannot understand me, but I wish to thank you," Neek said, smiling at his mushroom friend. "My strength is greatly renewed, and I will surely need it during the travels ahead of me."

Neek fell over once more, this time from shock rather than exhaustion, when he heard in his mind the tiny mushroom reply! "You are very welcome," it told him. "My name is Mohmoh. May I join you on your journey?"

CHAPTER 7
SENSE OF DIRECTION

It was a strange sensation. The words didn't reach Neek through his ears. No, they were spoken inside his mind, directly to his brain. Mohmoh's soft, sweet voice had a lilt and an accent to it, and his words conveyed emotion. But if Neek covered his ears, the message came through all the same. Somehow the mushroom was communicating without what would normally be called speaking.

Mohmoh understood Neek in the same way, but it took the young Rockling a while to comprehend this. Neek continued to speak out loud, asking Mohmoh about his life and his world, while the mushroom answered him with words but no sound, connecting directly with Neek's mind.

Mohmoh's stories were so fascinating, and the life he was describing so different than Neek's, that it took a while before the Rockling asked his new friend about the peculiar way he communicated. All Pluffstacks share thoughts this way, Mohmoh explained. Pluffstack was the name he gave for his people. He was a Pluffstack just as Neek was a Rockling.

Apparently, by Pluffstack standards, Mohmoh was quite young. This meant that Mohmoh could move around quite quickly, and for great distances if he wanted. Mohmoh could go for days, he claimed, without nestling in the earth. Older

Pluffstacks, like the ones who showed up later to the meal, were very slow and less limber, unable to leave their roots out of the ground for more than a few minutes.

In their youth, Mohmoh explained, Pluffstacks like to travel. They go by any means they can, and try to get as far away from where they were born as their limbs and ingenuity will allow them. In this manner, Mohmoh explained, with noticeable pride, Pluffstacks were making their way all across the world, building their homes in new and different places, and enjoying the sights along the way.

"Don't you miss your tribe?" Neek asked. For a Rockling, the thought of venturing so far and for so long from their warren was a dreadful notion. Even those who took it upon themselves to explore the uncharted caves of their underground world were not as directly excited by the prospect of discovery itself as Mohmoh seemed to be. In Rockling life, exploration was a necessity for self-preservation, the need to have an escape plan if intruders came calling. For Mohmoh, clearly it meant something else, something joyful and hopeful.

The Pluffstack explained that as they moved around, members of his community left tiny traces in the ground they touched, and that other Pluffstacks could read these traces and experience them as memories.

"The ground is covered with my ancestors," Mohmoh shared. "I am almost never alone. And the farther I travel, and the more traces I leave, the more pathways I will open for the Pluffstacks that follow."

"We sense through one another," he continued. "We share in what we experience even though we are not physically present at the same time. Our world is made in the company of those who go before, as we accompany those who come after, so we are not confined to just our own imaginings and ideas. We sense through other consciousnesses, sometimes many of them, all at once. My mind is full of the thoughts I am lucky enough to inherit, and the ones I discover in my journeys. If I stayed in just one place, I

SENSE OF DIRECTION 119

would never meet all my unknown cousins, and the palette of my thoughts would be too limited. It would be like living in a world without shape or color or reason."

Neek nodded. It seemed wonderful, to never be alone. How he longed to hear the voices of his family. But when he touched the wall of the tunnels he walked down, they were silent, and cold. Still, he supposed there were some ways Rockling life shared a similarity to what Mohmoh was describing. He thought of the stories Malika told him, or Altak's jokes.

Mohmoh chuckled. "That's quite funny," he remarked, clearly hearing the joke Neek was remembering in his mind. "I'll have to share that one." And he touched the floor with his wispy white tendrils, writing Altak's joke into the ground for all future Pluffstacks to enjoy.

Neek asked Mohmoh how he had healed the young Rockling's foot so quickly. If there was anything Neek himself hoped to communicate to his tribe if and when he ever returned, this certainly was it. He had never seen anyone so miraculously or quickly fixed as he had been by his little friend.

The Pluffstack hesitated. Perhaps they had secrets after all, Neek thought, wondering if that was even possible given their special means of communication.

"I'm happy to tell you," Mohmoh responded, smiling, "I am just trying to find the concepts that will make sense to you." After a moment he continued, "My people live on the edge between life and death. Just as we transfer the energy from creatures that are no longer alive into ourselves to give us energy, so we can transmit that same energy back out, to help others. We feel this back and forth movement, the directions that the life force itself takes as it meanders through the world all around us. We use this knowledge to try to turn it back on itself in times of trouble, to show the body the road from illness back to health. Do you understand?"

Neek nodded, though inside he wasn't so sure. He certainly wished that he did. Neek suddenly felt very small next to the

Pluffstack, even though his little friend was far less imposing in stature. Whatever he had been told about the wisdom of the First-Mother, clearly there were a great many things he didn't know. Perhaps no Rockling had ever been introduced to such knowledge before. The feeling Neek had was almost as strange as when his skin changed color for the first time. This was a different kind of magic.

"And on the subject of secrets," Mohmoh said, interrupting Neek's reveries, "don't worry. If you wish to hide something, you can. It is taking me a few moments to figure you out, but I am starting to feel whether you want to share your ideas or not as you have them. I won't look at anything you don't want me to. My people tend to share everything, as sometimes the things you feel should be hidden are often quite useful, and make solving problems much easier, especially between two individuals, but I can understand that other creatures don't think as we do." He reached for Neek's hand and squeezed it softly, communicating the unmistakably clear signal of reliable friendship.

"Why did you help me?" Neek asked. "You didn't even know me."

"You fed my family," Mohmoh replied. "And I could feel you were connected to the flow of good things. You pulsate life as I do."

Neek wasn't sure what to make of Mohmoh's words. He understood them in some basic way, but they hinted at greater things that Neek felt he could only catch a brief glimpse of from his limited understanding. If this wonderful creature felt they were in any way similar, however, that in itself made Neek happy.

"And, how is it that we can speak, in our minds?" he asked, finally overcoming his embarrassment on the subject. He wanted to ask Mohmoh sooner, but he was overwhelmed by a new sense that the world was far larger than the maps in his home warren hinted at. "Do you speak with all creatures? No one in my tribe has ever told a story of such a thing."

"No," said Mohmoh, "I sometimes try to share thoughts with

the creatures I see in my journeys, or at least to understand what they are thinking, but I have never been able to share as clearly with anyone before as I can with you, except with my ancestors and people of my own kind, of course. I could hear your thoughts quite plainly before you ever spoke to me," Mohmoh explained.

Was this another strange aspect of his mysterious skin, Neek wondered, another gift from the First-Mother? He would have discussed it with his new friend but there were far more pressing matters to attend to. Where was this place he had ended up? Which way was his warren? How far was he from his home?

"You say you wish to travel with me," Neek indicated, "I would enjoy that too. Sadly, I don't know which way I am headed though. I need to return to my tribe. They will be worried for me. But I have no idea which way my home lies."

Mohmoh looked and him and smiled. "No problem," replied the little Pluffstack, who took Neek's hand and gently began to guide the young Rockling to his feet, "we will find a way together."

~

Whizzle and Barnag were miserable. They had so little with them. Only a few days worth of food. Two meager sleeping bags. A few simple tools. Two skins of water. No tribe. And absolutely no idea what they were going to do next.

In other circumstances they might have been happy to have each other for company, but they had bickered and argued all morning, and if they hadn't both been so scared, they might have dumped the other and headed out alone.

Barg had been very fair to them. He had checked the surrounding caverns for danger. He had given them the meager supplies they had. He had even helped them craft a small, makeshift camp with a crude door so they could sleep in relative safety.

Despite these kind gestures, Barg was obligated to follow the orders of his Chief, the voice of his tribe. And so, after the boys were situated, he bid them good luck, and collapsed the tunnels behind them. There was truly no way back. Even if they could find another way home, they were no longer welcome there.

"It's all your fault," argued Barnag. This was the most common thread of disagreement they had been circling around all morning. "Why did you push Neek down that hole? You know that is wrong, don't you? What did you think would happen?"

Whizzle was getting tired of hearing it. "I've told you already. He almost got you killed. He lied about the Boar. You hated him. You wanted him gone. Well, now he's gone."

"In case you haven't noticed," Barnag barked in reply, "we are gone too. And there's no going back. They would throw a festival for Neek if he returned, but they'll kill us if we show our faces again. That's on you. You!"

Despite his angry words and loud screams, Barnag knew there was really no difference between them. He had tried to cave in the tunnel on Neek. Maybe that wasn't as deadly a threat as pushing him in a river, but Chief MakMak would have been just as angry if she had known. The only true difference between them was that Whizzle couldn't keep his mouth shut and ended up getting them caught. It must be hard to keep a mouth like that shut, he though angrily, looking at Whizzle's overfull cluttermouth of jumbled teeth. He had started to hate those awful teeth.

"Ok. So, there's no going back," Whizzle chimed in. "What do you want to do about it? You want to head off on your own? Go. Go on! I'll be fine without you. I'll just . . . " Whizzle stopped midsentence. He heard a scuffle of movement just around the corner. They both heard it.

They were consumed by fear, not just of the sound they had heard, but more deeply at the prospect of months, perhaps even years alone, in this alien place, devoid of anything familiar. And so, the two brothers, having argued all morning, held each other close, hiding behind the makeshift stone doorway Barg had assembled for them, that thin slab of rock their only protection against the dangerous, unknown world around them.

"The ground has a voice. Many voices. And if you listen closely, you can distinguish the contours of one patch of ground from another, and what it is telling you." Mohmoh was attempting to explain, as clearly as he could, how the special ability of Pluffstacks played out in the landscape. They used it to communicate with each other via special chemical traces their tendrils left in the ground. These traces were in the dirt and rocks left behind by his people. Pluffstacks could read some of the traces left by other creatures as well, but these lacked the intention and clarity of those etched by their own kind.

"I can read the bits of dirt and rock you have on your body," Mohmoh continued. "Even after your time in the water, there are tiny, microscopic particles all over you. I could read them earlier, when I was healing your foot. The journey you have taken, Neek, it is written all over you. The dirt from your home hasn't washed away completely. So, as we travel, I will listen and compare the voices we find with those you carry. It will take time, but there is a logic in how our voices work and what they say. I can map where we need to go, though it might take us time to find the right tunnels to get there."

"I am lucky I met you," Neek smiled. "I might never be able to retrace my steps with my own limited abilities. How will I ever repay you for your kindness?"

"I believe with you, I will walk places my people have never been," responded Mohmoh. "That will be your gift to me."

"Then we will walk together until that happens," Neek promised him, "and long thereafter if fate allows. Thank you, my friend."

Neek looked at his new companion, silently thanking the First-Mother for all the things Neek knew, and all the things he now knew he didn't. He was grateful for this kind creature who might not only help him find a way home, but who was also introducing him to a new way of seeing the world, a new way of living. Neek sensed that the kind of traveling and exploration his new friend valued so much appealed to the Rockling on some deep level he couldn't yet fully understand, so different as it was from typical Rockling life.

The two new friends gathered up some of the remaining food from the chamber floor before heading off in the direction indicated by Mohmoh's ancestors' voices.

∼

It is a shame they were exiled so young, otherwise Whizzle and Barnag might have attended enough Warrior lessons to learn a few words of Goblin. That would have been quite useful as they hid trying to avoid the Goblins that were searching their cavern.

"I can smell them, two dragon-mice," one Goblin spoke, using the derogative word for Rockling so common in the Goblin language. "They are younglings, fresh."

Perhaps if they had learned some Goblin, the boys would have understood that these were two Goblin trackers, their sense of smell and direction among the finest in the Goblin world. Any well-trained Rockling Warrior would know there was no chance of hiding for long from creatures such as these. You could run, or fight. Hiding was not an option.

Their Rockling Warrior training would have also taught them that if you hear Goblins talking, and then they stop talking for no particular reason, you should be very careful. But the boys, untrained as they were, assumed that after the noise stopped for a few minutes the Goblins had moved on.

"Do you think they've gone away," whispered Whizzle quietly. Not quietly enough.

Within seconds the Goblins were on them, binding them and covering their mouths so they couldn't cry out for the second time that day. The Goblins snatched up the supplies that Barg had left the younglings, and carried them, supplies, Rocklings and all, back toward the Goblin camp.

Whizzle, when will you ever learn to keep that mouth of yours shut, Barnag thought to himself silently.

Mohmoh's talent for communicating with his ancestors turned out to be much more useful than Neek had even imagined. Not only was Mohmoh able to discern whether they were going in the right direction or not, he could also gather information from the traces about what had happened lately in the area. The tiny pieces left by his Pluffstack relatives seemed to have an almost eternal life, sensing the world around them and relaying the information to any passing Pluffstacks that were inclined to listen.

At one tunnel junction, Mohmoh insisted they change direction, not because it was a more direct route, but because he was alerted by the traces to the presence of a gigantic snake in the caves ahead. Similarly, another passageway was skipped due to Orcs having travelled there some hours earlier. If they had bigger bodies, and were ambitious, Neek thought, these mushroom creatures could rule the world. Perhaps they already did, but preferred a form of rulership that didn't entail the things Neek associated with dominion. The young Rockling didn't know what to make of his friend in any number of ways. Sometimes the Pluffstack's thoughts were all around him, sometimes there was silence. Occasionally Neek even felt that he himself was starting to read in the rocks what had happened in the hours or days before they had arrived. In this manner, for more than a week, Neek and his new companion travelled slowly and cautiously, back and forth, following a complicated route that few maps could hope to capture, making their way back toward Neek's home.

Despite the dangers they faced, Neek had rarely felt such joy as during his days with Mohmoh. If he had been traveling with Rocklings, they would have marched on relentlessly, focused only on achieving their immediate tasks or reaching their established destination. Rocklings were highly successful, to be sure, due to their social organizing, but sometimes their isolated focus on a goal failed to appreciate the other things life has to offer. Mohmoh was not so burdened. He would have Neek stop and put him down so his tendrils could explore anything particularly interesting they passed. Mohmoh touched the wet surfaces of especially colorful stalagmites. He dipped his tendrils into strong-smelling mineral pools. He hugged the corners of brightly glowing crystals, feeling the intricate patterns their edges made and their wonderful shapes. There was no phenomenon that Mohmoh didn't seem to find joy in investigating at length.

SENSE OF DIRECTION 129

"Just as my ancestors speak to me, so I speak to them," Mohmoh explained. "That way, even after we are gone, as the new ones pass over us, we will continue to discover and enjoy all this world has to offer through them. I must leave my marks, and make my stories rich by examining every wonder the world puts before me."

Neek found himself following suit, only it was Mohmoh's lead he took as guidance, not the traces of any ancestor. He would sometimes caress the sides of the caves as they walked past, just to feel the arrangement of stones there. He would run his fingers through cave moss, and catch water droplets as they fell from the ceiling. None of this had any purpose, but it made him feel happy as few things had before.

Mohmoh could walk quickly for a Pluffstack, but he moved much slower than Neek was capable of. So, for much of their journey, Neek would carry Mohmoh in his hand or on his shoulder. Mohmoh liked to sit where he would be close enough to the tunnels' walls to hold his tendrils out to brush them as they moved past. Sometimes, when the cave tops were low enough for him to reach, Mohmoh would sit on Neek's head and run his tendrils along the ceiling. Very often, in these locations, there would be no traces at all. No traces until of course Mohmoh himself had been there. How long would it be before other Pluffstacks stroked those surfaces? Mohmoh didn't mind. All good things in time.

Rumbletum, the Goblin Chief, was rarely confused. He had risen to the role of Chief due not to his physical might, which was ample, nor to his viciousness, which was proven, but primarily due to his clear thinking. Many Goblins lost their heads in pursuit of treasure, or other base desires, or gave in to their anger and jealously, making poor decisions. Rumbletum's will was stronger than that, and so in every situation, he could suppress his emotions and see clearly what had to be done, pleasant or otherwise.

This situation made no sense though. Emotions weren't getting in his way, but the facts didn't line up. First, his people had found two of the dragon-mice younglings, out in the remote reaches of an area far from the nearest Rockling camp. Rumbletum knew enough of Rockling society to understand that they valued their young. They overvalued them from Rumbletum's perspective. One could always make more young.

He knew this was not how the foolish dragon-mice approached such matters though. They held their children to be their greatest treasure. So why had they let them travel so far away, and unescorted? Surely, they hadn't just gotten lost. No two young ones would venture that far on their own. Yet there they had been found, in the middle of nowhere, with a crude carved door and camping supplies. Had the rest of their group been consumed by monsters in the area? There was nothing to suggest as much. Just two young Rocklings, far from their tribe, with only some basic supplies and a crude shelter. Strange.

Stranger still was the response Rumbletum got when he sent an emissary to the Rockling encampment asking a ransom for their return. The Rocklings had asked only a few questions before making it clear they weren't interested. A Rockling tribe abandoning two younglings? It didn't make any sense at all. These two had similar markings to members of that tribe. They must be theirs. Yet the answer was no. Not even a negotiation, just a flat no. Strange.

So now here he was, with two young dragon-mice to feed. Two creatures with no apparent value at all. It would pain him to harm two creatures so young, but he would do what must be done. Rumbletum never let his emotions cloud his thinking.

The Goblin Chief had requested the services of an Orc interpreter as well. There were a few among them with knowledge of the Rockling language. No one within Rumbletum's tribe had ever bothered to learn the Rockling tongue. Perhaps the boys could answer some of his questions and help him understand what they were doing out there alone. There might be some value that could be gleaned from this yet. It would likely take a while to get an appointment with the interpreter here though. Big things were happening with the Orcs and all their travel tongues were occupied at the moment.

Rumbletum wanted to know more about all the recent commotion around his caves. What were the Orcs up to? He had heard rumors about connections to surface-dwellers above. The Chief didn't like the idea of waiting, but he had learned that even during times of desperate need, sometimes one had to be patient and allow the things in the dark to show themselves. All good things in time.

CHAPTER 8
FOOTPRINT

Mohmoh's keen senses, augmented by the trails left by his Pluffstack ancestors, were able to guide Neek to a great many wonders in their initial travels together. Glowing waterfalls were illuminated by flashing rocks that burned like stars. Bright flowers with intricate patterns uncurled from dusty rocks when you blew on them. Special holes in the stone emitted strange, delightful sounds that seemed to come from a long way off.

Neek had never heard stories of any of these marvels, and was unsure how his people, so at home in their underground caves, could be unaware of their presence. Perhaps he was still a long way from home. Or perhaps the elders did know of these things, they just didn't believe the younglings needed to be familiar with them yet. The clever traps and cooking tips from his lessons seemed far less interesting now by comparison. Even the dramatic adventures of the First-Mother seemed less spectacular somehow.

Of all the wondrous sights he had recently encountered though, this one was by far the most spellbinding. Mohmoh and Neek sat on the floor of a medium-sized cavern with a small pool in the center, the chamber's only entrance. They'd had to swim for almost an hour through a complicated maze of twisting, water-filled passages to reach this place. If it wasn't for Neek's special ability to turn silver, and therefore no longer need to breathe, he would never have been able to remain underwater long enough to reach this cavern. Mohmoh, thankfully, was also well-suited to aquatic travel. Like a fish, he could pull air from the water itself. Mohmoh glowed and pulsed in the water, tiny internal strands shining with a soft blue light as he swam.

The tiny pool in the center of the chamber was not what made this place special though. It was the crystals. This entire chamber was covered in brightly shining crystals. From floor to ceiling, they blanketed the walls, their translucent bodies pulsing with colors that changed softly and slowly over time. To a surface dweller, this might have looked like a spiky sea of glass, with clouds of color washing through it. Neek had never seen clouds of course. He had no words for what was all around him.

The glow had been so bright when he initially climbed out of the water that it had stung Neek's eyes, especially when he reverted to his normal, reddish-brown form. As Neek gradually adjusted to the crystals' brilliance, he was overwhelmed by the emotions he felt due to the beauty and mystery of the display before him. All of the strange twists of fate that had to come to pass for him and his little friend to even be here, seeing this wonder, boggled Neek's mind. Despite all the attention he had received from his tribe for his special, colorful skin, Neek had never really taken the ideas of prophecy or destiny that seriously. Yet here he was, in front of this pulsing marvel, and felt that surely some force beyond him was guiding his path. Reality itself was like these crystals, seemingly changing color, tone, and shape with each passing moment as he experienced a universe much grander and more marvelous than he had ever imagined possible. He could feel his heart beat with the rhythm of the colors around him, and tears filled his eyes.

Mohmoh tickled Neek's ear with his soft white tendrils to get his attention, so lost in thought was the young Rockling. "Sing to them," Mohmoh suggested. "Those thoughts you are feeling. Turn them into sounds and share them with the cave."

"Sing to them, are you sure?" Neek asked. He wondered how

his little friend even knew what singing was, given that Pluffstacks seemed to make no sounds themselves. Mohmoh nodded and smiled.

Neek paused for a moment. Focused as his people were on survival and practical matters, singing was not a frequent activity in Rockling society. He thought back to his lessons and struggled to recall even a single tune he had been taught. He then remembered the lullabies Dragon-Mother Malika would sing as she rocked new hatchlings. They were slow melodies, interlaced with tales of the First-Mother.

In stops and starts at first, as well as he could, having never actually tried to sing before, Neek mimicked the Dragon-Mother, breathing out slowly and widely to make deep tones, telling the story of the First-Mother and how she carved the world. As he began to sing, tentative at first, and then a little stronger, the crystals seemed to come to life. They shimmered with fluctuating color in response to his sounds, shaking and vibrating, creating pleasant harmonies with their movement to accompany his voice. Mohmoh sat on Neek's shoulder, swaying and pulsing with color to the rhythm of the music. The sound began to flow through Neek, to wash over his scales and down into his blood, wrapping his very heart in its tones.

When he finished Malika's song, Neek began to make up his own. Having started singing, he now had no desire to stop. He enjoyed the feeling of the air in his lungs, and the vibrations in his chest. His emotions were pouring out of him. He sang of his travels with Mohmoh, and his family back home, and of all the wonderful things he had seen, and how lucky he felt to have this moment and this friend beside him. And when Neek ran out of words, or had feelings no words could convey, he just chanted tonal sounds, finding whatever notes pleased his throat and his heart.

When Neek finally stopped singing, the crystals continued to vibrate for a moment, their fireworks of color gradually dimming back down to floating pastel clouds. His whole life, Neek would remember this chamber. He would dream of it. This wonderful music. This glorious feeling of peace as the music filling the chamber in turn filled Neek himself. Sitting there, next to the pool, the surface of the water flowing in rhythmic patterns along with the music. His new friend Mohmoh perched on his shoulder, swaying back and forth, and gently holding his ear.

This feeling of complete tranquility would sustain Neek in the face of impending events he could never have imagined, but nonetheless were already written in the stars, already decided and awaiting him. Neek couldn't possibly know what a rare and precious thing these moments would become in his memory, how unlike so much of his future this sense of connection across time and place would feel. He hated to leave it, hated even to stop his song, though he was hungry and tired, and the crystals themselves had dimmed as if they were drifting off to sleep.

It is hard to return to ordinary time when one has been somewhere extra special like this, and Neek would have stayed here forever if he could, but Mohmoh had new tunnels to find, and the young Rockling needed to return to his people. They must be worried sick, he thought, shaking free of his reverie, and feeling the magic of the moment slipping away.

Neek sang one last song, thanking the crystals for their gift of color. He was dismayed to hear a cracking noise as one of the crystals split during its vibration, a small tip falling from the cavern ceiling to the ground before his feet.

"Oh no, I have broken them," Neek thought, tears welling up inside him.

"No," Mohmoh responded. "They have given you a gift, as you gave them the gift of your songs." Then, as if the cavern itself had heard Mohmoh speak, it pulsed in agreement, a warm yellow glow filling the room, and dimmed again, back to the walls of floating clouds. "Your songs will live in them, and this piece will help them live in you. I brought you here because your spirit is like my spirit. Like their spirit. We must share our light and our songs with the world."

Neek hugged his friend, thankful for the kind words and this glorious experience. He then picked up the small piece of crystal on the floor and tucked it carefully away. He would cherish the gift though he would not need it to remember this place. No, this was one of those moments that never leaves you.

This was the third time the search party had doubled back. There were many exits from this chamber and they had tried only a few of them. Unfortunately, no matter which they tried, each tunnel turned out to be a dead end eventually. The number of search parties looking for the lost youngling had been recently reduced. Bodies were needed for other things. Many of those that searched had given up hope, believing it to be a hopeless quest.

Inko though, perhaps driven by the shame he felt about being on Guard duty when Neek was lost, refused to give up. He was determined that the boy would be found, alive or dead, even if he had to search the entire belly of the earth. It was beginning to feel to Inko, however, that he might sooner find the First-Mother, trapped in her cave deep below the world, before he found Neek. It had been many weeks now, and they had been through thousands of passages like this one, winding and weaving, hour after hour, with no sign of the young Rockling.

Though he wasn't particularly hopeful when it came to their mission, Nani, the Explorer assigned to this search party, found Inko's determination inspiring. Inko should have been an Explorer, he thought. He had the required patience, and a good sense of direction. The Trials, that set of tests young Rocklings endure to help identify their appropriate role in the tribe, were good, but they sometimes made mistakes. Why was someone like Inko wasted as a simple Cave Guard? It was possible, of course, that this had been Inko's own decision. Perhaps he had chosen this path.

At that very moment, Inko was also questioning his path, but in a far more pragmatic way. The latest turn resulted in an impasse. This too was a useless branch. "Blocked!" he called back to Nani, alerting him not to waste any more time on this particular tunnel. Inko hung his head. The journey seemed endless. His footsteps, usually so quick, began to slow just a tad.

Out near the branch entrance, Nani crossed the tunnel off of the map. From a lifetime of exploring unknown caves, he had guessed based on the shape of the tunnel's mouth that it would not lead anywhere. Certain types of rock had tell-tale signs. Explorers learned these shortcuts to speed up their work, otherwise you would spin forever in the endless maze of the underneath. Nani walked the twenty or so paces to the next tunnel, which at least had a more promising look to it. As he poked his head in to have a closer look, he spotted something on the ground. Many Rocklings would have missed it, but Nani, seasoned as he was from a lifetime of studying caves, saw it easily. There was a footprint in the soft ground near the tunnel's wall. A small, Rockling footprint.

"Inko, come quick!" he yelled, feeling hopeful for the first time in days.

The journey back through the watery maze they had followed to the singing crystal cavern was a lengthy and arduous one. But, just as with most journeys, the way back didn't seem quite as long as the way there had been. This was due in part to the continuing euphoria Neek felt after his experience in the cavern of living music. He imagined he could still see the crystals' shimmering patterns as he swam through the winding tunnels of water.

When they finally emerged from the labyrinth, Neek and Mohmoh followed the same routine they usually did after a long swim. Mohmoh could not communicate as fully with the traces left by his ancestors when he was wet. Traces in the water he could read, but when sopping wet, traces on the rock or in the soil were muddled. It was similar to how Neek couldn't hear very well while swimming. The young Rocklings used to play a game where one of them would shout something underwater and the others would try to guess what they were saying. They almost always got it wrong.

And so, after getting wet, the two followed a procedure where Neek would put Mohmoh on his shoulder to dry off, and carry him until Mohmoh felt that he was back to normal. During these times, Mohmoh could not pick up clues, so the friends usually planned the direction they would take before they entered any water, as it might be an hour or more before Mohmoh could get in touch with his ancestors again.

It was a shame they had to do this now, otherwise Mohmoh might have sensed the two adult Rocklings who had been through this area just a short while ago.

Still, the unknown is unknown, and thus is not to be worried about. Neek and Mohmoh headed northwards through the tall tunnel they had decided on before their swim. It was the opposite direction Inko and Nani had taken just a short time earlier.

Tizzo and Shaka, another search party to the west, had also found footprints. These were far less inviting, but similarly had to be followed. They appeared to be Orc prints, walking side-by-side with Humans. Tizzo and Shaka were searching for Neek, but a sign like this could not be ignored. They must investigate, cautiously, and report their findings to the tribe.

Orc footprints were fairly common, and not particularly a cause for concern. The Rocklings had nothing the Orcs wanted really, and they would help the Orcs occasionally with trap craft and stonework, so the two races for the most part got along perfectly well. They tolerated each other, and were seldom active enemies. Human footprints though were extremely rare this far down, and a dire sign.

Humans only travelled this deep for two reasons. First, they might be miners, looking for deposits of ore to tap and take back to their surface world. Miners were bad news, as mines were highly-valued treasures to the surface dwellers, and they were often ruthless in extracting that value, pushing out whatever creatures might call nearby caves home. Miners usually travelled in groups though, and never alongside Orcs. Besides, there were no veins of ore in this direction, so why would there be miners here? Miners could also be reasoned with, some of them anyway. Many of them spoke the language of the underneath, and they were not particularly violent. All they wanted was the ore. As long as you let them have that, and stayed out of their way, you'd be ok. You might lose your home, but you'd keep your life.

A second, and far worse option by comparison, was that these footprints might have been left by adventurers. If these were adventurer prints, no one was safe. Adventurers were greedy like miners, taking whatever they wanted, but they were also over-eager to show their prowess in battle. Wizards and Warriors seemed to think of the underneath as a place to experiment with their newfound weapons and spells, to revel in the damage they could wreak. All too often, the quests these adventurers were on involved decimating whole tribes of creatures to ease the fear of some minor lord or another, acting on incomplete information, hopped up on ale, with little regard for anything other than the treasures they could pilfer and the glory they would receive in the eyes of their masters above.

It was unlikely to be adventurers, however. To see adventurer prints and Orc prints in the same place usually involved finding signs of a struggle, and the corpses of one group or the other. They usually were at each other's throats, not walking side-by-side like this as friends. What were the Orcs up to Tizzo wondered, following the trail of prints slowly and with great trepidation.

~

The Wizard was annoyed. They had journeyed for hours, broken into a long-unused temple full of monstrosities, and fought off numerous dangers, only to find that the main reliquary had already been ransacked. The rumors the Orcs had provided about this place had been exaggerated, and none of the artifacts he was seeking could be found here. The looting had been done long ago, perhaps during his grandfather's lifetime. Had grandpa ventured this far down,` he wondered?

There was the wand, of course. He had sensed it below the ground, carefully hidden during an ancient age. This wand was the only bit of treasure with which he would be returning to his King. He could tell from his somewhat limited knowledge that this wand would spit fire, a skill he had long wanted, but not yet mastered in his magical studies. Other court Wizards were true masters of flame, so he imagined the King would let him keep this wand for himself. If only he had found one of the birthing artifacts instead, the real reason he had expended the effort coming to this awful place, then glory truly would have been his.

Aleric Merrilthin, this young Wizard, despite his meager talents, was held in high favor by King Blackburn, due mainly to the relationship he had forged with the Orcs. His fellow mages had mocked him for studying Orcish rather than one of the proper magical languages. It was bad enough that he had focused on mental magic, the art of manipulating the thoughts of others, which many mages felt was invasive and more than a little creepy. Studying Orcish on top of that, well, it just proved how odd this young mage really was. They were always mocking him about the many spell books he couldn't read. Well, books eventually get translated, he thought. And he knew that the bowels of the earth held great treasures. And in this part of the world anyway, when it came to the underneath, the Orcs were the dominant group.

Aleric knew their language and their weaknesses. And so, in just under a year, a year full of negotiation, flattery, well-placed threats, and even better-placed bribes, he had developed a kind of friendship with the Orcs. It was the kind of relationship where you gave the other party something important to them and they did what you asked. Most friendships could be purchased for the right price, the Wizard knew. And King Blackburn had many things the Orcs wanted. Stronger weapons, veins of silver ore, food supplies, fishable waters. In return they promised to find Aleric the thing his king most desired, a magical solution to the Throne's lack of an heir.

So far though, his friends weren't delivering as well as Aleric had hoped. The King, while supportive, was starting to lose patience. The young Wizard needed to produce results. That, or he might have to use some of his mental magic to rearrange the King's expectations. That was a dangerous road to travel, however, and punishable by death. There were limits to the freedom granted to Wizards, even brilliant ones.

Just as Aleric's thoughts started to turn to worries about what might happen if he couldn't solve the King's problem, he felt a distinct ringing sensation in his head. Someone or something had triggered a magical tripwire Aleric had placed behind them in their journey. The signal alerted him to the presence of something very close behind them now. He picked up his newfound wand, eagerness in his eyes. Let's see what you can do, he thought. Perhaps today wouldn't be a waste after all.

∽

They had walked for hours, scouring every direction around the footprints that had so tantalized them earlier, but to no avail. Nani would remember this place so they could return tomorrow. It was important though that they head back now to their camp to rest and resupply. "We'll concentrate all the search parties in this area tomorrow," Nani promised a dispirited looking Inko. "We will go back and get more of the tribe to help us, and we'll find him. I promise you."

Inko knew Nani was right. If they kept going like this, with no rest, no food, and no more clues to go on, they'd end up in real trouble. If something happened to them, it would be of no help to Neek. Inko nodded and followed Nani's lead, heading back toward the warren. It would take a few hours still to reach their home, even if they followed the straightest path, and they were both exhausted, having gone well beyond their limits during the frantic hunt around the footprint.

They had shouted for Neek, a risky choice in an unknown area like this where anything might lurk around the next corner, but there had been no response. It was frustrating to turn back when they were seemingly so close, but Nani was correct, with more searchers they might find him. It had been a fresh print. That meant Neek was alive. Yes, that was what he should focus on. As they trudged along, tired and hungry, this kept Inko's spirits up. Neek was still alive!

~

At least they were still alive, Barnag thought to himself. And they were being fed well for the last few days. At first, it had been miserable, stuck in these awful Goblin cages, choking down food scraps not fit for a cave lizard, much less a Rockling, descendant of dragons. For two days now though the exiled boys had been eating even better than they would have in their home warren. Fresh meat, crunchy Goblin bread, and even wine had been provided to them. The young Rocklings had never experienced anything like it, and it made their heads swim, taking them away from their dim surroundings. They were, after all, still in chains. Still prisoners in a Goblin camp. But they were eating like kings. And they were alive!

Whizzle had warmed to his captors. "They treat us better than our tribe did," he remarked to Barnag. "They haven't harmed us. Haven't abandoned us in the wilds. They saved us, if you ask me."

"But for what?" Barnag responded. "Why are they treating us this way? Goblins kill our kind. They must want something." Try as he might though, Barnag could not figure out what his captors were after. He ate his dinner slowly, scanning the room outside their cages for any kind of clue.

∽

Rumbletum was pleased. He could tell his plan was working. In learning to master his own emotions, he had become an expert on dealing with the emotions of others. *Too many creatures misunderstand this,* he thought to himself, watching the two Rockling boys chatting through his secret hole to their cells. *Most Goblins believe that you can control others through fear. Rumbletum knew better.*

Fear makes you see phantoms in the night. Fear makes your soul lie, and as your soul does so your tongue will follow. Torture a prisoner and they will tell you whatever you want to hear, even if it had no resemblance to the truth. A tortured Rockling would tell you it was a rat to make the pain stop. This Rumbletum knew from first-hand experience. Fear makes you careful. Fear makes you run.

Greed, though. Comfort. False security. These will make a beast spill all its secrets without thinking. There would be lies, of course, but truths as well. Comfort made creatures lazy. Comfort made you sleep. Comfort made you thankful. And though he couldn't speak their tongue, Rumbletum could tell, watching these boys bicker, that they were thankful for the food they were getting. Far more thankful than they were likely feeling toward whomever left them there, alone in the empty darkness. Yes, it was working. When the interpreter arrived, these boys would tell him everything.

The Wizard Aleric was pleased. The wand had been far more powerful than he had anticipated. Rather than a tiny tongue of flame as so many wands were apt to shoot, his newly found wand had sent a massive ball of fire, wide as a throne room, engulfing the two Rocklings in flames so hot there was hardly anything left when the fire died out.

He had tried reasoning with them first of course, in the guttural tongue of the underground dwellers. They had tripped his invisible magic signal, and he and the Orcs had surprised them. The beasts wouldn't listen to reason though. He and the Orcs had threatened them. Told them what they would do if the Rocklings didn't lay down their arms and surrender. But the two pathetic creatures had run. Fearful beasts. I can see why they cower down here in their holes, he thought.

They probably could have been captured. The Orc Guards he was escorted by were strong, and fast. Even as sneaky and quick as they were, the Rocklings likely could have been caught. Aleric could have been more diplomatic too, he supposed. But was there really any point reasoning with such low creatures? More to the point, he really did want to test out that wand before turning it over the Council of Mages when he returned home. Despite his favor with the King, he was worried the Council would take it from him without even letting him study it properly.

Well, what the Council didn't know wouldn't hurt them, not yet anyway, he thought, slipping the wand into a hidden pocket in his robe. "Search them for gold or treasure," he told the Orcs. "Keep what you find." And with that, the Wizard walked back up the tunnel, heading home, tapping the wand in his robe, smiling from ear to ear.

The Orcs followed quickly, eyes looking away from the pitiful burnt creatures on the ground. The sight gave them no comfort, and they knew better than to look for gold on the bodies of Rocklings. Experienced soldiers, veterans of many a bloody war, even they were shocked by the savagery of this young Wizard.

CHAPTER 9
REUNITED

Neek's dream must have been glorious, because as hard as he tugged, Mohmoh couldn't wake him. It was strange to watch his big friend curled up and locked in this unconscious state. Rocklings, it seemed, spent large parts of their lives in this manner, something passing through their minds, turning from side to side, sometimes muttering, sometimes calling out in fear, but remaining all the time in that somewhere else, a place the Pluffstack could not follow.

Mohmoh didn't need to sleep. He would usually wander about as Neek slumbered, scouring every inch of the nearby caves. He wanted to experience everything. To learn everything. And to share his memories with future generations. Mohmoh recognized the soil here as being close to what he had found under Neek's claws. They must be nearing the Rockling warren.

Mohmoh sensed that the tunnels nearby were well-traveled. There had been many pairs of feet walking these halls in the past few days. And now, as the vibrations of the floor were making clear, someone was coming, more than one creature in fact. They were moving swiftly. Neek was not that well-hidden, and he had been humming in his sleep. Mohmoh had to wake him, quickly. They had to go.

Distraught at Neek's slow progress, Mohmoh's tendrils sent

forth not their usual yellow aura of healing energy, but a strange black-spotted light that shocked Neek's ear.

"Ouch!" Neek shot up and yelled. "What are you . . . "

"Quiet," Mohmoh quickly interrupted. "Creatures approaching. They are close. They are armed."

Neek sprang up. "Which way should we go?" he asked. Mohmoh gestured with a wispy tendril toward the nearest exit and Neek grabbed him, jumped up, and ran off in that direction. He held Mohmoh in one hand and his newfound crystal in the other, going as rapidly as his little legs would take him.

If he had been in his home warren, running through familiar tunnels, Neek probably would have been just fine. He was a nimble youngling, well-balanced and good on his feet. But these passages were unknown to Neek. These were bumpy, winding pathways with rough floors and many folds and crusts to leap over. There were no branches here though. No alcoves to hide in. He ran for a few moments, clearing most of the obstacles successfully, until he sprang over one particularly large bump and found the floor beyond was much lower than he anticipated. Neek lost his footing and toppled to the floor. He hit the side of the tunnel wall with a bang, dropping his cherished crystal and his new friend. The crystal was easy enough to retrieve, but Mohmoh had fallen down a hole, and was too far away for Neek to reach.

"Leave me," he heard Mohmoh tell him. "Leave me and run."

But Neek had no intention of abandoning his new friend. "Climb up," Neek insisted. "Come on, hurry."

Mohmoh inched his way along the wall toward Neek. His progress was agonizingly slow, and Neek could hear the footsteps behind them growing louder. "Hurry," he told Mohmoh. "Hurry!" Mohmoh climbed into his hand just as Neek felt someone grab him from behind.

∾

The hand on Barnag's shoulder made him jump, even though it had only touched him gently. Barnag was in the middle of a terrible dream. He had been running through a maze of tunnels, all of them filling up with scalding red rocks. He had reached a dead end, and felt the burning rocks collapsing upon him just as the hand grasped him. Barnag gasped and opened his eyes to see Rumbletum, the Goblin Chief, looking back at him with a big smile.

In his other hand, Rumbletum was holding a roll of Goblin Sweetbread, offering it to Barnag. Made with the rare honey of the Cave Bee, these delicious treats were a Goblin specialty that Barnag had only experienced since his captivity. He saw his brother Whizzle was already awake, chewing busily on his roll, bits of sticky honey running over the edges of his many misaligned teeth.

The Goblin smiled and said something Barnag couldn't understand. If he had been older, he might have recognized the kind greeting Rumbletum was addressing him with. But Barnag did not yet know the common tongue of the underneath, speaking only his native Rockling dialect. Yet the pleasant smile combined with the offer of the sweet roll made his meaning clear enough, the Goblin was trying to be kind. But why, Barnag wondered?

This Goblin had visited them many times. From the way he spoke to the other Goblins around him, Barnag guessed he was their leader. He would bark loudly, and the other Goblins would run off and do things, things that presumably he had asked for. Though he was by no means cruel to the other Goblins, he never seemed to smile or to show kindness to his followers as he was doing to the boys at the moment. Barnag didn't trust him or this unexpected generosity.

The Goblin leader had some pieces of parchment with him. While the boys enjoyed their food, he sat on a stool outside their cells and showed them various documents. They were pictures. Pictures with bits of writing the boys couldn't read. Most of the things shown in the images were completely unknown to the

Rocklings. There was something that looked like a dagger, a necklace of some kind with a round jewel on it, and a variety of other artifacts pictured on the parchment that meant nothing to the boys.

One object depicted though was clearly recognizable. It was a drawing of the hat worn by Malika, their tribe's Dragon-Mother. Most Rocklings didn't wear anything on their heads. Malika, however, almost always wore a distinctive headdress that looked identical to the illustration on the paper before him. Barnag wasn't sure what to do. He appreciated that the Goblin was being kind, but they were still locked in a cell, and Barnag had no idea what the Goblin's plans for them were. Not wanting to give anything away, Barnag tried to keep his expression from showing there was anything different about this image from the others they had seen.

Whizzle on the other hand, excited from the sugar filling his body after eating the sweet roll, foolishly poked his arm out of the cell and started tapping on the picture and chattering. He was explaining what the hat was, but the Goblin Chief didn't seem to be following his words.

Rumbletum smiled. He couldn't understand the boy, but that didn't matter. His reaction was easy to read. The boy knew this artifact. The Rocklings must have it. The Rocklings have it and the Orcs want it, he thought. This will be a great boon to the Goblins. And the interpreter would be there in just a few short days. He smiled and offered the ugly, snaggle-toothed boy another sweet roll. "Good boy," he said in Goblin. "Helpful boy."

∾

Neek's heart beat out of his chest as the hand on his shoulder spun him around. He pictured a wide range of creatures in his mind but was surprised to find himself face to face with a Rockling! It was Inko, the Guard that had been so kind and let him go back for his necklace all those weeks ago. He wrapped his arms around Inko's neck and hugged him fiercely.

"Neek, I can't believe we found you," Inko declared, hugging the young Rockling in return. "Come, we must flee these tunnels quickly," he signaled. "We have heard sounds of fighting. It is not safe here."

And with that, Inko picked up Neek, still holding his crystal and his dear friend Mohmoh, and sprinted back down the tunnel toward the warren. Though he was exhausted, his legs on fire, his eyes heavy, Inko ran as rapidly as he ever had in his life. Even Nani, experienced Explorer though he was, had a hard time keeping up with him.

The boy was alive. They had found him!

∾

Underground, there is not always a clear night or day. Life continues on, hour by hour, in many subterranean communities without ceasing. Without light and dark, and the daily rise and fall of the sun to guide their actions, underground creatures tend to make up their own rules about when to rest and when to be active. So it was in Rockling society that life went on mostly around the clock. There were certain times though when things were more quiet, when a larger part of the tribe would sleep, and life would slow down around them to allow them to do so in peace.

Inko's group, with Neek in tow, arrived during this quiet time. Despite the customs about not disturbing others during this period, Inko and Nani were shouting noisily to wake everyone up. "We've found him, we've found him!" they yelled, shuttling him to the great chamber, the center of Rockling life.

The whole warren quickly sprang to life, filtering into the grand hall to get a glimpse of their special boy, returned at last after so many feared him dead. Rocklings were hugging and grabbing him from every direction, some touching him just to make sure he was real. Neek carefully put Mohmoh on a high shelf out of harm's way, afraid he might be crushed in the celebrations. Chief MakMak, all the caste leaders, and nearly every member of the tribe greeted Neek and wished him well. Dragon-Mother Malika held him for a long time, weeping tears over his shoulder.

The Cooks sprang into action, whipping up a feast, and the whole warren celebrated the triumphant return of their blessed All-Shade. Inko sat close by, a careful watchdog at Neek's side. If people asked Neek too many questions, Inko would tell them to leave the boy alone, insisting that he was tired and needed rest. Many hours of celebration passed, however, before the tribe finally allowed Neek to return to his bed, so long deserted, with Mohmoh at his side.

Neek quickly fell into in a calm, deep sleep, the kind you only achieve after returning home from a long trip. If Neek's dreams had shown a mixture of wonder and terror during their time down in the tunnels, now his mind seemed to exhibit nothing at all. His body lay still. Mohmoh had never seen Neek rest so peacefully.

Despite the celebrations, Chief MakMak was concerned. The return of Neek was an unexpected and welcome relief, of course, but sadly the search party with Tizzo and Shaka had not been heard from. Backup Scouts had gone looking for them and returned with the grizzly news of their demise. MakMak had lived long enough to know what the fiery mess they had found meant. There was magic being used underground. Against Rocklings. That was surface dweller magic. Human magic. There were adventurers in their caves. May the First-Mother protect us all, she prayed.

Since he had no plans to share his new wand with the Council, the young Wizard Aleric would have been returning to court empty-handed, if not for the good news recently delivered from one of his Orc spies. One of the fabled fertility artifacts he had been seeking had finally been discovered. The Orcs had located it for him through their shadowy network of underground contacts. After the recent disappointment at the temple, Aleric had made it clear to the Orcs that he would suffer no more failures on their part. Despite his warnings, which they certainly respected after the terrible demonstration of his cruelty upon the poor Rocklings, the Orcs insisted that this time they were sure the correct artifact had been found. To get it though meant circumnavigating a huge tunnel complex, a deadly set of caves full of traps and creatures who would fight to keep their home. It would be no simple matter to retrieve the magical helm.

The Orcs apparently had a source of information that would help them piece together maps and other information on the complex to make their assault easier. This was a good plan, the Wizard agreed, and very welcome timing. Sure, if he involved the Council and an army of the King's soldiers, he could go and clear those warrens easily, no matter what they contained. However, armed with maps and knowledge instead, he could use his Orc allies, a few trusted friends, and go and retrieve the artifact himself. This approach would yield the most glory, and would give him another chance to use that lovely wand of his as well. The King would be so pleased with him, Aleric would soon be a member of the Council of Mages, even leading it perhaps.

That would certainly be a good start, Aleric decided, daydreaming of future power.

CHAPTER 10
DIFFICULT CONVERSATIONS

Neek was happy to be home. Mostly happy anyway. But lots of factors conspired to make his return a difficult one, despite the merry mood of everyone around him.

He was greatly saddened by the loss of the other Rockling patrol that had been looking for him. If only he could go back and tell them not to seek him out, tell them that he would be fine on his own with his new Pluffstack friend who could safely navigate even the most treacherous depths. They had traveled weeks by themselves, just Mohmoh and he, easily avoiding danger nearly the entire time.

He was heartbroken too to learn what had been done to his brothers, Whizzle and Barnag. He understood the Chief's decision in the matter, but he wished he had been there to argue against their exile. Even with what Whizzle had done to him, Neek had no lingering anger toward him. If Whizzle hadn't pushed me in that river, Neek thought, I might never have learned of my new abilities. I might never have met my friend Mohmoh. I wouldn't have seen that glorious crystal cavern with its colorful music. Neek was starting to believe that perhaps the First-Mother did have something special in store for him, and perhaps it was she who had guided Whizzle's hands.

Barnag was gone now too. Neek had saved Barnag's life only

to have him exiled to certain doom. Such an outcome didn't sit well with Neek at all. It didn't feel right.

Neek had never enjoyed the special attention he received from the rest of the tribe. The stares. The constant questioning. The smiles he often felt he didn't deserve. Now, even more than before, everyone seemed to be watching him. The round-the-clock escort Chief MakMak had assigned to him only intensified this feeling. No matter where he went now. To dinner. To bed. To the bathroom. There were Guards following him, making sure he didn't somehow manage to get lost again. The tribe's treasure must be secured.

To keep him safe, they also restricted Neek's activities. No more hide and seek sessions in the caves. No more wandering alone with Mohmoh, experiencing unknown joys. He was always in the warren, always being watched, and almost always being examined it seemed by one tribal elder or another. All the endless questions. The physical tests. Constantly asking his thoughts on every subject imaginable. It was suffocating.

Beyond all these minor annoyances, in the back of his mind, the sorest disappointment he felt in this new life was that home no longer satisfied him as it once had done. His warren, the lessons, the day-to-day activities of Rockling life, they all seemed dull in comparison to the things that he and Mohmoh had seen together. And they had been traveling mere weeks. What might they find given more time in the tunnels, more freedom? Neek had the unpleasant feeling they might never let him venture out past the borders of the warren again. He wasn't exactly a prisoner, but he felt like one, confined both by the elders' admiration and their fear.

He felt bad for Mohmoh too. His little Pluffstack friend seemed happy regardless, and never complained. But after scouring every inch of the warren, Neek knew Mohmoh must be thirsting as he was to explore new places. He often suggested Mohmoh go off at night, as he didn't need sleep anyway, to explore on his own. Neek would have been worried, but he trusted that Mohmoh could protect himself, thanks to the wisdom of his ancestors, likely better than anyone in the whole tribe. He had given Mohmoh a mission too. A mission that so far was going poorly.

～

The Wizard Aleric wore his finest cloak, his grandest hat, and his shiniest shoes. An audience with the King was an important occasion, especially for someone so young as Aleric, and King Blackburn was famously impressed by the well-dressed. "Slovenly men sully a kingdom," the King used to say. A well-kept appearance signaled attention to detail and careful, methodical calculation, two qualities highly revered by the King.

Aleric had made a good enough impression thus far to be trusted with responsibilities far beyond his years, but he needed to be careful. The young Wizard did not yet have any treasures for the King, and the Queen was progressing quickly in her pregnancy. A fact the King reminded him of constantly.

"It has been two months, you realize that, I trust," the King remarked, as much to signal his frustration with Aleric to the others in the room, others who at any minute might take Aleric's place in the King's favor. The King could be as fickle as he was determined, except that is when it came to the Queen and her well-being.

Of course I know that, Aleric thought to himself. The King and every one of his advisers began nearly every order, every letter, every speech with a reminder that within the fourth month of her pregnancy, the Queen had in the past grown ill and lost her child. Sometimes it felt like this was all Aleric or anyone else in the kingdom was permitted to think about.

"You made me promises of magical treasure underground," the King continued. "That's why I allowed you to bargain with those awful beasts, the Orcs. I hope to see that treasure soon, before another child is lost."

"Yes, your Majesty, of course," Aleric apologized. "I'm sorry the temple of Hyramin turned out to be empty. The false creature who lied to us has been dealt with. I assure you, my Lord, a few more weeks and I shall have something even better than Hyramin's belt. The Helm of Life, my Lord, I have located it."

DIFFICULT CONVERSATIONS

The King's eyes grew wide. The Helm of Life. Could it be, finally? "Well, if you know of its location, let me gather my Knights and take it. How many days ride is it from here?" Blackburn asked.

"Apologies, my King," Aleric continued, "but where it lies, no horse can tread. It is deep down, far below the surface, in a foul, dangerous place. We would lose many fine men seeking it there, my Lord, were it not for our relationship with the Orcs. With their help, we shall have it, and have it soon. We shall gain it without substantial loss of life," Aleric noted, directing his attention to those in the chamber who might be thinking to use his returning empty-handed to their advantage. "Well, our lives anyway," the young Wizard smirked, his the only smile in the room.

King Blackburn was not quite sure what to make of the news or of Aleric. He disliked the young man and his methods, but he could read between the lines, and the plan, while distasteful, was a good one. Let the Orcs die retrieving the thing, the King thought to himself. He had spent a great deal training his faithful soldiers, and though he hated to deny them the glory of a victory, it would be a shame to lose them underground, in that cold darkness.

At the same time, he wasn't so sure he trusted the young mage to manage such a momentous task himself. True, the Wizard had come through with his promise to tame the Orcs. This had solved a great many problems for his kingdom. The boy's potentially overdeveloped ambition was clear though in everything from his grossly fawning looks to the gaudy rings he'd jammed on his stubby fingers. Was he trying to impress the King with such a tacky display? Possibly. And despite the alliance with the Orcs, none of the precious artifacts the Wizard had promised had yet been found. He would give the upstart boy a few weeks to retrieve the helm. And if the boy failed, well then, the King's men would have to hunt beyond the sunlight after all, marching as deep down into darkness and its many dangers as was necessary to save his beloved Queen.

"Weeks I will give you," ordered the King, "but no more. You are to provide the details to the Mages Council, and if by the new moon you haven't brought the helm to me, then other plans will be made. This is good work, young Aleric. See it completed and your name shall be the stuff of stories and song." The words hurt the King's mouth even to suggest. He detested braggarts of any stripe, and loathed the endless drinking and storytelling of tall tales so common at court. There were limits even for what a King could change in the world he'd inherited though. Plus, he knew what would move an ambitious young Wizard like Aleric, and King Blackburn needed him to move quickly. Looking fondly at his Queen's face, he knew the smile he saw there would not last long if they lost another child.

"Thank you, my Lord," Aleric replied before turning to leave. "I will inform the Council immediately." Heading out of the royal chamber toward the Wizards' tower the young man's lips parted again in one of his unpleasant smirks. Yes, he thought, I'll tell them and everyone else in this accursed place the story they need to hear now. And when the helm is mine, well, then perhaps the story will be quite different indeed.

Soon after Neek's return, he was called in to see Chief MakMak in a private chamber. Rocklings conduct most business in their great halls, out in front of the whole tribe. This builds trust amongst the community. At certain times though, things must be done more discretely. This was one of those times.

When Neek arrived, he saw Malika was already there, as were a great many of the Rockling Priests, and many of the senior caste leaders. They sat or stood, gathered around a great table. In the middle of the table was a block of black rock, and the statue of the Rock Boar he had carved the day of his disappearance. He was surprised, but also a little pleased to see that Altak had decided to keep it.

"Have a seat, Neek," Malika asked of him, and Neek joined

them at the table.

"Neek," asked Altak, the wise old Carver, "could you please use your claws to carve this piece of stone as you carved the Boar for me before?"

Neek hesitated. He knew he would be expected at some point to share the things he had discovered about himself with others from the warren, but he had hoped to do it more privately than this. He was in front of all the tribal elders, and these were powers he didn't fully understand yet. The whole thing made him very nervous.

"Please, Neek," Altak continued, gesturing to the stone block. "Show them your gift."

"What would you like me to carve?" Neek asked, trying to buy himself a few moments to remember what exactly he'd done that day at the Carver's.

"Make anything you wish," Altak replied.

"Anything?" Neek asked, awkwardly.

The Carver looked deep into Neek's eyes, nodding and twisting his mouth with a deft subtlety that communicated it had not been his idea to bring the youngster before the group in this manner. He knew better than most the damage it might do to put pressure on a young one's talent too soon. Many a fine Carver had been lost to the community through impatience, both the Carver's and the community's.

Neek turned his attention to the black stone. Concentrating, as he had done that fateful day, he activated the green glow around his nails and starting digging into the surface of the black block. Bits of rock fell away as he worked the stone, cutting its surface as easily as a sharpened knife though a fresh loaf of bread.

The crowd in attendance muttered quietly to each other as he worked, marveling as the hard stone fell away. I suppose it will be like this from now on, Neek thought to himself, people watching me and saying things as if I'm not really here. Getting stared at was bad, but having everyone talking about you and not being able to make out what they were saying, that was torturous.

Malika spoke next. "Neek, my dear. Have you noticed any other gifts like these? Anything else you wouldn't expect a Rockling to be able to do?"

She hadn't mean to be aggressive with her question. It was innocent enough, but being asked to expose himself like this, being asked to take what was most private and mysterious and put in on show for the world, to Neek this felt shameful and humiliating. No other youngling was inspected in quite this manner, other than at the Trials, one of the most frightening moments of a Rockling's life. He looked around the room for someone, anyone, to rescue him from what was being asked of him, but they were all staring in his direction, every one of them with an intense and demanding curiosity. The room had gone completely quiet now. It was as if they could read the hesitancy in the sculpture of himself he had unconsciously carved while he was hiding in his thoughts.

Neek put down the self-portrait, and without a smile, without a hint of pride, or a sense that any of what he was to show them might be something to admire or even acknowledge, he went through the motions, showing them what he had discovered about himself over the past few weeks.

He turned his skin silver and let them hit him with a stone to demonstrate its strength. He turned bright red and lifted up the massive stone table that would normally require a group of adult Rocklings to inch across the floor. He even told them about his friend Mohmoh, and his gift of healing, describing the yellow glow that had extended from his friend's tendrils to heal his foot after being attacked by the rats. "I can also breathe fire from my mouth," he explained, "but I haven't done it very often, only once in fact, and I worry I would burn you all."

With the revelation of each additional power, the entire room looked increasingly shaken. Their eyes grew wide, but whether from awe or fear he wasn't quite sure. Neek was no longer just the center of attention, he was isolated in a spotlight in a way he had never felt before. He felt so different. So completely alone. It was awful. I wish I could just go and hide, he thought, playing a special round of Secret Treasure that would only end when people gave up looking for him entirely and recognized he had well and truly disappeared.

He just wanted a few moments of peace. A brief respite from the attention. At that moment though, another of his abilities, one that he had not even known about yet, revealed itself to the crowd, before Neek himself recognized what was happening. As he had wished for, the youngling disappeared suddenly, right in front of their eyes.

His invisibility so completely unnerved those in attendance there was a temporary panic. "Where has he gone now?" one elder shouted. A few of them darted forward, as if perhaps he had run from the room. The big Warrior Bartok stumbled into him, knocking him to the ground. Neek was so shocked by the collision that he turned visible again. The crowd wasn't amused. They glowered at him, overwhelmed by anxiety.

"I guess I can do that too," Neek joked sheepishly. It suddenly struck him that there was nothing terribly impressive in his wonderful performances during the hiding game. No wonder no one could find him.

"There's one other thing you can do, isn't there?" he heard Malika ask. Like with Mohmoh though, this was communicated, not with her voice, but with her mind.

"Yes Dragon-Mother," he replied, after a moment, silently, just as he had done so often with his Pluffstack friend. He started to tremble. These revelations. This attention. He was frightened. It was too much.

Malika stood up from the table, came over to him, and held his shaking hands. "I think that is enough for today everyone. Neek has been through a lot, and this is difficult for him. We must let him rest."

Chief MakMak nodded, and Neek was excused. Malika led him out of the room, toward his old nursery.

"I'm sorry," she said softly. "It was unkind of us to push you."

DIFFICULT CONVERSATIONS 169

Neek was relieved to be away from the eyes of the crowd, and calmed by the kind tone of Malika's voice. The smile in her eyes took him back for a moment to his early childhood, to the warmth of being wrapped in a blanket, fond memories of the vibration of her voice as she sang and held him close.

His daydream faded as he suddenly wondered, how was Malika able to communicate silently to his mind like Mohmoh did? If Malika had special powers like his, maybe the other elders did too. Perhaps he was just as clueless about his own people as he had been of the strange wonders he had discovered wandering the tunnels with Mohmoh. He felt increasingly small in a growing world of endless mystery, and again he sensed the eyes of the crowd upon him, drowning in feelings of shame about how little he understood of his universe.

The remaining elders in the great hall were all talking quickly, with great excitement. Nothing like this had ever been seen in any Rockling tribe, much less among the Hardhands. The Priests were insistent that the representatives from Kindlehoof be summoned immediately. Neek's magic must be assessed, right away, by the Great Priests of that renowned clan.

"Yes, summon them," MakMak agreed. "But go, now." She loved her tribe, but the sight of all these elders chattering like confused children bothered her. We knew Neek was special, she thought. We should not be so shocked when we find out what we thought is actually true.

As the other Rocklings filed out of the room, MakMak did see something that surprised her. In all the confusion caused by his display, the elders had not paid much attention to what he was actually carving. It was the chunks of stone falling away so easily as he passed those green claws along them that had so preoccupied their view. Looking now at what remained of the chunk of black stone, she saw Neek had carved a rendering of himself, but on its side, the faces of his exiled brothers, Whizzle and Barnag. Had she done the right thing sending them away, she wondered, picturing the young boys out there alone in the dark. She wasn't so sure.

∼

Rumbletum's spies were making great progress. Slowly, and carefully, they had been creeping around the periphery of the Rockling warren, mapping tunnels and observing the behavior of the creatures living there. His orders had been very clear. Don't be seen. Don't steal anything. Don't fight anything. Just watch, take notes, make maps. The Goblin mages had even given them some potions allowing them to walk invisibly through the Rockling camp. Their reach was limited, so there were many places they could not examine. But they could certainly probe farther than they ever had before. Tempting as this power might be to a Goblin, the orders remained firm. No violence. No looting. And above all, no getting caught. Like the snails and the rats of the dark, they scurried about, alongside their enemies, making a comprehensive picture of their world.

Soon the young ones will fill in these gaps, Rumbletum thought to himself, as he watched them talking to each other and laughing, eating their daily sweet rolls, oblivious to their upcoming role in the tribe's destruction. The Orc interpreter was on his way. He would be here soon. Soon their secrets would be his own. Soon it would be done. And he could be done with these ugly beasts once and for all. He was getting sick of watching the toothy one eat.

∼

In the nursery, now devoid of eggs, this season's clutch already popped and running about, Neek and Malika were finally alone. Neek supposed, given her ability to mind speak, as he could with

Mohmoh, they could have talked in the main cavern and no one would have noticed. How many others had this power, he wondered? Neek had so many questions.

"Yes, I can feel your questions, all of them," she spoke, in the silent mental language. "I have many of my own," she continued, "and we will try to answer them all in time. But before we get there, I must warn you to be careful with this particular gift."

"Why?" he asked out loud, out of habit, though he need not have done so. He had grown accustomed to this silent speech with Mohmoh. Why was it so hard doing it with another Rockling?

"This gift is not just an extension of your mouth," Malika explained, "or of your ability to speak and communicate with others. It is a gift to your eyes as well. If you concentrate carefully, you can see inside someone's heart, whether they want you to or not."

Neek pondered this for a moment. He supposed it was true. He knew what Mohmoh was thinking, and Mohmoh knew the same of him. It had never worried him. His sweet Pluffstack always thought such happy things. And there was nothing he had to hide from his friend. Besides, there were only a few people he seemed to be able to communicate with this way. Other than Mohmoh and Malika, nobody else had this power. Not yet anyway.

"Not all thoughts are kind," she continued, clearly reading his own. "Even with those we love, we sometimes make mistakes, and can even be cruel."

He thought of Whizzle, with sadness, and Malika nodded, clearly understanding.

"And this sight we have," she explained, "gives us great power. You can see through deception. You can pry hidden secrets from the mind. Just because you can though doesn't mean you should do so. It is like those miners that rip ore from the earth, with no care for the collapse of the caves they despoil. You must be careful with this gift, Neek."

He understood and agreed. It wasn't fair to eavesdrop on someone who didn't want you in their mind. There was something precious in what we kept to ourselves that was lost when privacy wasn't respected. He, under constant watch these days, and seemingly always the center of attention, knew this all too well.

"Good," Malika told him. "I tell you this Neek because I wish to teach you how to use this gift fully. To both speak and to see. It may be the greatest gift the First-Mother has given you, as it will enable you to unlock the world. Language will no longer block your way. Any creature that has a mind can be your companion, and you will be able to converse with them as you do with me now. You will not be held back by the boundaries that so often keep Orc from Rockling and rats from men. You can move between and among them all. You are not confined like most of the people you know to only a single world, with only hints of the many others."

"How do you know all this?" he started to ask, but Malika was already sensing and answering his request.

"This gift of silent speech is given to many Dragon-Mothers. It is helpful to be able to reach the minds of the young before they are able to speak. Your friend Mohmoh, his gift of healing, I share that too, to some extent thanks to this relic," she explained, pointing to her headdress. Malika made a yellow aura extend from her hand and stroked Neek's brow. He felt soothed.

"I use this energy to keep the eggs and the newly born healthy," she continued. "I do not share the other gifts you have shown us. They are beyond anything I have ever seen in our people. But there are tales, tales of the First-Mother, that mention abilities like yours. The Great Priests of Kindlehoof are being summoned, and they may be able to help you. Then again, they may not. There may never have been another Rockling like you, Neek. Try not to be afraid. It is a beautiful thing, even if none of us fully understand it yet." Malika hugged him for a long while and gave him a kiss on the head.

DIFFICULT CONVERSATIONS

"And now you need rest, Neek. This is too much for any boy to handle, even one as special as you. You will sleep here tonight." She made him a special bed there in the same room where he had first climbed out of his egg. She brewed him a warm mug of Rockling tea, earthy and strong, and put some of her special Red Nightroot in it. "This will calm you," she promised.

He drank his tea slowly, his mind ablaze with the revelation that Malika, like him, had powers. How many others, he wondered? But his thoughts already had slowed. After a while, his eyelids became heavy also. He closed his eyes, and as he tried to hold onto the warmth he felt in Malika's words and the feeling of her arms encircling him, sleep took him.

Neek was asleep again, so Mohmoh was off on his own, exploring. Neek had entrusted him with an important mission that even for someone with Mohmoh's gifts was quite challenging. If only Mohmoh could move faster. With Neek to carry him, they had made their way great distances, and could reach anything, high or low, they might find. Neek was an excellent climber and swimmer, and could help Mohmoh get anywhere so quickly it was dizzying. On his own, Mohmoh moved much more slowly. He didn't want to disappear longer than Neek slept, as he knew, when Neek awoke, he would need his friend. He could sense Neek's sadness, and wanted to help take it away from him. But unfortunately, Mohmoh's healing yellow aura only healed the body, not the heart. So Mohmoh stayed with him, sensing that his presence made Neek feel better.

That's not to say the mission he was given was impossible. No, he had made some progress. He had picked up the initial direction the two boys had been taken, and had followed their trail for a while. But they had been taken so far, it would take little Mohmoh days to follow them all the way to where Barg had left them.

He would keep searching until he found a way. His friend Neek needed him and he wouldn't let him down. Perhaps he could use the waterways to get around more quickly. He thought about it for a long while, ambling slowly over the rocky ground on his spindly white leglings. He could sense the water in the rocks below him. Water moved, unseen through the rocks like the trails of memory and the pictures from other's lives. It was wonderful to live in such a vibrant darkness.

CHAPTER 11
SPECIAL VISITORS

When the much-anticipated Great Priests of the Kindelhoff tribe first arrived, Neek had been quite excited. These were the foremost experts in the various fields of magic known to Rocklings, and Neek wanted answers. His gifts were so new to him, and nobody in Neek's own tribe seemed able to help him understand them. Malika shared his telepathy, but otherwise Neek was on his own.

The Priests looked quite promising when they finally appeared, bearing great sacks of rolled up parchments, and weighed down with a vast array of strange and intriguing artifacts. The Priests were very different in appearance from those in Neek's tribe. They wore elaborate tattoos on their bodies, bright robes, and spoke to each other in unusual tongues the young Rockling didn't recognize.

Many of them also had gifts of their own. Brodana, most senior of the group, had the ability to send sparks shooting through the air. Dimaad, a broad male with one bright yellow eye, could change his body so that his nails grew long, like tiny swords. And Fraga, who looked to be the youngest of the trio, could levitate several inches in the air.

Despite his initial impressions though Neek soon became frustrated with his new companions. They took up much of his time, pressing him to demonstrate his abilities over and over again. They prodded, poked, and measured, constantly, and they would observe him for hours at a time. It was all more than a little disconcerting.

SPECIAL VISITORS 179

What stones could he cut? How much could he lift? Would anything damage or pierce his skin when he activated his strange silver armor?

The tests of this last ability were particularly draining. While it didn't hurt him to be hit with swords or clubs, even to be subjected to small drips of acid, it exhausted him to maintain the armor, and he ended his days aching and tired.

He could tell, from the elaborate notes they took, that they were learning things from their experiments on him, but they seemed unwilling or unable to teach Neek much in return. The majority of the powers he possessed were unknown to them. Their own abilities, it turned out, were mostly adapted from the magical studies of other races.

Instead of the answers Neek wanted, the Priests offered him instead tome after tome of stories about the First-Mother. Neek enjoyed reading these, seeing resemblances between many of the things she could do and his special gifts. But these stories were from a time long before now, and having been told over many generations had been altered and simplified. They were often quite abstract, and didn't answer most of the questions Neek had about himself. So, he was like the First-Mother. Why? What did it mean? What was he supposed to do or think about the gifts he shared with her, that were increasingly feeling like a burden?

Nobody seemed to know, and so he endured endless hours of testing with precious little time for play. When the Priests weren't examining him, it seemed the whole tribe was continuing their work. Everyone had questions. Everyone wanted to see what he could do. They would ask him about his future. What role did he expect to take? What caste would he join? The list of questions about his life grew endlessly, with precious few answers in return.

～

As fascinated as everyone was with Neek, among the youngest Rocklings at least, they were starting to move on to other things, much to his relief. It was nearly Trap Week, and the Trials were just around the corner. The Trials are a pivotal moment in a young Rockling's life. A series of complicated, dangerous coming-of-age rituals that every Rockling would be put through near their first birthday, the Trials consisted of a variety of tests designed to illustrate the strengths and weaknesses of each young Rockling. Upon turning one, they would no longer be considered children, but the yearlings were not fully developed adults either. The Trials were part of a transitional period during which the tribe and the individual came to a consensus regarding each Rockling's future.

The elders of the tribe would look at the yearlings' behavior during the Trials in combination with the history of how they had performed in their various lessons to help decide what role the Rocklings would play in the tribe, which caste they would join. Those showing strength and quickness of limb might become Warriors or Explorers. The quick-witted might be anything from Trap Makers to Tunnel Wardens. Some who possessed social intelligence or a special connection with their peers were given tasks to train them for leadership. Whatever your gift, be it cooking, fighting, trickery, or leadership, the Trials were supposed to expose those gifts to help place you where you would be well-suited to succeed.

The Trials were a source of great stress to most young Rocklings, not, as some outsiders presumed, because the yearlings were unaware of their future place. No, for most, they already had their lessons tailored by their elders to certain subjects and had a good sense of the role each would ultimately play. The reason the Trials were so stressful is that if you weren't careful, they could kill you.

To those unfamiliar with Rockling ways, who may know little about them except that they are fiercely protective of their young, to subject those same young Rocklings to life and death challenges might seem contradictory. There was a cruel logic in this testing, however. Rocklings develop quickly, and by the end of their first year, though young by other race's standards, they were considered mature enough by their fellow Rocklings to begin fulfilling their duties to the group. This meant the risks they were exposed to in the Trials were about to become very real to them in their everyday lives. What's more, the most dangerous Trials had alternate, easier solutions that their training should have helped the yearlings identify, solutions in the future that would keep them alive. Other challenges, which you could not avoid, were suitably crafted so that any reasonable Rockling, though pushed close to their limits, should be able to survive.

In truth, only the overly ambitious or the truly foolish were likely to get seriously hurt during the Trials. The dangers were in part exaggerated by the older members of the tribe to keep the young Rocklings on their toes, and to give them a sense of pride and a stronger connection to one another once they had completed the challenges. It was important that the yearlings try their best and come to understand that they were each of them a valuable member of the tribe. How better to do this than to put them through experiences where they came to depend upon one another?

To combat the stress of the Trials, the young ones were given ample playtime in the weeks leading up to them. Lessons were relaxed, focusing mainly for each individual student on those things they were planning on trying to excel at in their Trials.

From most young Rocklings' point of view, the greatest thing about the Trials was it meant they would get to enjoy Trap Week beforehand. It was a special time they looked forward to their whole first year.

Rocklings are notoriously clever at protecting their warrens with clever and dangerous traps. They have a great regard for deception and trickery. A carefully concealed pit can slay as many foes as a strong sword, with far less danger to the one wielding it. So, from an early age, all Rocklings are taught about springs, latches, trip wires, and all the secrets of trap craft so cherished by their people. While traps were used by and large for protecting their warren, or catching food in the desolate underground, Trap Week was a light-hearted affair, where Rocklings played tricks on each other, setting up traps to tease and embarrass each other, set to cause laughter, not death.

It was such a beloved time that the older Rocklings would not scold the young even if they themselves sat on a bum chomper, found their tools hidden in a trap door in the ceiling, or were caught in a clever toilet explosion. Trap Week was a time to revel in the joys of life. Nobody was safe from the pranks, young or old.

Margle, one of Neek's favorite younger sisters, had been the victim of three different traps already that day, but rather than being angry about it, she was overjoyed. With an inventive treatment to her washing soap, another sister of hers, Talma, had tricked Margle so that all her scales had turned bright green. Margle also had a colorful cloth attached to one of her wrists with a difficult to remove tumble lock. And that morning, she had found nipper beetles in her pillow case. She seemed to have really taken to the beetles, and was sharing her dinner stew with them.

It made Neek happy to see Margle smile and hear about her elaborate plans for revenge. Talma was certainly going to regret the soap trick the next time she went to the toilet. Margle had been sharing her moss water drink with her all dinner, enticing her to need to go. Pripo, the Tunnel Warden teacher, was going to regret assigning her all those landforms to study. She went on and on about the pranks she had planned. Neek could see she had a gift for this.

Neek would have enjoyed all of this a great deal under normal circumstances, but these were not normal times. Would they ever be for him again, Neek wondered? The Great Priests from Kindlehoof were not only pestering him with their daily interviews and examinations, they had also severely restricted his activities. The tribe had clearly been informed that under no circumstance should anyone play a trap prank on Neek. His powers were still too much of a mystery. They're worried I'll blow fire on someone by mistake, Neek supposed, or tear them to ribbons with my claws. He was allowed to prank others, they told him, but Neek didn't feel right doing so when they couldn't retaliate. And so, one of the happiest weeks of the year went by with Neek having to watch from the sidelines, his only companionship the continuous prodding and questioning he faced from his magical examiners.

Neek was worried he wouldn't even be allowed to take part in the Trials. He had heard them talking about it, out loud, and sometimes silently in their thoughts about him. He's already proven himself, some thought. Between the cave in and the journey through the underground river, he's shown he will be an asset to the tribe. We shouldn't risk losing him through some unfortunate mistake. Even a clever Rockling occasionally lost their footing and thus their life in the Trials. With all of Neek's unique gifts, allowing such a risk was out of the question.

Neek had talked about it repeatedly during his sessions with Malika. He had been fine-tuning his mental powers, working with her nearly every day to extend and control his gift. He could pick out images, memories, almost anything from her mind now, if she let him. His mind grew tired though and sometimes he couldn't avoid hearing other people's mental voices when he didn't want to. At the moment for example, he could hear the joyfully devious schemes running through his brothers' and sisters' heads, as they planned their next great trick.

Neek had insisted he be allowed to take part in the Trials, just like any other Rockling. Over and over he had brought it up until Malika promised him that he'd be allowed. Chief MakMak took much convincing, but in the end, she relented and agreed to the request. He would be permitted to participate. But not in Trap Week! She had put her foot down there, mainly to appease the visiting Great Priests.

Neek felt no need to prove himself. He wasn't looking at the Trials as a chance to show off. He had other plans, plans that involved his little Pluffstack friend, Mohmoh, succeeding in the mission he had given him. Mohmoh was gone all that week. Neek had agreed to give him time away from the warren so he could track the trail of the exiled boys as far as it led.

So there he was, missing out on the most fun week of the year, without even his favorite little friend to keep him company. Somehow the stew just didn't taste as good today.

∽

Neither Whizzle nor Barnag had ever seen an Orc. Certainly not an Orc with reading glasses. The food they had been given was more extravagant than normal today, and they sat on comfortable chairs, covered with warm blankets, rather than shivering in their Goblin jail cells. The Orc spoke a remarkably formal version of the Rockling tongue. It was like listening to the Dragon-Mother again, with her extreme politeness. He spoke it with more dexterity than either of them possessed, using a number of unusual and impressive sounding words that they didn't know the meaning of themselves.

The Orc had certainly made it clear what he wanted. The Goblin maps, so painstakingly crafted over the past weeks, lay before them on the great table in Rumbletum's personal lounge. The Orc pointed from tunnel to tunnel, cavern to cavern, asking the same questions over and over.

"What does the tribe use this cavern for? Is there another way to get from this room to this room? Are there hidden tunnels we aren't seeing? What traps are there here?" the Orc asked, pointing at each bit of the map, on and on for hours.

Whizzle shared all he knew without reservation. Thankful for the food, and the comfortable chair, he was happy to help his new friend with whatever he needed. Barnag was unsure whether Whizzle grasped what the Goblins and this Orc might be planning, but then after what happened with Neek, perhaps he understood clearly and simply didn't mind.

Thankfully, for the Rocklings, Whizzle's knowledge, which he was indeed happy to share, was not particularly vast or accurate.

Whizzle never had a mind for traps, so he had stuck mainly to those areas without them, and certainly if he did know of a few of them, he couldn't explain to the Orcs how they might be disabled. Rumbletum, watching them attentively during the entire interview, clearly could tell the boy was not living up to his expectations. He began staring fixedly at Barnag, a wicked look in his eye.

Barnag tried to be clever, providing misleading information about what a room was used for or whether there was a trap somewhere. But the Goblins knew more than he had expected, having scouted some of these locations already. The Orc, privy to this information, corrected him when Barnag lied and prompted him to tell the truth. The anger in Rumbletum's eyes grew, and the young one's bravery evaporated. In the end, Barnag told them what they wanted to know. Mostly.

Strangely, the main focus of their efforts seemed to be on the Rocklings' birthing chamber and nursery. While they both knew where this was located, nobody except the Dragon-Mother herself and some of the senior Trap Layers and elders knew all the secrets of those hallowed chambers. There were many traps, the boys could tell the Orc that much, but they honestly knew nothing about how to disable or avoid them, having always been shepherded in and out of the chamber by the Dragon-Mother in their infancy.

After hours of interrogation, Rumbletum and the Orc clearly decided they had gathered everything useful these young Rocklings had to offer. Whizzle and Barnag were sent back to their cells without any food that evening. "Work on your memories if you want to eat," they were told. Barnag understood now why they had been treated so well. He also knew what was likely to happen to them when they were no longer useful. Even Whizzle seemed to understand their adventure was coming to an end.

~

When he arrived in Malika's chamber for his evening lesson, Neek was surprised to find there an unusual kind of Rockling he had never seen before. Most Rocklings, viewing the good of the society as paramount, and the importance of the individual to be secondary, don't tend to be flashy or showy. Even prominent leaders like Chief MakMak wore only minimal ritual jewelry and similar signs of power. This Rockling was certainly cut from a different cloth. And well, cloth was a big part of it. He was covered in clothing from head to foot, like the Humans Neek had seen in the Rockling scrolls. He wore an elaborate hat that covered his horns and gave him the appearance of long flowing hair. He had tattoos and marking around his eyes, on his hands, and even on his neck. And he had a giant gold hoop ring pierced through his snout. There was something about the way he stood that made him seem taller than other Rocklings. He was a curious sight.

"Neek, this is Reginald Herringbone," explained Malika. "I'd like you to speak with him." And with that, the Dragon-Mother left him alone with the unusual looking stranger.

"Charmed to know you, my boy," said Reginald, grabbing Neek's hand and pumping it up and down for a while for some unknown reason.

Reginald Herringbone? Neek had never heard such a silly Rockling name. Why not have a normal name like Bugo, or Orpa, or Gingan?

"Are you a magic expert?" Neek asked, fully expecting this to be another visitor from Kindlehoof, here to poke and prod him some more.

"No, my dear lad, I am no Priest or Wizard. I am a Wanderer," Reginald replied. "Do you know what that is?"

"Is that a kind of Explorer?" Neek suggested.

"Good guess, my boy, but no," Reginald explained. "An Explorer searches tunnels and pathways, looking for something specific. A Wanderer, on the other hand, travels the world, meeting people, searching for wisdom, for allies, and for things unknown."

To Neek, this sounded very like what Explorers did, but he figured he would humor the stranger. There was something in his manner that was intriguing, even if he was usually dressed and disturbingly tall.

"An Explorer, however brave they are, however far they might go, seeks to return to the tribe to share their discoveries soon thereafter. And usually, an Explorer is sent by the Chief or some such elder to complete a particular purpose," Reginald continued. "We Wanderers return very seldom to our original tribes. Instead, we head onwards, here and there, guided not by the orders of our elders, but instead directed by the clues and mysteries we find in the world. The Tunnel Wardens and the Explorers and the Cooks and the Chiefs and the vast majority of our kind labor for our survival, the survival of our knowledge, the maintenance of our ways. A Wanderer seeks to look beyond this wisdom to find the pieces that don't fit, to find new directions, new paths for our people."

"Is that why you look the way you do?" Neek asked,

embarrassed as soon as the words came out of his mouth. If he was honest, Neek would have liked to try on the man's hat, to feel what it was to wear boots. This was a kind of difference the stranger chose for himself, not like the things that set Neek apart, which were just an accident of birth.

Reginald smiled. "I suppose I must look quite peculiar to you. Most Rocklings live with other Rocklings, under the earth. But I have lived in Human towns, in deep Dwarven halls, in pixie tree homes, on sailing ships, in a bear's den, and a great many other places besides. When you learn to make the whole world your home, you tend to look as varied as the great world is, and nearly as strange."

It had taken a moment, but Neek noticed that Reginald's lips had stopped while his words continued on. He too had the gift of silent speech.

"You can speak to minds," Neek observed, using his silent speech. "Is that why the Dragon-Mother wanted me to meet you? Are you here to help further my mental training?"

"No, dear boy," the Wanderer responded. "She summoned me because she sensed in your heart the desire to lead a life like mine. Malika sees your unhappiness at being stuck here. The Trials are almost upon us, and she wanted you to understand that this was a choice. We are a caste unlike any other. This is a choice few are offered, and even fewer are suited for. But from what I hear of your adventures," Reginald smiled, "you are a Wanderer already."

Neek thought immediately of his friend Mohmoh. Mohmoh was a Wanderer, wasn't he? He thought of their travels together and the joys they'd experienced. The more Neek thought of the times they'd had beyond the warren, the warmer he felt, and the wider Reginald's smile grew, until it spread from his mouth to his eyes, and then his whole body. He recognized a heart similar to his own.

The two stayed up late into the night talking. Neek wanted to know about life on a sailing ship. He wanted to hear how one slept soundly in a bear's den. Neek asked about the world of men, of Orcs, of all things that traveled below and above the earth, even of things he had heard about that lived in the sky, a place the young Rockling had only ever experienced in stories. Reginald happily told him tale after exciting tale, different than the stories told by the Dragon-Mother and the elders, as they took them far beyond the caves, the pools, to places only imagination gets to visit, places past where even our bodies can go.

Reginald wanted to hear Neek's stories as well, which Neek excitedly told him, culminating in his favorite, the one about the cave full of musical crystals. They shared stories back and forth until it grew late and Malika finally came back in, insisting Neek get some sleep.

The next morning Neek learned Reginald was gone. He had left a note. "Dear Neek, Thank you for listening to my stories, and for telling me yours," it read. "They are all but the beginning to a tale you must continue and shape to be your own. Happy wanderings, Reginald Herringbone."

Happy wanderings, what a strange and wonderful thought that was. Something the youngling had begun to get a taste for but had never imagined could be the basis for a life. Neek spent the afternoon weaving his singing crystal into his relic necklace. It wasn't exactly a giant gold nose ring but it was a start.

~

To say Mohmoh was easily distracted was a gross understatement. Mohmoh could, in the right circumstances, spend ten hours going five feet. He never bored of talking to his ancestors, observing the minute details in the world around him as if each one was singular and precious. His nature was open, ready to accept whatever the world had to offer.

Neek was depending on him though. He had given him this mission and let him leave for days now to complete it, even though Neek was clearly saddened by his departure. And so

Mohmoh ignored a great many things along the way and had followed the trail as clearly and directly as he could, working at great speed to try and locate Neek's bothers, Whizzle and Barnag.

Mohmoh had been nervous when he first sensed where the Goblin and Rockling trails met. He had expected to find a short, one-sided battle ending in the boys' demise. But instead he was thankful to discover the Goblins had spirited the boys away, very much alive, clearly headed to the Goblin base. A great many ancestors knew all about the Goblins' home. About Rumbletum. About the Orc that had visited. These were all troubling and confusing signs. What was coming? The ancestors were not quite sure, but they seemed confident the boys were still alive.

Much as Mohmoh wanted to explore the base himself, to verify the information and experience the Goblins' world firsthand, he wouldn't be able to return in time for Neek's upcoming Trials if he did. And so, summoning all the willpower his Pluffstack body could muster, he pushed away his curiosity and headed back to the Rockling warren as quickly as his little pseudopods would take him.

First an Orc with glasses and now a Human? It was truly a special week. Too bad it would be their last, Barnag thought, remembering the past few moments where the Wizard's magic had probed their brains, double-checking the truth of what they had told Rumbletum and gathering up any details they might have left out.

"There isn't much left for them to give you," the Wizard Aleric told the Orc and the Goblin Chief, speaking the common tongue of the underworld. "There were a few traps the thin one left out, but otherwise your notes look correct. You should have brought me here earlier."

Rumbletum wasn't sure whether he should have brought the Human here at all. This one had a look the Goblin knew well. He could not be trusted. Still, the deal was done, and would have to go forward now.

"Time runs short. We go this week," Aleric continued.

"We are ready," the Orc emissary agreed.

"We can go today, if you'd like," the Goblin Chief offered, keeping his reservations to himself.

"I will gather my party and meet you at the Orc stronghold shortly, Goblin. We will march from there to the Rocklings' lair. Glory will be ours," the Wizard said, smiling. Glory shall be yours too, thought the Wizard, slowly rubbing the body of the flame wand he carried beneath his robe.

CHAPTER 12
THE SERPENT

Mohmoh returned earlier than Neek had expected, a full two days before the Trials. Neek was thankful to have his friend back, as the pressure of the upcoming tests, his sadness from being banned from Trap Week, and the emptiness he felt when Mohmoh was off journeying without him were all dragging on the young Rockling's spirit. Mohmoh had returned with the vital news they sought, but what he had found was both hopeful and troubling. The exiled boys seemed to be alive, and Mohmoh knew where to find them. They appeared to be locked up in a Goblin camp, however, and therefore were in terrible danger. He and Mohmoh had to act quickly.

Neek's initial plan had been to sneak away during his turn in the Trials. Young Rocklings are left alone at certain times during the tests, to see if they can make it through particularly clever traps unassisted and unlock complicated puzzles by themselves. Neek had thought to use one of these moments to get away from the Guards that constantly shadowed him. Ever since he had returned, he had been something between an honored guest and a prisoner.

But strange as it was to admit it to himself, he hadn't felt he was home really, or one of this tribe any longer. He had become something quite apart from them, despite their kind words and gestures of affection. Much as it would pain him to break the rules of the warren and go against the commands of the elders, he couldn't just leave his brothers to the Goblins. Neek was sure he would be punished, perhaps even exiled himself for abandoning the warren when they had gone through such great trouble to find him. He would also be turning his back on the Trials, one of the Rocklings' most sacred rituals. But he was already an outsider now, and almost an exile himself. His brothers were in some ways more like him than the others in his tribe.

Neek went cold at the thought of this. He felt his chest tighten. Even if he could free his brothers from the Goblins, which Neek felt sure was possible with Mohmoh's help, he feared none of them would be able to return here. Home was lost to them. It had been lost when Neek was pushed down into that stream, perhaps even earlier than that when these special powers began to show themselves. He cursed his gifts at that moment. They had ruined not just his life, but his brothers' as well. How much more damage would he do to the warren if he stayed?

There was no time to wait. I must go today, Neek thought, as soon as possible. But how?

He remembered the Nightroot, that red herb Malika had added to his tea to help him sleep. Neek had a lesson later that day in Tunnel Craft with the elderly Beemo. During such teaching sessions there was usually only one Guard in the room. Neek had a plan. He'd have to get his gear ready to go though, and let Mohmoh in on what was happening. And he'd have to somehow take the Nightroot from the nursery. That was the tricky part, but perhaps not so difficult given one or two of Neek's particular talents. Neek found he was already packing his bag in readiness before he completely recognized that he was in fact leaving. It seemed that catching up with his own decision-making was another thing the young Rockling would need to work on. At least this time he could properly ready himself for the journey and bring along a few things he really treasured from the warren.

THE SERPENT

The Goblins were leaving. Barnag wasn't exactly sure what this meant for him and Whizzle, but he had a pretty good idea what it would mean for the other members of their tribe. The Goblins will be taking the maps we helped them make and clearing out our warren, he figured. There was no satisfaction in the thought that the tribe who abandoned him and his brother would be getting punished. All he felt was shame. Shame about trying to trap Neek with the cave in. Shame that he had lied about Neek saving his life. Shame that he and his friend would not even be remembered by the tribe in a year or two. If there still was a tribe by then. The catastrophe was on such a scale that Barnag felt almost numb at the thought of it. He knew what was coming, and now, when his actions might actually have been able to have some positive impact on things, now he could do nothing. The cage he was in felt like a structure Barnag had built himself out of pride and stupidity.

Even slow-witted Whizzle seemed to regret his own actions now. Regret them, not just because where they had landed him, here in a cell with nothing to eat for the past two days, but also because he had come to understand that Barnag had lied to him, and that Neek, far from the monster he had thought him to be, had actually rescued his friend.

He and Barnag deserved to be banished, Whizzle thought. Banished from the world entirely. He looked at Barnag, and for the first time in all that they had been through, he saw something new in his brother. We are just alike, he thought. We are the same. And he hated that sameness. Whizzle had never had much pride in himself but he had always admired his friend. He was proud to have a friend like him, proud that out of all the Rocklings who were younglings that season Barnag had chosen him as a companion. There was a bitterness in that now, something almost laughably cruel about the two of them stuck together like this.

Well, not for much longer, he supposed.

Their thoughtful melancholy was interrupted as Rumbletum, the Goblin Chief they briefly believed might be their friend, entered the chamber dragging a length of thick chain. All other thoughts they were having disappeared in an instant when they saw, slithering at the end of the chain, with a thick, metal ring around its neck, the largest snake Barnag or Whizzle had ever seen. It was easily ten times their length, with a wide, round body that undulated back and forth, its sickly green and orange stripes flexing and twisting as it crossed the floor.

"This is Malgotha," Rumbletum gestured to the young Rocklings, the smile across his face almost more menacing than the monster next to him. "My Warriors have important work to do, so she will guard you, and more importantly, guard my vault in our absence." The boys were housed along with all the other important items the Goblins wanted to protect such as gems and weapons and their other spoils. Whizzle and Barnag could not understand the words the Goblin Chief spoke, but the menace in his tone was clear, matched perfectly by the wicked expression on the snake's face.

Barnag looked at Whizzle, the cluttermouth trying for a smile in response. He loved his friend, even if he hated what they had done. It's my fault, Barnag told himself, putting his hand on his friend's shoulder. There was fear in Whizzle's eyes, fear and anger. I put those there, Barnag thought, and he gripped his friend more tightly.

Rumbletum attached the chain to the far wall. Barnag nervously tried to measure the length of chain in his mind. Was it long enough for the snake to make it to their cages? The bars surrounding him no longer felt tough like iron. He imagined the snake could swallow their cages whole if it wanted to.

THE SERPENT

"When I return," the Goblin continued wickedly, an evil glint in his eye, "Malgotha will eat you. She will be starving by then. Thank you for your help boys." And with that, the Goblin Chief left with his Warriors, chuckling as he walked, as the awful serpent coiled itself up and watched the boys through its sparkling, hungry eyes.

Malika was surprised by Neek's visit. It was welcome, of course. She always enjoyed spending time with him. They had been seeing one another nearly every day, sometimes multiple times a day recently, as she worked to help him hone his mental abilities, the one power she shared in common with the boy. He was progressing quite well. He could read and project thoughts, images, even memories quite successfully. Feeling pity for him about the ban on Trap Week, she had even allowed Neek to project a false impression upon her as a prank, making her believe her feet had turned into mushrooms like his friend Mohmoh. They had laughed about it. It was good to see a rare smile upon Neek's face. The young Rockling might imagine he was good at hiding things, but Malika could see the pressure he was under, and how badly it was bothering him.

He would have made an excellent Dragon-Mother, she thought, although by custom that job usually went to a woman. Male Rocklings rarely possessed the gift of silent speech, her friend Reginald being a notable exception. Like Reginald, Neek had a caring nature, and like Reginald, Malika knew Neek would likely never be happy spending his whole life in one warren. Neek's future lay in other places, places Malika knew she would never see herself. She was sure he would travel the world, as Reginald did, witness to wonderful sights and exciting adventures. She would love to have been by his side, seeing what Neek brought to the world with his gifts, but she knew it was not in her future to see much of the young Rockling's life going forward. There was so much that was hidden from her despite her own gifts.

The Trials were just days away, and soon the whole tribe would know Neek's choice. Would they respect it though, she wondered? Would they allow him to wander, if that ultimately was his choice? The Great Priests were very insistent that after his Trials, Neek should go with them to Kindlehoof, to further explore his magical powers.

Were their examinations doing him any good though? She wasn't sure. It was clear the Priests themselves were learning a lot from Neek. He had abilities the Priests had never seen before, even despite their deep knowledge of magic. In talking with Brodana about it one evening, she had explained that though some of what Neek could do they had seen before, such as turning himself invisible, the actual source of his power was a mystery. Neek hadn't studied runes or sigils or potions, or any of the other paths of magical lore which gave some of them their power. Neek's colorful scales linked him to the First-Mother, but there had been no All-Shades in living memory, so the Priests' understanding of what that actually meant or how the connection granted power was unfortunately thin and largely theoretical.

Some Rocklings had limited magical talents, such as Malika's own ability to summon fire in her hand, but they had never seen anything like Neek's gifts, so varied, so powerful. There was disagreement among the Priests about many things, however they all seemed to agree that as amazing as his powers were, for Neek, this was only the beginning. There was more to come. To their way of thinking, it would be best if that development happened in Kindlehoof, where they had the knowledge and the skills to allow him to study his powers safely, alongside well-trained magical minds.

Their argument had some merit, but she felt strongly that Neek should have the final decision in the matter. Thankfully, Chief MakMak shared her views. The Great Priests were respected, but they would not be allowed to take a young

Rockling away with them without permission from his tribal leader.

In any case, his future was not the issue at the moment. She was curious why he had joined her here now in the nursery.

"Your friend, Reginald," Neek asked "how did you summon him? I mean, if he is a wanderer, freely roaming the world, how is it that you were able to bring him here to meet with me?"

"A fair question," she responded. "Come with me." She opened a sliding wall behind the egg chamber.

A tribe's younglings are its greatest treasure. But Rocklings have other treasures too. Try as they might not to hoard gold or gems or other such goods that would only have deadly thieves and enemies trying to rob them, Rocklings like all beings have things that are important to them. Things of value they must protect. And so, it made practical sense, Rocklings being an eminently practical race after all, that a tribe's treasure is generally stored in close proximity to their eggs. The Hardhands tribe followed this practice, with a hidden chamber just off the nursery floor.

Neek looked around in wonder at the strange artifacts lining the walls of the tiny chamber. Malika reached up and grabbed a red globe from the shelf. "This is a sounding stone," she told him, showing him the crimson orb. It was a dark burgundy color, shiny and semi-translucent like volcanic glass. "If you hold it in your hands like so," she showed him, "and chant the right words, it sends out a pulse. All Wanderers wear special rings. Do you remember Reginald's ring?"

Neek nodded, yes. He was quite sure he would always remember every detail about the strange Rockling who led a life so like the one he wanted.

"Those rings are tuned to these stones," Malika continued. "If they receive a pulse, their rings allow them to track it. We generally leave Wanderers alone, calling on them only when a tribe is in dire need, or has a special request. I used this to bring him here to meet you, so you would understand what a Wanderer was and could consider it as a choice during your upcoming Trials. I'm surprised he didn't tell you about the rings actually."

"Thank you, Dragon-Mother," Neek told her. "I have been very curious about that. I'm sure he would have told me if I didn't ask so many other questions," Neek joked. "I must go to my other lessons now." And the boy turned to leave.

Reginald had told Neek all about his ring, of course. But that was the best excuse Neek could think up to explain to Malika why he had come to see her like this.

The Dragon-Mother put the sounding stone away, closed up the chamber, and went back to the work she was doing. A new clutch of eggs would be arriving soon, and the chamber would need to be prepared. She had to review what supplies she needed. Analyzing her stocks, she decided she must procure more anti-itching salve, some Tingle Leaves to help with laying pains, and clearly a lot of Nightroot. She was nearly out it appeared.

Malgotha's life had been quite a roller coaster. Lying there, however, coiled up and chained to a wall, she felt like the ride had reached a pretty dull stage, and she would very much like to try something different for a change.

Her early life had been glorious. Stronger and larger than her other snake brethren, Malgotha had flourished in the tunnels. She had slithered fearlessly along cavern floors, swam through underground streams with no worries at all, hunting and eating all manner of prey. She was the envy of all serpent-kind, a true marvel. She had a fine lair, full of food, and a hunting ground where no snake, or any other beast to be honest, would dare challenge her.

Then somehow, it had all gone wrong. The Goblin Chief had captured her, smuggled her to his domain, and now she was a glorified pet. What a humiliating fall from grace, she thought. How the other snakes would laugh at her if they could see her here, chained up like this, guarding these frightened, overgrown lizards.

At first, captive life had been acceptable she supposed. She was the Goblin's latest toy, and so was treated to fine food and given the freedom to roam. She had only eaten one or two Goblins though before he started treating her like this. Chaining her up. Starving her to make her fierce. As if she needed the motivation! There was more hunger inside her she guessed than in that whole stinking Goblin tribe. But there were so many of them. She could swallow them whole, but if enough of them beat her with their swords, well, there were limits, even for a legendary creature like herself.

She eyed the Rocklings closer, sliding her body over the floor until she was within striking distance of their cages. She pulled against her chain as hard as she could but it held firm. She looked at the caged Rocklings hungrily and pulled again with all her might. Soon enough, she thought. Soon her captor would be back and she could at least see if these lizards were tasty. Or this chain might eventually give way. And then who knows what she might eat?

All good things in time, she thought, struggling against the chain that held her collar with all the force her massive, thick body could produce. The pin shifted, just slightly.

~

Beemo, the elderly Tunnel Warden, already looked tired. Neek thought he might not even need to use the Nightroot on him at all. Dida, the Guard, however, looked bored, but very awake. He was playing games with his claws, tapping them one against the other to keep himself entertained through the Warden's lengthy lecture about tunnel safety. Even Neek felt bored by the elder's droning. No, not bored, anxious. Anxious to get going. He was fairly sure he had heard this particular lecture before though, soon after the cave in. He knew how to spot weak tunnel walls, and how to reinforce them or rupture them as circumstances called for. Neek tapped his leg, waiting for a break in the lecture.

Beemo paused for a breath, and Neek hopped at the chance. "I'm sorry to interrupt, but I am desperately thirsty, may I grab us all some tea from the kitchen?" Neek asked.

Beemo, after speaking for quite a while about types of rock with long, complicated names, honestly thought the idea was a good one. His parched throat could use it. "Yes, of course, Neek, I'm sure we'd all like some tea."

Dida nodded. Anything to get a break from all this tunnel talk. Besides, Dida thought, Alakoo, the female Chef, might be there today. Perhaps he would have a moment to chat with her while the boy made tea. "Come on then," Dida told Neek, motioning him forward.

Neek's heart raced. He had to be careful. Dida was a bright Rockling, keen eyed and alert, and if he spotted Neek putting something funny in the tea, his whole plan would be ruined. Luckily, for Neek's sake, and Dida's, Alakoo was indeed in the kitchen, preparing stew for the dinner that evening. She was bored too. As thankful as she was to the First-Mother for all this fish, she really wanted something new to cook with. It was hot standing over the huge kettles all day, stirring and tasting as the liquid bubbled.

And so, Dida and Alakoo chatted happily, uttering the familiar, soft tones of young creatures who cared for each other, while Neek carefully took some of the Red Nightroot from his hip pouch where it was hidden, and stirred it into two cups of tea.

He waited for the herb to dissolve, took his third cup as well, and rushed back to the room where he swore he saw Beemo with his head hanging down, eyes closed.

"Thank you, Neek," Beemo said, as he snapped awake, trying to hide his napping, disappointed the boy had returned so quickly. The tea was tasty. Earthy. It reminded him of his younger days for some reason.

Done so soon, Dida wondered? He bid Alakoo farewell and followed the young Rockling back to the study of the old Warden, tapping his claws and praying the rest of the lecture would be brief.

CHAPTER 13
BEDTIME

Mohmoh was inching slowly along a wall near where two tunnels met. He felt unusually impatient. Normally, the Pluffstack would have been happy to spend several hours crisscrossing a room, absorbing every inch, every detail, all the while communing with his ancestors. There was no natural hurry in a being whose sense of time was shaped by an almost infinite lifespan.

Today though was different. Mohmoh knew the great risks he and Neek would be facing at the Goblin camp, and even here, so close to the Rockling warren, the signals Mohmoh was receiving from the traces on the tunnel walls were distressing. There were all kinds of creatures moving through these passages. Orcs. Goblins. Even Humans! There was so much activity in the communication network Mohmoh depended on for guidance that it was nearly overloaded with messages. All of them pointed to some form of danger nearby. Mohmoh was eager to get moving.

Finally, Neek appeared, lifting the anxious little Pluffstack from the wall and placing him on the young Rockling's shoulder. Mohmoh loved traveling like this. Now they could move quickly, and today that was vital. Even on Neek's limber legs, it would take them nearly a dozen hours to reach the Goblins' base. "Let's go!" he signaled forcefully to Neek's mind. "There are lots of strange legs in the tunnels today. We must be quick."

∼

The Wizard Aleric had selected only his closest, most trusted friends to take with him. This meant that the list of people to choose from had been quite short, and dotted with oddities.

There was a cultist, Erawynn, a healer and worker of dark magic. She worshipped a strange earthen deity known only to a few secret societies in the kingdom. Her habit of covering her body in dirt and mud before battle disturbed him, especially given the fondness he had for his clean, bright robes. She was powerful though, and ruthless, so he looked past her grungy exterior. That god of hers must be a stern one, he thought.

Erawynn seemed like a delicate flower though in comparison to RockLopper, a hulking, wild Warrior who lived it seemed only to fight other creatures to the death. Can you truly be a friend to someone who hardly ever speaks, Aleric wondered? The Wizard supposed though, given the dark thoughts likely to fill RockLopper's meager mind, the less the big brute spoke, the better. His rippling muscular form and his ferocious battle axe spoke volumes. Aleric wasn't bringing him along to negotiate anyway.

Of all his friends though, Aleric treasured Grutch the most. Grutch was a wiry, battle-marked bandit who could solve any problem you put before him. There seemed to be no locked door, no maze of secret passages, no heroic Guard that could stand in Grutch's way. Whatever the obstacle, Grutch had seen it before a thousand times or more. And when well-paid, Grutch was as loyal as an old dog. A particularly vicious dog, to be sure, but loyal nonetheless.

Like Aleric, they were all ambitious. Self-interest would keep them on task. Erawynn dreamed of elevating the reputation of her muddy god, hoping to bring the cult out of the shadows and into popular view in the kingdom. RockLopper lusted for bloody struggle, and daunting challenges sufficient to earn him a heroic reputation in the songs of wandering bards. Grutch had plans for a grand estate surrounded by a wide moat with a pool of gold to swim in. And so far, in their time with the young Wizard, they had all found Aleric to be useful to their ends. As they stood there now though, deep in an Orc stronghold, with a small army of Orcs and Goblins all around them, all heavily armed, listening to Aleric's dangerous plan, the adventurers hoped their trust in the young Wizard was not misguided.

"Your Scouts," Aleric motioned to the Goblin leader, "will go with Grutch here and remove the traps we've identified, clearing the outer passageways so we can get your Warriors," he now indicated to the Orc general on the map, "in through here and here. They will clean out the warren, with our help, of course."

212 BEYOND SUNLIGHT

The Goblin Chief, Rumbletum, smirked at Aleric's choice of words. Clean, Rumbletum thought to himself, there's nothing clean about what we'll be doing today. It would take months to clean up the mess we'll be leaving when we visit the pitiful home of the dragon-mice. He spoke none of this out loud though. The plan was clear enough. The Goblins would be risking their lives removing the traps, the Orcs would battle the Rockling Warriors, and the Humans would come in at the end to grab all the glory, and whatever meager treasure the pathetic Rockling tribe had amassed. Rumbletum felt a brief pang of regret about his subjects that would fall in the effort, but when he looked over at the plentiful chests of gems and gold the Wizard had brought in payment, these thoughts quickly passed. One can always make more Goblins, the Chief reminded himself.

Rumbletum could see on the Orc leader's face that he was likely having similar misgivings. Rumbletum trusted the Orcs to do as they were told. They weren't as imaginative as his kind. It might just be that misplaced Orcish bravado, the Goblin thought, their seeming need to show how the Orcs could overpower anyone, that kept their leader silent in the face of what was obviously a poorly thought-out plan. It was the scheme of a young Wizard with precious little battle experience, and seemingly no regard for protecting his soldiers' lives.

After the plan was agreed to, the various commanders went and gave the final orders and rousing speeches to their troops. The whole camp feasted and drank heavily, bolstering their spirits and cleansing their minds of any doubt about the dangerous work ahead.

~

It was supposed to be a celebration. But it certainly didn't feel that way to most of the Rocklings in the great hall.

Neek was gone again. Not lost. Just gone. Neek had left a note next to a sleeping Guard and the old Tunnel Warden explaining his actions.

"I have gone to save my exiled brothers from a Goblin prison. They are in grave danger and I will not abandon them. Please do not follow me. I will return when I am able. Good luck to all the yearlings in the Trials. I am sorry to miss out, but I must do what I can to help my brothers," the note read.

The elders were in fervent debate about how the tribe should proceed. The Kindlehoof Priests, and others, were adamant that a group of Warriors should be sent to retrieve Neek immediately. This group argued that Neek was a precious gift to all Rocklings and must be saved at any cost. Some of the senior tribe scholars argued that the Trials were a vital ritual in Rockling life, and must proceed as planned for the good of the tribe. The community was fiercely divided, with views and suggestions of all kinds being put forward as to how to proceed.

Chief MakMak considered all of their arguments carefully. She knew that if the Goblins had Neek, it would take all of the Warriors the Rocklings could muster to get him back. This was a huge risk, especially because the tribe was not even certain where the Goblins' camp was located. She also realized how much work had gone into preparing the Trials, and how disruptive it would be for all the yearlings if these were cancelled or postponed. There was no path forward that didn't seem treacherous for her tribe.

In the end, it was Malika, the Dragon-Mother, normally so protective of her young, who swayed the group. "Neek seemed lost to us after the cave in. Yet, he returned, unharmed. He seemed lost forever to the underground stream. And again, he came back to us," she spoke imploringly. "Now he is not lost. He has left willingly, gone to do what he sees as right. He is with that strange little friend of his, on a mission to save his brothers, the two boys we cast out. If Neek truly is a gift from the First-Mother, if she is guiding his destiny, perhaps this choice is part of that destiny. This is his Trial. We should trust him to face it alone, as we do of all younglings."

Shortly after Malika's stirring words, a compromise was reached. The tribe would continue with the Trials, as scheduled, giving Neek two days to complete his mission. If after that he had still not returned, they would gather their forces and go after him.

And so the community sat in the great hall, as they did every year before the Trials, and feasted to celebrate the yearlings. Never before were so many meals left unfinished. Little music was played. Few laughs were heard. Most Rocklings went to bed early that night, their hearts heavy.

Malika sat up, all through the night, praying to the First-Mother for Neek's safe return.

Neek's plan to escape the warren had worked perfectly. He had used his talent for invisibility, combined with his knowledge of daily Rockling life, to slip past the perimeter defenses and the Rockling Guards undetected, racing to the meeting point where he quickly swept up Mohmoh. They hurried north through twisting cave passages toward the Goblin camp. Neek hurtled along at top speed as Mohmoh clutched Neek's ear, holding on for dear life as the little Pluffstack bumped around on Neek's shoulder.

The young Rockling knew that his plans, while so far successful, extended no farther. What would Neek do when he reached the Goblin camp? How would they get through the Goblin defenses with no special knowledge of Goblin life or the complex itself to guide him?

Neek hoped that Mohmoh's special gift would protect them. Perhaps the little Pluffstack ancestors knew the caverns where these Goblins lived, and could help guide them past some of the dangers there. Unfortunately, Mohmoh's talent was not working as well as it normally did. Mohmoh had mentioned something about too many ancestors speaking at once in the thought stream, and Neek was worried. Oh well, he would just have to be flexible he supposed.

~

Whizzle and Barnag were not being held in an established Goblin warren, but instead inside a temporary military camp. The main difference, other than the complexity of the structure, was that in a warren there are usually Goblins of all ages, doing all kinds of jobs. There are the young, old, healthy, sick, and everything in-between. In a Goblin war camp, on the other hand, one would only find Warriors, and the few functional service Goblins such as Cooks and Animal Handlers who were needed to attend to the other details of day-to-day life. With all the Warriors currently away at the Orc stronghold, there were precious few Goblins remaining at camp. This was why Rumbletum had left his precious snake, Malgotha, there. An intruder might get past the Cook, or the few remaining Goblin sentries, but anyone foolish enough to venture into the treasure room with the two boys and the serpent would never leave alive.

So, relatively empty as it was, it shouldn't really be surprising then that no Goblins noticed when the massive snake finally pulled the final link of her chain free from the iron ring on the wall. The great metal link fell heavily to the floor as Malgotha's grin widened to both ends of her terrifying jaw.

The young Rockling boys heard the clatter. Rousted from an uncomfortable slumber by the noise, Whizzle and Barnag cried out, and began rattling the doors of their cages with wild abandon. The Goblin cell was quite good however at masking their noise, its thick stone door blocked out the sound from the chambers beyond. You wouldn't want the cries of prisoners waking you up in the night, would you?

Malgotha looked at the little lizards, trapped in their metal cages. She would come back for this meager snack. There were other, tastier treats to be had next door. She could smell them.

And so, Malgotha slithered toward the door, her massive form covering half the width of the passageway. She pushed herself out of the storage cell and into the sleeping quarters beyond.

~

Neek was young and fit, but even so, after running nonstop for hours now, he was reaching the limits of his endurance. He paused for a moment to rest, hunched over, his hands on his thighs, breathing heavily. Neek put Mohmoh down on the floor to test the soil. "What are your ancestors saying?" he asked.

"We are close," Mohmoh told him, smiling warmly as always. "Just a few more miles."

Just a few more miles, Neek thought. He had a hard time matching Mohmoh's optimism. Neek's legs ached and his lungs were ragged after so many hours of sprinting. He could make it, Neek knew he had no choice, but even then, he and Mohmoh would immediately have to face whatever Guards the Goblins had posted, find his brothers, and get out safely. Even if Neek and Mohmoh could accomplish all that, the group of them still would have a long journey back home, with who knows what kind of danger on their tail.

Neek also suspected that if he wasn't quick to return, the tribe would come searching for him, despite the request he had made in his note. He couldn't bear the thought of leading the tribe into greater danger. The Rocklings might already be on their way here.

If only Malika were here, Neek thought. She could brew him a special tea, or rub a special oil on his scales, or use her yellow aura to restore his energy. While Mohmoh possessed the power to heal, it seemed to be only for injuries, not the kind of exhaustion Neek was currently feeling. Neek's heart continued to pound rapidly in his chest as he struggled against his growing anxiety.

Just then, Neek felt Mohmoh's touch near his ear, as the Pluffstack began to caress Neek's face in long, calming strokes. "You must use your power," Mohmoh told him. "That will sustain you." Clearly his little friend had been following Neek's cluttered thoughts.

"None of my abilities can help me with this," Neek responded dejectedly. "I can't lift this pain away with strength. I can't cut it away with my nails. None of my gifts work here. I just have to rest here a moment." With that Neek slumped to the ground, his knees up, panting and desperately trying to summon the necessary strength to continue onwards. His brothers needed him. What terrors might they be experiencing at this very moment?

Mohmoh slid down slowly from Neek's shoulder onto his chest. Milky white tendrils reached out to Neek's necklace, toward the singing crystal Neek had recently tied there, and the little Pluffstack extended his familiar yellow aura out around the stone. As a yellow glow enveloped the stone, the crystal began to shine with great intensity. The light gradually but consistently grew until it was so bright that Neek had to squint to protect his eyes. Neek felt strong vibrations, much like the ones that had experienced in the wonderful crystal cavern where he sang his songs. The vibrations penetrated his entire body, sinking down even into the depths of his mind. The waves of pulsing color that washed through him were silent, but his whole body tingled as they passed through him. It was an exhilarating and startling sensation, but his legs continued to ache, and his lungs still panted for air.

"This is wonderful Mohmoh, but," Neek began to complain, but Mohmoh pressed on Neek's chest, strongly interrupting his words.

"Now you must extend your light," Mohmoh insisted. "Those shaking vibrations you feel deep inside yourself, you must use them. Let them flow out of you, toward your pain. Hold the crystal while you try. It will help you." Mohmoh guided Neek's hand to the glowing stone hanging from the Rockling's neck.

Neek clasped the bright crystal and closed his eyes tight, concentrating on the vibrating hum inside himself. He used the silent voice in his head to sing along, chanting tones that matched the rhythms of the pulsing light. Gradually, Neek found a harmony between the lights and the song inside his head. The light in the chamber flared even brighter now, so bright that Neek could see it through his closed eyelids. Neek held on even tighter and let the energy flow outwards from his mind, pulsing along with the shining stone to the beat of the sacred song inside him.

When Neek opened his eyes, he saw that Mohmoh was no longer touching the crystal. The yellow glow coursing through the stone was coming solely from Neek's hand, wrapped firmly around the stone. The light covered his body and the entire tunnel chamber around them in a powerful yet soothing glow.

Neek released his grip on the crystal and relaxed as the pulsing light and the song in his head began to fade. The tunnel chamber gradually returned to darkness. Neek was no longer panting. His heart beat at a comfortable pace. His legs and lungs no longer bothered him. Somehow, this release of energy had restored Neek's strength.

"You see now," Mohmoh explained to Neek, smiling, "how much you and I are alike. You can channel the energy of life as I do, back and forth between the light and the darkness. We must continue on now though, danger is all around us." With that Mohmoh climbed back onto Neek's shoulder and grasped his ear tight.

Neek bent his neck toward his friend, and reaching up with his left arm, hugged the little Pluffstack tightly. What would I have done without Mohmoh by my side, Neek thought to himself, thanking the First-Mother for bringing this miraculous companion into his life.

Then, after that brief moment, Neek stood up and grabbed his things, preparing to move on. They hopped back onto the trail and Neek raced off at top speed, renewed by the lesson from his friend. In less than an hour, they reached an intersection near a crude door cut into a cave wall.

"This is the place," Mohmoh indicated.

Well, what now, Neek thought? What would they face inside? Whatever it was, Neek felt ready.

∽

Malgotha had started by eating the Goblin Cook. He was disappointingly bland. She could tell from the smell in the air there were at least two other Goblins somewhere in the complex. Having been starved for nearly a week now, even a whole Goblin did little to satisfy her appetite. She had almost nabbed one of the remaining sentries, but she had accidentally knocked over some pots and the Goblin had spotted her, running off screaming in an instant. She heard more footsteps, and some unintelligible chatter in the distance. Then more running. They've both gone now, she assumed. What a shame.

Malgotha's belly grumbled with anger. It called out to her to be filled up. I will have to pry those scaly lizards out of their cages, she thought. A talented constrictor, she supposed that if she wrapped herself around the cages and squeezed hard enough, the bars would eventually break and pop out those two tasty snacks. It was still a disappointingly small dinner after so long a break. Oh well, she would just have to be flexible she supposed.

And then, she smelled a new smell, coming from the other entrance to the camp. It was similar to the lizards in the cages. But it was free. It was moving. That meant a hunt. Feeling like a young viper again, back in her childhood tunnels, Malgotha made her way quietly toward the cells. One lizard seeks another after all. She would hide around the corner and wait, just like the good old days.

∽

Neek's heart was still racing. He had been standing just south of the entrance to the war camp when two Goblins burst out, running and yelling loudly. They found us so quickly, Neek thought. My plan is already ruined. Neek started to turn invisible and raised his claws for a fight, regretting that he had not brought any other weapons, when he noticed that the two Goblins were actually headed away from him. They looked terrified.

Confused, Neek backed up against the wall, slowly and carefully easing his head around the corner and peeking inside. There were a few torches burning on the walls. Several pieces of furniture had been knocked over, likely by the fleeing Goblins. But otherwise, Neek saw no signs of life. There were no voices here.

Mohmoh, who hadn't been turned invisible by Neek's power, still sitting on Neek's shoulder, seemed to float through the air like a funny mushroom bird. "Do you sense anything?" Neek asked him.

"No," Mohmoh replied. This was a new set of passages it seemed, only recently crafted by their Goblin inhabitants. Mohmoh was the first Pluffstack to travel these halls. Neek and Mohmoh were walking blind, with no one to warn them about the monstrous serpent on the other side of the adjacent room.

Neek put Mohmoh down on a nearby shelf. The little Pluffstack hid himself in a water jug while Neek explored the camp, one soft, slow footstep at a time.

Where were all the Goblins, Neek wondered? He saw many beds in this room. Dozens of Goblin Warriors could have slept in this warren. Yet, there was not a single body to be found, nor the sound of any movement nearby. Neek continued forward.

The next chamber was a kitchen. The cooking tools had been knocked over and littered the floor in disarray, showing clear signs of some kind of struggle. There was soup on the floor and the walls, and bits of beetle everywhere. But still, no Goblins.

At end of this chamber, another room held one much larger bed, covered in plush, comfortable skins. This must be their leader's chamber, Neek guessed. But this room was empty of life as well. Neek saw only a few more passages to try on the other end of the barracks. Were his brothers gone as well, Neek wondered? Had he come too late?

And so, emboldened by the lack of Goblins about, Neek began to walk quickly toward the few remaining unexplored passages. His quiet footsteps became louder by the moment, sending soft vibrations across the floor of the camp. Even the most sensitive Rockling feet would not have felt these tiny tremors through the earth. To the broad, fat belly of the snake though, a vast sensitive ear to the ground, they were like drums playing. Sweet music. A dinner bell ringing.

Just a few more rooms, Neek thought, turning toward the cell where the boys were kept.

Closer and closer they came. Louder and louder the vibrations sounded, and then, nothing. They just stopped. It had been years since Malgotha had hunted the tunnels of her youth. She had been a captive of the Goblin Chief for longer than she cared to remember, and so she was ready to admit that her talents for catching prey, once so expertly honed, might be somewhat diminished. She could swear though, by the vibrations, that the lizard she could hear and smell walking the halls should be just in front of her.

It must be just outside the passageway, she thought, waiting patiently for the noises to resume.

It was enormous. Neek had seen cave snakes, sure. They were a delicacy in Rockling life, and a danger as well. Many of them were venomous. Even if they didn't poison you, their fangs were long and sharp, and you would long regret it if you didn't look where you stepped in the world below.

But this beast, easily twice as wide as Neek himself, and ten times as long, was like nothing he had ever seen. And it was inches from him. Neek knew it must smell him. It must have felt his footsteps. It was coiled, ready to strike, its killer's eyes poking daggers into the dark. What could he do?

∼

It was excruciating. She had heard the footsteps. She could smell its oily lizard skin. But her eyes showed her nothing. Where was the lizard hiding? She had waited, patiently, coiled, ready to strike, and yet there were no more sounds. Only that strong, musty smell. Her belly gurgled.

She inched forward slowly.

∼

Barnag was hungry, tired, and terrified. But beyond all those more pressing concerns, he was also extremely confused. First, the gigantic snake had slithered back into their room. He figured this surely meant that this was the end of them. But the awful beast had paid Barnag and his brother no mind, coiling in the corner on the far wall and staring out at the passage opening.

Then Barnag heard soft footsteps. Someone was outside. Had the Goblin Chief returned? He doubted the Chief would be so quiet about it. And why would the Chief be alone? No, it must just be an unlucky Goblin Guard who'll soon be a snack for this massive beast, he assumed. Yet the footsteps had stopped, right in the doorway, and there was no one there. The snake looked nearly as confused as Barnag was, and its eyes moved about, frantically searching the empty doorway.

Then, most confusing of all the events so far, Barnag thought he heard a voice. A familiar voice. It was Neek's voice!

"Make noise," Barnag heard the voice tell him, seemingly from inside his head. "Barnag, make some noise, now!" the voice insisted.

At first, Barnag thought that this must be the Rockling gods teasing him again. Or maybe his guilt was talking to him. But as the snake started to slither slowly forward, the voice screamed inside his head. "Make noise now, or this snake will eat us all!" and Barnag decided that crazy or not, he would do as he was told.

Barnag grabbed the bars of his cage and shook them as hard as his tired arms could, yelling at the foul serpent in his native Rockling tongue. "Come over here, you smelly cave worm! Your fangs are pathetic, you lousy grub!" he yelled, along with a great number of other insults that should not be repeated in a civilized story.

Thankfully, Barnag could hear him. And his brother was doing what Neek had asked. While Barnag shook the cage and screamed, Neek was able to turn and run from the passageway, back to the sleeping chamber beyond. Neek hopped up onto one of the beds. I must keep off the floor, he realized, or the serpent will find me.

Neek's footsteps caused Malgotha to turn and slither quickly after him. The hidden creature was there, she knew it, angry at the little lizards in their cages for distracting her. She rounded the corner, her massive body flowing over one of the beds and out into the middle of the room. The bedframe broke into splinters as Malgotha smashed through it.

Malgotha still had the creature's smell in her nose, but the noise of its movement stopped. Where are you, little snackling, she wondered as her belly continued to roar at her. Enraged, Malgotha bit through another one of the bedframes, snapping it in half with her massive jaws, beads of green poison showing through on the blankets below.

Thankful that he hadn't picked that particular bed to stand on, Neek had formulated the beginnings of a plan. He would have to be careful though, one wrong step and the snake would certainly catch him. Slowly, slower even than Mohmoh on a lazy day, Neek crept, climbing from one bed to the next, as quietly as he could, carefully off of the floor to avoid making any vibrations the snake might notice. When he reached the bed closest to the Chief's room, Neek quickly picked up a blanket and threw it against the far wall.

Malgotha lashed out at the sound where the blanket fell, catching nothing but a mouthful of wall and fluff as she slammed into the side of the cave closest to the kitchen. Neek jumped immediately, hurtling into the Chief's room and vaulting on top of his large, plush bed.

Malgotha was behind him in a flash, her huge form filling the doorway and the only exit from this room. She realized that she had him now. There was no other way out. The sneaky lizard was in here somewhere. She needed only to wait and he would reveal himself.

Neek too realized the flaw in his plan. How would he ever get past that massive wall of teeth and flesh before him? He tried to breathe as quietly as possible, unmoving on the layers of fur covering Rumbletum's lavish bunk.

How had the lizard eluded her in the room of beds, Malgotha wondered? No matter, she wouldn't let it trick her again. Dinner was hiding somewhere in front of her and she was blocking its only exit. In the old days, she might have gone to sleep, just to taunt it, and snap the lizard up when it finally worked up the courage to try to jump over her. But Malgotha was older now, and her belly was rumbling, and she would never be able to sleep without a good meal.

Malgotha stretched out the back end of her tail, trying to use it like a long finger, feeling around the room for any signs of life. She brushed along one wall, over a chair in the corner and the little table next to it, prodding and probing to find her prey.

Neek realized to his dismay that the serpent was long enough to reach over the whole length of the room in this manner. She would find him soon if he didn't act.

The tail made its way toward the bed. It lifted over the side, creeping toward him in a sick, lumbering motion.

Neek tried as quietly and carefully as possible to move to the other side of the bed. The tail stopped.

Malgotha's tail, now on the bed, clearly felt the motion of Neek's feet moving, even as careful as he was being. Her eyes, fixated on where her tail was exploring, also saw the blanket move. So, there you are, Malgotha thought. She spread her jaws wide and lunged forward as fast as lighting toward Neek.

He had nothing against the snake. They were all over the tunnels of the underneath, and they certainly played their role in the ecosystem. You had to be careful, sure. But thanks to the snakes, the rat population was kept under control. The diseases the rats carried on their teeth were often even more deadly than a viper's poison.

He really didn't want to hurt her. But when that awful mouth flew toward him, a wall of painful death, what Neek wanted didn't really matter. His instincts took over. Quick as a flash he dropped his invisible form, opened his mouth, and bathed her in his fiery breath.

As much from shock as from pain, Malgotha reared back, hissing, her scales smoking, her eyes damaged from the heat. The serpent instinctively slid away, underneath the bed, to escape the flames. Cave snakes fear few things, but they know fire has an even sharper bite than they do.

Neek jumped off the bed, leaping farther than he had in his whole life, making it nearly all the way to the Chief's door.

Malgotha, her scales still hissing from the flames, was slow to react, and by the time she slithered forward, Neek had slammed the door shut and barred it closed.

Malgotha banged her heavy frame against the door, thumping on it with all her might. But she was not strong enough to break the heavy slab, and so there she lay, trapped. Her skin was hot with pain. Her belly was still empty and angry. She would have wept if she could.

∽

After taking a few deep breaths to compose himself, Neek grabbed Mohmoh and rushed to the room where his brothers were still screaming. When Neek entered their cell. Whizzle and Barnag both started babbling apologies, thanking him, and praising the First-Mother he was there. Unable to find any keys, Neek activated his glowing green claws and slashed through the bars of their cages, freeing the boys.

"Hush now, brothers," he told them. "We must go. The Goblins may be back any second." He hugged them both in his arms. They hugged him back, long and intensive hugs. Neither Whizzle nor Barnag had ever expected to be embraced by the Rockling community again, much less the brother whom they had so badly wronged. "I am sorry I could not find you sooner," Neek told them.

"Our warren, that's where the Goblins were headed, Neek," Barnag warned him, excitedly. "We have to return home and help them. A war is coming."

Neek nodded. He grabbed Mohmoh from the jar where the Pluffstack had been hiding, and in a flash, the group was out of the complex, running at top speed back toward their home.

CHAPTER 14
THE TRIALS

It was considered rude by Rocklings to compare the Trials from one year against another. Manners aside though it was clear that this year the bar had been lowered. Quite literally, the bars they had to jump, the locks they had to pick, the traps they needed to diffuse, these were all somewhat simpler this year than in the past.

Perhaps the elders in setting up theses course over the past few weeks had decided to reduce the risks so that nobody, especially not their colorfully-scaled prodigy Neek, would be hurt. Of course, Neek wasn't even here now. So, if that had been the elders' concern, their efforts had been wasted. More likely though these changes were guided by a collective sense that this had been a truly hard year for the tribe. Two of their young had already been sent into exile this season, a topic few discussed openly. Many Warriors had been lost, and Explorers too, from Goblin raids and whatever the source of that awful fire had been. In the Trials this year, it was clear that the elders wanted the youngling to achieve their successes as safely, soundly, and quickly as possible.

The tribe's mood was certainly more somber than normal. The recent disappearance of Neek weighed heavily on everyone's mind. There was less cheering and fanfare than usual as they watched the yearlings make their way through the challenges put before them. There were very few injuries though, and no loss of life, so as the day progressed the warren was infused at least with a mild sense of calm. The yearlings, excited to make it through the Trials successfully, celebrated their achievements as their elders gradually started to relax and enjoy the ritual. Whatever the recent hardships, the tribe felt safe for now.

The afternoon would be quite different though. Very quickly, no one felt safe at all.

∼

His brothers kept up admirably, Neek thought, as thin and sickly as they looked to him. When was the last time they had eaten, he wondered? How had the Goblins treated them? The young Rocklings spoke little, the only conversation being Neek telling his brothers which way to go at the various intersections they passed through on their way back toward their warren. Neek supposed that after their terrible time with the Goblins, his brothers' legs might take them all the way across the earth if needed. Finally, despite Whizzle and Barnag's silence, Neek could see overwhelming exhaustion on their faces. He could hear them panting heavily, and he suggested they all stop for a moment to rest and recover.

Neek had brought with him some water, and a bit of dried meat. Whizzle and Barnag consumed all of this quickly in the dark, their eyes hardly looking up at him. Neek examined the brothers as they ate. There were marks around their wrists and ankles where they had been shackled. The scales were loose there, and their skin was bruising. Neek could see Whizzle was favoring one leg and walking with a slight limp.

"Come, let me try to help you," Neek told them both, holding his crystal and activating the vibrations inside himself to bathe them in the golden healing light. The sore marks on their ankles and wrists began to fade.

"Neek, what is this?" the boys started to ask, looking at him with eyes full of thankfulness and wonder.

"Hush my brothers, save your strength," he told them. "I will tell you all about it later. After our tribe is safe."

Barnag took his hand. Looking Neek in the eyes, he wept. "I'm so sorry Neek. For everything I've done."

Whizzle was weeping too. "I shouldn't have pushed you, Neek. I . . . ," and Whizzle's tears overwhelmed him before he could complete his words.

Regretful thoughts were emanating from Whizzle and Barnag's minds so strongly that they didn't really need to say anything. Neek could feel the difficult emotions they were struggling with. He could hear their misery, their shame. And beyond it all, he could read their true love for their people. They were sorry not just to Neek, but to their whole community. His two brothers clearly longed more than anything to be reunited with the tribe.

"I love you, my brothers," he told them. "Save your tears. You may need them. Everything will be alright, but only if we are strong now. Let's go." Neek smiled, and helped his brothers to their feet.

They all looked brighter now. Refreshed as Neek had been, the goodness he felt from his rescued brothers gave him even greater hope. The group still had a long way to go, but Neek knew they would make it. And whatever lay in store back home, they would all face it together.

∼

The carefully constructed coalition of Human, Orc, and Goblin forces, forged over months of scheming and plotting by the young Wizard, were already at each other's throats before the battle even started. Quite literally.

Grutch was holding a long, thin blade to the neck of an Orc swordsman whose argument with RockLopper, the axe wielding barbarian, about who was stronger, had escalated to an ugly stage with the Orc promising to "show him the truth" in the Rocklings' warren.

"If you want the truth," Grutch was warning him in a rough, low voice "I can spill it all over this floor right now and we can be done with you."

"Leave him be, Grutch!" the Wizard Aleric barked at him. "Save your energy for the real enemies ahead."

Slowly and reluctantly, the thief lowered his blade. Grutch was getting tired of hearing the young Wizard talk to him in such a condescending tone. "He robs a few tombs and thinks he's a grand mage," Grutch muttered under his breath. "I could teach you a thing or two, boy".

But Aleric didn't hear his quiet threats. The Wizard was too busy settling a dispute between some of the lower-ranked Goblins and Orcs about who was going to carry the many empty treasure chests Aleric had demanded for the expedition.

"We can't carry heavy chests while we are gingerly dancing around their traps," the Goblin Scout was protesting. "We have to walk lightly or we'll trigger something dangerous."

"Well, we are Warriors, not beasts of burden," the Orc argued in response. "We have better things to do than carry a bunch of fancy boxes for you."

"You aren't doing it for them, you are doing it for me. You are doing it for King Blackburn, and for the all the gold and supplies he will give you that will grow your people's power in this region," Aleric snapped at the Orc, trying to quell the argument. "You are being handsomely rewarded, with riches suited to the great Warriors you are. So please just carry the chests and stop complaining about it."

The Wizard turned, and headed off toward another group that was bickering. Maybe I should have just used the King's Knights after all, Aleric thought to himself. They at least would follow orders without all this quibbling. If only the Knights weren't so attached to that strict code of ethics, Aleric thought, then they might really be useful.

NibCrusher, the Orc leader grunted and commanded his troops to pick up the heavy, ornate treasure boxes and bring them along. If this King has so much gold already, the Orc wondered to himself, why are we even bringing these chests to fill? Those savage little Rocklings will have nothing useful to fill these with, he thought. If they did, we Orcs would have robbed them already.

The brothers continued on at a brisk pace. A few more miles and they'd be back at their warren. How would the tribe react, Neek wondered? He had defied the wishes of the Great Priests, his tribe's Chief, and every elder in the tribe. Even Malika would be upset with him, he was sure. How could he face Beemo, the wise, old Tunnel Warden, or Dida, the Guard, when he had knowingly tricked them into sleep with medicated tea? He had even missed the Trials. How would the elders be able to decide on his place in the tribe?

Neek hoped his people would forgive him. But it wasn't just Neek that required forgiveness, was it? The tribe had exiled

Whizzle and Barnag. Would they ever accept them back? Being branded a clan cleaver was one of the worst offenses in Rockling life, and Neek had never heard of anyone being forgiven of this dire crime.

Neek hoped that the elders might agree that if Neek himself could forgive his brothers, the tribe should too. Hadn't their crime been against him?

Neek had explored deep inside his brothers' hearts, reading their truest thoughts. He couldn't avoid it honestly, their thoughts were so strong and their emotions so overwhelming. Whizzle and Barnag were deeply sorry. They would be loyal to the tribe from now on. They would be a benefit to the warren. Hopefully the elders could see that.

Neek knew that very soon, just a few more miles down the tunnels, he would have his answer, one way or the other. The boys raced on, seemingly gaining pace now with every step.

∾

Despite all the early hiccups, when the army finally got down to the "real business" as Aleric liked to call it, the combined Orc and Goblin forces were more focused, and started to work together. As they arrived on the outskirts of the Rockling warren, the two groups stopped bickering, and quietly went about their grizzly work.

The Goblins led the way. Their mission was undoubtedly the most dangerous of the day. The Goblins had to clear all the traps out of the various tunnels the army hoped to bring the Orcs through later. The Orcs, with their bigger, heavier bodies, would undoubtedly trip over the wires and depress the pressure plates that could send poison darts shooting at them, or mountains of rock tumbling down on their heads. The nimble Goblins had to work quickly, and in tight coordination, for as soon as a single trap was sprung, the Rocklings would be aware of their presence, and would start fighting back.

This great danger was why Rumbletum was risking so many of his forces at once. There were nearly a hundred of his finest Scouts and soldiers here today. They moved noiselessly, keeping in visual communication by signaling each other with silent gestures to ensure their timing was in sync. A great many fine Goblin minds would be required to undo the defenses of the dragon-mice.

Ironically, it wasn't any of the expert traps, set by the wisest and most experienced of the tribe, that gave the Goblins trouble. No, it was the work of little Margle, Neek's younger sister, that frustrated their well-laid plans.

Margle had planned to prank one her teachers, Pripo, during the joyful chaos of Trap Week. Pripo had injured his back in a tunnel cave in a number of years ago, so when he gave his lectures in the tunnels, explaining the various natural formations in the rock, and what could be learned from them, he often resorted to leaning up against the wall to stretch out his back. The younglings were supposed to study a particular type of limestone the week prior, so Margle had devised a special sticky material that she attached to a clam shell and suctioned to the wall of the limestone column. When Pripo brushed against it, the clam shell would be knocked free, producing a loud, rather embarrassing sound, that Human children might refer to as a raspberry. Pripo had changed his lesson plan that day though, taking the younglings to see a different chamber instead. So the trap went undiscovered, and its hidden surprise remained there still.

Ripplerip, the Goblin Scout, was busily disarming a pressure plate, when his elbow accidentally brushed against the forgotten clam shell, and its naughty noise rang out in the hallway. Margle would have been proud. The noise was much louder than even she would have expected. Ripplerip was temporarily startled, and just that flicker of doubt was enough to make his hand flinch, triggering the tripwire he was currently undoing. The pressure plate in the floor dropped downward, followed by several tons of rock from the cavern ceiling. The noise was deafening.

THE TRIALS 237

Rockling feet were soon running everywhere. The Goblins couldn't see them yet, but they knew the Rocklings were preparing their defenses.

∼

Noise travels a long way underground. The sound waves bounce from cave wall to cave wall, winding and twisting their way through the darkness. And so, even though they were still a fair distance from their warren, the boys clearly heard it. There was a cave in. A big one. As far as they could tell, the sound was coming from one of the largest main tunnels outside the warren entrance. Those tunnels were regularly checked and secured by the Wardens. If there was a collapse, it could only mean one thing. Trouble! The Goblins' attack must already be underway, Neek thought. The boys ran faster, preparing themselves mentally for whatever danger lay ahead.

∼

Like a line of falling dominos, one small problem in life can, if you aren't careful, easily escalate to create another and another until, in total, you have far too many problems to deal with any of them effectively. And the Goblins, after the initial cave in, quickly found themselves with problems arising in every direction.

The Goblins who were desperately trying to disarm the remaining traps were hurriedly rushing through work which just shouldn't be rushed. When they worked too quickly like this, they made mistakes, and the Wizard Aleric could hear the results from those mistakes all around him. He heard more cave ins, small explosions, the screams of Goblins falling down pits, and many other such signs that the traps were being removed "the hard way."

The Orcs didn't seem to be faring much better. Several of the passages they had planned to ferry armies through had been collapsed already. The alternate tunnels the Orcs were finding turned out to have many hidden protections. In one, small holes opened up and Rockling Warriors were shooting darts with blowguns through them at the Orcs. The darts, poisoned with some foul spider venom were causing the Orcs to get violently ill, which made them easy work for the Rockling Warriors waiting at the other end of the tunnel, who jabbed and poked and beat them with their clubs until the Orcs were retreating.

The Orcs were strong, and some progress was being made, but they were losing lots of troops, with only minor losses on the Rockling side. Oh well, that's what we are paying these savage beasts for, isn't it, the Wizard thought to himself.

There is, during times of danger, an impulse that is triggered in all creatures called the fight or flight response. Hyped up with energy, during a time of stress, you are primed to combat the danger, if it is beatable, or run away quickly if it is not. Rockling warren defense strategy was built upon the related philosophy of fight and flight. Their Warriors and their Trappers would bravely do their best to delay the enemy's advance while the rest of the tribe shuttled the younger, the weaker, and the more fragile members of the group away from the fighting to safer burrows down below.

The heavily fortified nursery and birthing area was by far the safest place in their warren, and Dragon-Mother Malika was hurrying the young and the vulnerable there as fast as she could. Other elders were taking different groups in other directions, splitting the tribe into a number of factions. Breaking up into different clusters was safer than keeping everyone together in one large group.

There was another set of caverns, not too far away, deep underground, with only few known tunnels linking to it, where the various Rockling factions would reunite. The different groups would drop the ceilings of the tunnels behind them as they fled, ensuring it was increasingly difficult for the invading army to follow them. Secret stores of supplies were already housed there, to assist the tribe as it began its difficult and dangerous search for a new home. Many of the elders had been through this process of home-finding several times now. It was an unfortunate part of Rockling life. Something the tribe was prepared for.

The ferocity of this raid was alarming though. Never before had the tribe ever been attacked by a combination of races like this. Orcs and Goblins working with Humans? What did this army even want from them? These were dark times indeed.

Thankfully, Bartok, Inko, Barg, and many of the other Rockling Warriors were holding their own in the fighting. Some were hurt, but many were still healthy, stabbing and kicking and clawing and dropping the walls on their enemies.

With her group safely locked away, Malika began the process of closing up the tunnels to the nursery. For some reason, the fighting was particularly fierce here, and she wasn't going to take any unnecessary risks. As soon as the mechanisms were ready, she dropped the celling, closing the chamber off from the rest of the warren.

Despite how it probably looked to the Goblin and Orc leaders, the fight was, in the Wizard Aleric's eyes, going pretty much according to plan. His army was diminished, but Aleric would get what he wanted. The Rockling Warriors were retreating, leaving their warren and most of their possessions behind. The Orcs and Goblins were suffering losses, but this didn't stop the Rocklings from continuing to flee, down into the darkness. As the Goblins and the Orcs fought and fell, they were springing all the toxic traps and clearing out the deadly surprises that Aleric wished to avoid.

It was his friends' turn now. Time to show what the Humans

could do. Aleric pulled out his favorite wand and smiled. He was excited to show them all.

Rumbletum knew it was time to leave. The Goblins had earned their reward, paying dearly for it. The Humans were advancing. It was time to go. The Goblin Chief used his silent body signals to order his senior Scouts and Warriors to begin their retreat. The Humans wouldn't even notice their absence now. The Rockling retreat was well underway, and the Orcs would take care of any heroic standouts who refused to run.

Rumbletum turned and left, heading back to the Goblin camp. As he ran, followed by his remaining troops, out of the warren and back toward his comfy bed, the Chief could have sworn he saw, out of the corner of his eye, hiding behind a stalagmite, that strange young dragon-mouse with the awful teeth that he had left in a cell back at camp. That couldn't be true, he realized though, pushing back against what was clearly a trick being played on him by his worried mind. Malgotha, his precious pet, would never let her delicious snacks go. There must be many Rocklings with teeth like that, Rumbletum decided. Poor, foul creatures, he thought, as he jumped over the body of one of his fallen soldiers without even a second look, his mind clear, his heart empty.

They had expected to find Goblins, and were surprised to see a few Orcs as well. But the most shocking sight by far was the group of Humans Neek saw before him. Neek's blood ran cold. This was bad. Very bad. Neek noticed that most of the Goblins seemed to be fleeing the battle though. Were the Rocklings winning? His spirits rose.

Whizzle and Barnag both grabbed swords they found dropped beside the bodies of two fallen Goblins. The brothers may have been poor at many school subjects, but they had always been fond of swordplay, and clearly now the tribe needed their gift. The main entryway was packed with Goblins and Orcs though, and brave as the two might be feeling, they wouldn't do anyone any good charging into an overwhelming force like that.

"This way," Neek told them, pointing toward a tunnel mouth cut halfway up one of the walls ahead. Neek knew another way in. A secret way he had used during the hiding game of their youth. A time that felt so long ago now.

Up they climbed, into a hole in the side of the cave wall, through twisting passageways full of the sounds of swords clashing and Rocklings screaming.

Orcs, as a general rule, are loathe to retreat. They pride themselves on their bravery, and they prefer to finish off their enemies, or be finished themselves. If they are not strong enough, Orcs figure they do not deserve to live on. How these foolish beliefs took such strong hold on a whole race, we may never know.

In this case though the enemy wasn't really the problem. They were retreating. The Orcs' Human "allies" were the problem. Especially the young Wizard. The mage was obviously crazed to show off his power, with little regard for whoever was in the way. He was throwing great balls of fire all around the warren with reckless disregard. More Orcs may be cooked by those flames today than by all the Rockling swords combined, the Orc leader NibCrusher thought to himself.

If the Orcs hurt the Humans in return, they would have the King and his armies to deal with, and probably many more nasty Wizards tossing their deadly magics around. It would be better to just get out of here and let the young maniac have his fun, the Orc decided.

And so, like the Goblins, the Orcs began to leave as well. This would not be considered cowardly by even the most traditional of Orcish standards. This was basic common sense.

The boy was insane. That much was clear. There was no point in earning gold if you weren't around to spend it, and already the Wizard had scared off both the Goblins and the Orcs. Grutch had not attended a fancy academy like this boy had, but he knew enough of Warriors to guess that the Orcs would remember their losses at his hand. And they would be slow to forgive.

Even RockLopper, as brutal a killer as Grutch had ever seen, happily swinging his sword about with joy, as if he was dancing at a daughter's wedding, even he saw the boy was a problem. Perhaps his frustration was due to the Wizard wiping out too many Rockling Warriors before RockLopper could get to them. Whatever the case, it was clear, everyone thought the Wizard must be controlled.

"Aleric!" Grutch yelled, trying to get the Wizard's attention. But the Wizard was speaking to the strange woman covered in mud, Erawynn. The Wizard was commanding her to use her magic to break through one of the walls of this chamber. The little dragonlings had blocked off the tunnel, and they had taken the precious magical device the Wizard was after with them.

Grutch watched as Erawynn's hands began to glow with a brown throbbing aura. He body transformed, changing itself into a huge magical drill which began to bore a hole through the wall as Aleric had demanded. On the other side of this wall, Grutch, recalled was the creatures' nursery. It was a good distance from here, and would take some time, he was sure, but the mud-woman seemed to be making good progress. The Wizard was watching eagerly.

"Aleric!" Grutch yelled again, and finally the Wizard turned. "Calm yourself," Grutch warned him. "You'll burn these caves down around us with that wand of yours. Can't you see the Orcs and the Goblins have left us?"

"Even the little Rocklings have run off. Don't you see that, young one?" RockLopper added.

"Well, you can leave then, cowards," Aleric angrily responded. "If my flames frighten you, run away like the Goblins."

RockLopper, stung by the insult, started toward the Wizard, his knuckles holding his axe so tightly the ends of his fingers were white. "What did you say, boy?" he yelled.

"Fine, don't run," the Wizard responded, raising his wand in the direction of his companions. "Treasure goes a lot farther split two ways instead of four," the Wizard joked.

In his final seconds, as the wall of flame sped toward him, Grutch realized that of all the awful cut-throats and double-crossing scoundrels he had done business with over the years, this boy must be the worst. It was a lesson learned too late.

∼

Even hidden as they were behind a foot of stone or more, the Rockling brothers could feel the heat blazing in the chamber below them as they crawled quickly along. What in the world is going on down there, Neek wondered? What evil have these invaders brought against our tribe?

In a few moments, Neek's group finally reached the end of the tunnel, and emerged from another hole above a main chamber in the Rockling warren. The scene they saw before them was chaos. Small fires still burned all around the chamber. Burnt patches of black soot covered the wall and floor where the fiery blasts of the Wizard's wand had landed. There were many bodies littered about, but thankfully very few of them were Rocklings.

Neek climbed down the side of the cavern, his brothers following close behind. The hall, despite all the signs of devastation, seemed to be empty now. "We must check and see if there is anyone we can help," Neek told his brothers, sending

Barnag to the south tunnel and Whizzle to the east. "Rescue any survivors you find and help get them to the gathering spot," he continued. "Be careful. If you find soldiers or danger, keep hidden." Then the two exiled brothers ran off, eager to finally help their tribe.

Neek scanned the chamber once more. Everyone here seemed beyond helping. As he looked around in despair, unable to comprehend the horror that filled what had once been a joyful place of celebration for his people, Neek heard voices coming from the far side of the chamber. He noticed a jagged hole there, with a roughly cut new tunnel running beyond it. From all his trips to visit Malika during his recent weeks in the warren, Neek realized at once where that tunnel must lead. The noises were coming from the nursery!

CHAPTER 15
BROKEN

While in the strange, magically-altered form of the giant rock drill, Erawynn, the muddy cultist, was invulnerable to harm. So as she bore through the rock, grinding to dust the stones that Dragon-Mother Malika had dropped in her way, Erawynn was not bothered by any of the other traps installed in this treacherous passage. Acid sprayed on her. Poison darts pricked her side. Sharpened spikes sprang at her from every direction. Yet Erawynn didn't feel a thing. Her whirling copper cloud of destruction relentlessly cut a path forward until, at last, she reached the end of the cluttered tunnel and the cavern of the Rockling nursery opened up before her.

It seemed empty in this chamber. The lizard people must have fled, Erawynn thought. Aleric will be pleased. Somewhere in here the adventurers were bound to find that magical hat they were being paid so highly to retrieve. Erawynn changed back into her Human form and prepared to return through the rough tunnel she had carved to let the Wizard Aleric know the room was clear and ready to be looted.

She heard the Wizard's voice behind her. He was clearly hiding somewhere along the tunnel wall. "What do you see?" he asked her. "Is it safe? As we expected, is that the creche where they keep their young?"

"The chamber is empty," Erawynn replied. "And yes, it appears to be something related to children. There are carvings on the wall that show little lizards, held by bigger ones. Come and see."

She saw Aleric emerge from a hole in the rock. "I haven't yet seen the hat you are looking for, but I'm sure we'll find it here somewhere," Erawynn suggested.

The Wizard looked pleased. He walked swiftly toward the nursery, sidestepping the puddles of acid and hopping over the poison darts littering the passageway.

As Aleric passed her, Erawynn looked back toward the meeting chamber beyond him where she had started her drilling. The Wizard had clearly gone mad, she thought. Erawynn noticed tiny fires burning throughout the cave. She scanned for her companions, RockLopper and Grutch, and in a terrible moment of grizzly recognition, she spotted RockLopper's axe lying on the cave floor, awash in fire. She saw his body lying next to it, smoking. Grutch's familiar cloak was there too, fine lines of flame lacing it as well. This was clearly the work of the young Wizard, Erawynn realized. He wasn't just an idiot. He was dangerous. Treacherous. Anger welled within her. She walked back toward the great hall, leaving the Wizard to search about the nursery for his precious artifact on his own.

Erawynn had agreed to help Aleric with this mission, distasteful as it was, as she was sure the Wizard would gain favor in the King's court from assisting the Queen, and Aleric had promised to advocate on behalf of her deity, Thrubb, Lord of the Dirt. Aleric promised her that Thrubb would be admitted to the acceptable court pantheon of gods. Thrubb's worshippers, such as Erawynn herself, would no longer need to hide their beliefs or carry out their rituals in dark secrecy. They could build their churches to Thrubb, great adobe and mud mounds rising high in the sky, in the middle of towns now, not having to hide in the swamps and forests of remote areas. Aleric had promised as much.

Besides, Erawynn knew Thrubb would probably approve, or at least forgive the mission she was on. There would be death, yes, but also life. The Queen's child would be saved, at least temporarily. Thrubb valued balance above all things. Life in balance with death. Light balanced with darkness. Dry dirt balanced with water to make his glorious, holy mud. Brief hope balanced on the edge of a grim reality.

This was not balance though. This was slaughter. Having returned to the Rockling great hall, Erawynn looked down at the bodies of her two fallen companions realizing Aleric's promises were utterly worthless. The boy could not be trusted.

Thrubb will show me another path, Erawynn decided. She pressed her hands against the bodies of Grutch and RockLopper, whispered strange, mystical incantations, and the three of them transformed into puddles of mud. The puddles slowly sank beneath the cavern floor, out and away from this awful carnage.

The Wizard was now alone.

Malika couldn't avoid hearing his thoughts. They were shouted by the Human's mind at a volume that seemed louder than the clatter made by the rocky ceiling of the tunnel collapsing earlier. So clear was the invader's focused desire that Malika could not block it out if she had tried. But Malika wasn't trying to block his thoughts. She was desperately trying to understand their source and meaning. What were these Humans after? What did the Rocklings have that these brutes could possibly care about?

Malika was standing, hidden, on the other side of a sliding compartment of stone, mere inches from the room where the Wizard was walking around excitedly, turning over pots and beakers, frantically searching the room. Malika had sent her group forward, down into the tunnels, remaining behind herself as the last line of defense against the invaders. The Rockling Guards would be closing up the tunnels behind her. At least that's what

Inko had promised her. The younglings must be protected, and Dragon-Mother Malika knew that her silent speech, the ability to read minds and communicate with other creatures, had a better chance of protecting the ones fleeing below than the Rockling Warriors' swords and shields.

If Malika could figure out what the Humans wanted, and give it to them, then perhaps they will leave, she thought. That was usually the case. Some creatures could not be reasoned with. A Rock Boar only wants to eat you. You cannot give it what it wants and survive. These Humans clearly weren't hungry though, they had their vast fields of food above, in the sunlight. The Humans sought something else.

She was gradually beginning to grasp it. Her birthing tools. Her hat. That's what the strange man on the other side of the panel was hunting. Malika felt some relief. The Great Priests could easily craft her another helm. Every Dragon-Mother had one. They were helpful with simple healing magic, focusing a Rockling's thoughts. She paused though, taking a moment to prepare her words, as she was extremely worried about this frantic Human. She sensed a blood-lust inside him. Malika could feel waves of dark satisfaction coming from the man in regards to what he had apparently done to his companions. It was awful. She hated to hear such wicked thoughts. How could the Humans treat each other this way? But, despite her uncertainty, Malika knew that she must protect her young. Her people. It was her duty.

The Dragon-Mother pressed a hidden button in the wall, and the thin layer of rock between her and the crazed Wizard dropped downward. The man was looking at her with the eyes of a hungry snake. He was smiling at least. Malika hoped that was a good sign.

~

Oh, glorious day, Aleric thought to himself, marveling at the carvings on the wall, trying to make sense of the glyphs and markings there. He was enjoying himself. The new power he felt, commanding an army of troops, wielding walls of flame, it was all intoxicating. Even tough brutes like RockLopper and Grutch were no match for him now. Sure, bullies like that might have pushed him around as a child, but look at what short work he had just made of them. He chuckled to think of his former companions' faces as the flames hit them.

The information the Goblin Chief had provided all seemed to be accurate. Aleric saw the Helm of Life, as his people called it, carved in some of the pictures on the wall. It was nearby somewhere. He could feel it. He was close. So close.

So close to the helm, and so close to his ultimate dream. If he healed the Queen, he would soon be given a seat on the Council of Mages, he was sure of it. No longer would they mock him or his strange interests. The Council met regularly with King Blackburn, and that proximity, combined with Aleric's power to sway the minds of others, well, the possibilities were endless. He would finally have it all. Everything he dreamed about. If he could just find that helm.

Aleric looked about frantically for a few minutes but couldn't find it. The pots and jars here were full of pungent herbs and slimy jellies. The storage alcoves were cluttered with bits of cloth, presumably swaddling diapers, and all the other odds and ends you might expect in any nursery. Things were hidden, he supposed, in a secret chamber somewhere. These beasts were so clever that way. Aleric just needed to find the mechanism to open it.

Drat, he thought. I eliminated Grutch too quickly. The experienced thief's uncannily keen eye and subtle hands would have been useful here.

"Erawynn! Erawynn," he called out, turning to look for her, "come and help me." But it was soon clear to Aleric that just like the Goblins and the Orcs, the filthy cultist had left too. If you want a job done right, you have to do it yourself, Aleric decided, continuing his hurried fumbling about the chamber.

And then, just as his frustration was starting to overwhelm him, Aleric heard the soft grinding sound of stone scraping stone, and he turned. One of the little female lizards was standing there. And in her hands, she was holding the helm!

In Aleric's mind, he heard a delicate voice. "Here is what you seek," it told him. "Please, take it. We are no threat to you." And the little creature placed the Helm of Life on the ground and backed away.

Aleric raised his wand. "Be still!" he commanded her. "Sit down. Back there, against the wall."

The lizard did as Aleric commanded. He picked up the helm, finally holding it in his hands. I have it, finally, and someone who can teach me how to use it, the Wizard thought to himself.

Oh, glorious day.

∼

Malika understood what he wanted now, but she feared she couldn't give it to him. She wasn't capable of giving it to him. And she couldn't make him understand.

Malika had given the Human her headdress, the magical birthing hat crafted by the Great Priests for Dragon-Mothers to keep their Rockling eggs healthy. The Human seemed pleased at first. But he hadn't let her go. He was demanding she teach him how to use it. The man was pointing a wand at her as if it were a sword. It was far more deadly than a sword. She knew that.

The man put it on his head. That much he had figured out. It was ridiculously small for him, and in spite of her fear Malika wanted to laugh, though she could sense this man was not in the mood for laughter. The Human was getting angrier, she could feel it. She was trying her best to explain the process to him, to share Rockling secrets only a Dragon-Mother knows, but the Human didn't seem to have the ability to follow her teachings. Malika wasn't surprised. The Human didn't have the gift. There was no way she could give him that.

∼

The little lizard Witch was teasing him, Aleric was sure of it. She went on and on about vibrations in his mind. About listening to some inner tone that he had to bring outwards. At least that's what he could make of the images and words she was pushing into his thoughts.

But as he strained, and pushed himself, all he was succeeding in doing was giving himself a headache.

Deeper, you must go deeper down, inside yourself, she kept telling him. Was this a trick, Aleric wondered? Was she trying to get him to make his own head explode? That was the way with these cave lizards, wasn't it? Tricks and traps. Every fiber of Aleric's being pushed him to raise his wand and show the lizard a trick of his own, but he knew he had to be patient. If he couldn't control the helm when he returned, the Council might take it away. They would take the helm and the glory along with it. They would hog all the credit for the Queen's health. He would be thanked and forgotten. That wouldn't do. Aleric had to crack this mystery.

Aleric's anger grew until he did indeed, finally, hear a sound and feel a strong vibration inside himself. He focused on it as the lizard had instructed him, and after a moment, he could control it, pushing the vibrations outside himself. He watched as a dark cloud extended from his hand, enveloping the tiny lizard creature in front of him.

Instantly the lizard screamed and fell over. She lay motionless on the floor, as still as the stone around her. The delicate voice in his head went silent.

Aleric tried to rouse the lizard but she didn't move. Her body was cold. There was no pulse. She must be dead, he supposed. Aleric found this new power intriguing and exhilarating, but he knew he needed the helm to bring life, not death, to the Queen, and he was disappointed to lose the lizard Witch before she had properly shared all her secrets. Oh well, Aleric decided, perhaps there are other scrolls or carvings around here that will help me understand how this helm works. He walked out of the nursery and over to the egg chamber, searching that room instead.

∼

Neek heard a scream, an awful, ear-piercing scream, as he made his way invisibly through the rough tunnel toward the nursery. His stomach fell, and his heart stopped as he saw Dragon-Mother Malika lying on the floor. Neek could hear footsteps in the nearby egg room, so he tiptoed quietly forward, using only his gift of silent speech to try to wake her. But Neek couldn't reach her. There were no active thoughts in her mind. He feared the worst.

Neek dragged Malika quietly, deeper into the secret chamber she had hidden in earlier. He tucked her body behind a corner, as carefully as he could, hunching over her and trying to find some way to help. He pulled Mohmoh from his side pouch, placing his little friend on Malika's chest. "Is she dead?" Neek asked, tears filling his desperate eyes.

"No," Mohmoh told him "but she is close. Very close. We must heal her now. There is no time to wait." Mohmoh extended his tendrils to her face, and toward her heart, casting his golden yellow aura of life upon her. "You must help me, Neek," Mohmoh explained. "I cannot do this alone."

Neek wished they were better hidden. There was only a tiny corner of cave between the three of them and whoever or whatever was pacing the egg chamber next door. The urgency in Mohmoh's demand was clear though. They must act now or Neek might lose Malika forever.

Neek grabbed the crystal on his necklace with one hand and placed his other upon Malika's chest, right next to Mohmoh's tendrils. Neek tried to channel the inner vibrations Mohmoh had taught him about mere hours ago. The vibrations inside Neek were stronger than before. Every fiber of his being twitched and bent, pulsing in great waves. He thought of his time as a child, of Malika holding him and singing. The song inside his head built like a thundercloud until finally Neek poured the vibrations out of himself, blanketing Malika's motionless body in a dazzling golden glow. Wave after wave of light flowed from him, through Malika, through Mohmoh, and back again, the tides of a cosmic sea crashing against Malika's still heart.

Neek searched frantically for any signs in Malika's mind. Any speech. Any pictures. Any memories. Any sign of life. But she remained painfully dark. The waves washed over them all, pulse after pulse, until finally, a faint flutter of images began to appear in Neek's thoughts.

Neek was watching, he supposed, bits and pieces of visual memories from Malika's life. She was a child chasing a salamander with a bright green tail. She was a young girl talking to a handsome craftsman. She was balancing on the edge of a wall, completing her Trials. She was learning how to wrap up a youngling in swaddling from the Dragon-Mother before her. She was learning songs. She was singing songs. She was helping a youngling learn to eat. She was looking at her belly, fat and round, and smiling. She was straining, beyond pain, to push out a black, glassy egg. She was watching the egg, and the others around it, but especially that egg, with joy in her eyes. The egg was cracking. Tiny claws were cracking open the top, and out poked a head. She was staring at a boy with colorful scales. Every color.

"Neek," he heard Malika say gently. And between the images and the look in her eyes, he knew a secret that Rocklings are not supposed to know. But most importantly, she was alive. That was what mattered. There would be time for secrets later.

Or perhaps not. Neek saw someone watching them now, through the open tunnel door. The Wizard was watching them with a wicked smile.

～

There was nothing in the chamber Aleric was currently searching except strange curved basins, more baby supplies, and more frustrating pictures. The images showed lizard Witches, like the one who had given him the helm, doing various things with what Aleric assumed must be lizard babies. They were holding babies, cuddling babies, telling stories to babies. It was revoltingly cute, and as far as the Wizard could tell, absolutely useless. There were other carvings as well, showing winged dragons doing various things. Flying about. Cutting things with their claws. It was quite a mix, babies and dragons together. Only lizard creatures like this would combine such contradictory things, Aleric thought.

Unfortunately, there were no explanatory parchments, no helpful scrolls, and no instruction manuals for the Helm of Life. He searched and searched for hidden compartments, but found nothing. He really needed Grutch's assistance. Or the Witch's. But they were both gone now, due to him. The young Wizard made a mental note that he really must make better use of his resources in the future.

After a few frustrating minutes of searching, Aleric noticed a bright light begin to fill the chamber. The light was coming from the room beyond. The glare became quite blinding, filling the entire group of nearby rooms with a brilliant, golden glow. Aleric covered his eyes with his arm, and made his way slowly toward the source of the light. While he might have been more cautious in other circumstances, here Aleric could feel something special in that glow. Something warm, and calm, and inviting. Something unknown to him, but nonetheless not a threat. He followed it around the corner and squinting to shield his vision, Aleric witnessed a shocking scene.

There was another smaller lizard here, a male Aleric guessed, pouring light out of his body onto the dead lizard Witch. The boy had placed some kind of mushroom on her chest, and was clutching some kind of crystal in his hand which seemed to be the source of the light. After a few moments, Aleric saw the Witch open her eyes.

This is truly my lucky day, the Wizard thought, as the light faded, and the young lizard turned to look at him.

Neek felt exhausted. Completely depleted. However he and Mohmoh had managed to heal Malika, it had taken everything from him. Neek could hardly even imagine walking over to a bed in the next room and sleeping. He didn't have the energy. And yet, in front of him now stood a Wizard, a deadly Wizard judging by what he had seen in the other chamber, and Neek wasn't sure what he could possibly do about it. Had he and Mohmoh saved Malika from death just for it all to end like this?

The Human Wizard kept trying to scare him, telling Neek the awful things he would do to them, and demanding that Neek stay still. He really needn't have bothered. Neek hardly had the energy to breathe, much less fight this big Human or run away. Mohmoh climbed up on Neek's neck to comfort him. "I love you," Neek told him, using his secret voice. "I'm so thankful for our journeys together." Neek expected that all of their journeys would be ending soon.

Neek noticed the Wizard was wearing Malika's headdress. It looked ridiculous.

The Wizard reached down and ripped Neek's necklace from him, along with the singing crystal it held within it, the crystal Neek had had used to refresh himself and his brothers, and to save Malika's life. Neek wanted to fight him, but he couldn't.

The Wizard then reached down to pluck Mohmoh off of Neek's shoulder. Mohmoh held tight, grabbing Neek's ear, and Neek reached up to help his friend, but the Human tugged violently, and the little Pluffstack could not hold on. The Wizard put the necklace and Mohmoh into a velvet bag which he placed inside the pocket of his robe.

"No!" Neek screamed at him using his mental speech. "Not my friend. Leave him alone!" Neek even managed to inch his body forward, getting ready to use his last drops of life to leap at the Wizard and claw back his friend.

But Neek was so tired that the Wizard, even as scrawny as he was for a Human, easily pushed the Rockling back down to the ground with his foot. The Wizard raised his wand toward them. Neek closed his eyes and hugged Malika, the woman he had just learned was his mother, his true mother.

The Wizard Aleric was astonished. Do all these lizards possess the gift of telepathy, he wondered? Both the Witch and the young boy had been able to talk directly to his mind. Aleric had never heard this ability to be common to the Rockling race, and he resolved to research it in the archives when he returned to the Mages' tower. He had so much to research now. This strange, living mushroom. The crystal the boy had used to bring the Witch back to life. This helm which seemed to be able to channel the powers of both life and death itself. So many wonderful treasures. What a success this adventure had been, he thought.

Now it was time to return home. The Goblins and the Orcs and his companions had all left, and it was Aleric's turn to follow. The Wizard wasn't going to waste time with this boy like he had with the Witch. More lizards might show up and Aleric had no armies or companions to protect him if they did. One more burst on the old banjo, he thought, raising his wand, and it will be time to get out of here.

Barnag and Whizzle had not walked very far when they heard the awful scream Malika made from the nursery. Neither of them had found any survivors yet. The Rocklings had already fled it seemed, as had the Goblins and the Orcs. The brothers were alone. There was no one to help.

So when they heard the scream, the brothers decided to rush back to the chamber where they had left Neek. Finally they might serve some purpose. Earlier in their lives, the boys might have heard such signs of danger and fled from them. Now though, forgiven by Neek, and hoping again to return to the tribe they loved and were exiled from, the brothers were determined to be heroes. If there was a problem, they would help, no matter the risk. They hurried through the tunnel cautiously though. The brothers wouldn't be able to help anyone if they were instantly burned up.

As they reached the nursery, Whizzle and Barnag saw a Human, for some reason wearing a ridiculously tiny hat, standing over two Rocklings. They saw Neek on the ground. He was in trouble. The Human seemed to be threatening him with a fancy stick. What could they do?

For the first time in his short life, Whizzle had a really great idea. He explained it to Barnag and they crept slowly forward. Whizzle was smiling, curling his huge cluttermouth jaw full of mismatched teeth. It was a truly glorious idea.

All things are relative. One must be very thirsty to feel the true relief of a cool drink of water. One must be a long time in the heat to appreciate the kind reprieve offered by the shade. To feel the rush of a fall, one must first climb to a great height. In this way the universe balances itself. Our lives are governed by these movements. Up and down. To and fro.

And so it was, just then, at the height of his satisfaction, the Wizard Aleric felt a terrible pain in his backside, as if ten alligators were biting him at once. The shock of it sent the wand tumbling from his hand. He turned, and sure enough there was what he assumed must be the child of an alligator and a Rockling biting him from behind. It had an awful mouthful of jagged teeth that seemed to jut out in every direction. Another young lizard was heading toward his wand. No, he must not lose it, Aleric thought, desperately reaching toward it, but in an instant the beast was there, and with a quick flash it brought down a curved Goblin sword it was carrying and cut the wand in half. "No!" Aleric screamed. His wand was destroyed. If he didn't act quickly though, he would be cut in two as well by the awful creature biting his bum.

Aleric rapidly muttered a few arcane words, traced strange patterns in the air, and poof, in an instant, he was gone. He dematerialized, taking Neek's necklace, Malika's hat, and Neek's best friend Mohmoh with him.

Neek fell back exhausted on the stone floor and passed out. He didn't even have the energy to cry for his lost friend.

∽

Chief Rumbletum was tired. Exceptionally tired. True, he had done little of the fighting today, or the trap disarming, leaving it to his unfortunate soldiers to handle those grizzly jobs. Nevertheless, he still had to march all the way back from the Rockling hovel to his war camp, and that was a long distance. With all the Orcs and other creatures running about, it was not safe to rest along the way.

He had much to do. Many of Rumbletum's soldiers had been lost, and he would have to go back to the main Goblin warren now to recruit more. He would think long and hard before he worked with Humans again. They just couldn't be trusted.

His return to the camp had been a disappointing one. There was no food. The Cook and his two retainers had run off. The Rockling captives were missing, as well as his prized giant snake. And the entire place was a mess. Beds were smashed. Supplies were scattered everywhere. What had happened during his time away? Who knew? Rumbletum would deal with it all soon enough, he just needed some sleep.

Even his bedroom, with its famously giant, comfy bed, had been a source of disappointment. There was clutter everywhere. Someone had clearly been using his bed, seeing as it was unmade. There were burn marks and a smoky smell. Had a party gone wrong perhaps? The Goblin Chief vowed that if he ever found that Cook or those retainers, they would regret their insolence.

Still, those were problems for tomorrow. Tonight, he just needed some rest. Rumbletum climbed up on his massive wooden sleeping platform and pulled several of the thick skin blankets over himself. He closed his eyes. Finally, this was the relief he needed.

∼

Malgotha, the snake, had been patient. She had waited nearly a full day, coiled under the bed, for him to return. He will keep his promise, she thought, that nasty Goblin Chief. He had promised her tasty snacks, and they had all run away. No matter, who wants a snack when you can have a full meal?

She inched her way out slowly from below the bed, wrapping her body over the blankets and around the sleeping Goblin. He looked delicious.

CHAPTER 16
THE WANDERER

Neek opened his eyes. He was lying in his yearling bed, in the dormitory he had shared with the other young Rocklings just before the Trials. Inko, the Guard who had not left his side during the two long days Neek had slept, clasped his hand in excitement.

"Neek, you're awake! How do you feel?" Inko asked. The area around the Guard's eyes was dark from obvious exhaustion.

Neek could feel Inko's worry for him. It resonated from the Warrior's mind like a beacon. He knew what Inko needed to hear, even if it wasn't the truth. "Yes, thank you, Inko. I am fine," he responded. "I'm a bit hungry though to be honest".

Inko smiled and nodded, racing off to find Neek some food and to share the good news with the tribe that their young hero was awake again.

Neek was alone in the dormitory. All of the other beds had been empty since the day of the Trials and the awful disaster that followed. Mercifully, this room had been untouched during the recent invasion. Even if that awful event had never occurred, this room would have been unused. The Trials were over. The yearlings had completed their exams. They had selected their castes, and would no longer be treated as children to sleep in the dormitory, but were full, adult members of the tribe. They would share lodgings with their caste mates in other caves. Neek felt a bit foolish being stuck here, the only remaining child of the tribe. He supposed that without his role being chosen yet, the elders hadn't known where to put him.

Where he slept though meant little to him compared to the more pressing question of where his missing friend Mohmoh was right now. The terrible Wizard had ripped him away, right out of Neek's hands. Where had the foul Human taken him? Had he chopped him up and used him in a potion? Neek shuddered, thinking of little Mohmoh, desperately clinging to his ear. He could almost feel him holding on still.

As Neek sat, weeping for his lost friend, he began to recognize that the sensation of Mohmoh holding the Rockling's ear wasn't merely a memory. Reaching up with his fingers, Neek realized with a shock there was actually a piece of Mohmoh still there!

As Neek brushed the tiny white tendril that clung to him with his claw, it seemed to grip him tighter. The tendril felt like it was hugging Neek. Snuggling his ear. As Neek touched it, the little piece of Mohmoh emitted a faint glow, an impossibly soft version of his normal yellow aura, and Neek could feel, deep inside his mind, a beacon, signaling him from far away.

What did it mean, Neek wondered? Was this part of Mohmoh still alive? Was it trying to communicate to him? Neek noticed that when he touched it, his claws tingled, with a special sensation he had never felt before. The colors of the room around him seemed to grow brighter. He could smell the bowl of stew someone was bringing to him, far down the hallway. What is this gift you have left me, my friend, he wondered? I must find you so you can explain it to me, he vowed. Neek was determined to save his friend even if he had to circle the world ten times to do so.

All in all, the Hardhands tribe had been very lucky. The recent attack was a tragedy, of course. Many of their tribe were gone now, returned to the earth. But in consideration of the tremendous might of the army that had attacked them, many more Rocklings might have died. The tribe had performed admirably. All the Warriors and the Trap Builders and the Tunnel Wardens and the elders should be proud. Their clever strategy to carefully flee while defending had saved a great many lives.

Due to the awful infighting among their enemies, and the enemy's unexpected retreat, the Rocklings had even been able to salvage much of their warren, the complex of tunnels they called home. Most invasions like this one would have ended with the tribe wandering perilously through the underneath for months, looking for a new place to live. But the Goblins and the Orcs had fled, as had the Humans, and so the Rocklings were able to return safely, cleaning up and rebuilding, restoring their home as well as they could. The tribe had stood together against one of the fiercest trials in their history.

The Rocklings quickly went about the business of sorting the yearlings into their new castes. Neek's sister, Margle, had proudly joined the Trap Builders. She was famous now for her clamshell raspberry alarm. Without it, who knows how many Rocklings would have perished? Trap Master Mekani insisted it be added to the official list of traps that children would be taught in the future. Almost all of Neek's other brothers and sisters had made their choices as well. And all were approved by the elders, swiftly.

The only three Rocklings who still didn't have castes were Neek, who had been asleep for days, and his exiled brothers, Whizzle and Barnag. The elders wanted to talk to Neek before they decided on the fate of his two brothers. Feelings in the tribe were decidedly more positive now though toward Whizzle and Barnag. Malika had pleaded their case admirably, telling the whole tribe how Whizzle had bravely bitten the Wizard, saving their lives, and how Barnag had artfully sliced the Wizard's wand in two. The brothers were asked to tell the dramatic story repeatedly by the other young Rocklings. And this time, Barnag told the tale truthfully.

What caste Neek would decide to join was a popular topic of discussion. Would he be a Priest? He clearly had a gift for healing. Would he be a Warrior? He was brave and strong. He could be a Chief if he wanted, most of them would say, with all due respect to their beloved MakMak.

And so, the Rocklings carried on, clearing the debris, planning for the future, and working together as their ancestors had done for thousands of years.

~

When the stew arrived, it was Dragon-Mother Malika who carried it. Neek was pleased to see her looking healthy. She had seemed so close to death before, after the Wizard's attack, and only the combined power of his crystal and his friend Mohmoh's healing touch had been able to bring her back. He remembered the secret she had shared with him. She was his mother. His true mother. The egg he broke out of as a child. She was its creator. No wonder they had so many strange gifts in common.

Despite the Rocklings' fondness for their young, it is strictly forbidden in Rockling society to know which parents give birth to which children. The elders teach that the tribe is the father and mother of every child, and should therefore treat them all fairly. All the same. It is feared that knowing one's parentage, or who one's young are, will prejudice children in favor of particular castes, or cause the parents to favor one child over another. Only working together, in unison, can Rocklings survive the perils they face, and this secret protects that unity. This is, in any case, what most Rocklings believe.

It is the sacred duty of every Dragon-Mother to protect this secret fiercely. And so, Malika, having revealed her secret to Neek, was quite embarrassed about it. It was important that Neek understand the secret must be kept between them.

"I understand," he told her, speaking to her mind before she said anything about it. He could read her thoughts clear as a bell, and her shame hurt his heart. "You were my mother already. Just as you were the mother of all my brothers and sisters. I will treat you no differently. Love you no less than I love them all." He held her hand and smiled, looking deep in her eyes.

"Thank you Neek," she replied, holding in her tears of joy with great grace. "For everything." She thought back to that bright light, the healing light Neek had cast over her, bringing her back from the void.

They sat quietly together for a moment as Neek hungrily consumed the warm stew.

"I suppose the Great Priests are eager to see me," Neek guessed. "I'm sure they will want to continue their investigations. But, I don't wish to go with them."

"They have already been sent away," Malika explained. "Your

path is your choice, and it was clear you had no desire to be with them."

"But I missed the Trials," Neek pointed out. "How will the elders know how to judge me?"

"You have faced greater dangers than any of our other younglings. Greater danger than many of the elders of our tribe," she responded. "You, and your brothers Whizzle and Barnag, are all considered to have completed the Trials. What more could the tribe ask of you than what you did during the attack? You have all proven yourselves admirably. Especially you, Neek. The First-Mother has given you such glorious gifts that you could join any caste you wish. Do you know what you want to do?" Malika asked out of respect, knowing well-enough already what Neek's answer would be.

"I want to be a Wanderer," he replied, just as she knew he would. "I must find Mohmoh. I will explore the world. I will try to make the rest of the living races understand what Rocklings can be, and help our people understand what the world can offer us in return. There is so much out there, Mother, so many glorious mysteries, and I have seen so little."

"Dragon-Mother," she corrected him.

"Sorry," he apologized. "But how does it work? How do I join a caste with no members in our tribe?"

"You must excuse me," she explained, "but I guessed this would be your answer, and I have already activated the sounding stone. Reginald, or another like him, should be here soon. You will not be alone. Someone will guide you, Neek. And I know you will find your friend."

Neek went silent again, thinking of Mohmoh. He touched the tendrils near his ear and his claws tingled.

"So, if Whizzle and Barnag passed the Trials," Neek began, remembering his brothers and sitting up suddenly, "does that mean they have been welcomed back into the tribe? Surely the elders will not send them away again."

"I have argued as much before them already," Malika replied.

"But Chief MakMak and the others wish to hear your thoughts, Neek. They place great weight on what you have to say about it. But please, sit now. Enjoy your food. You'll be traveling again soon, as all Wanderers do. You need to build your strength."

And Malika left Neek there, with his thoughts, and his stew, heading off to tell the tribe of his decision.

∽

Malika had been correct, Neek thought, running his hand along the surface of the water. Chief MakMak had indeed agreed to let Whizzle and Barnag rejoin the tribe. They were the two newest members of the Warrior caste. His brothers were overjoyed to be reunited with their people. Whizzle even seemed proud of his jagged teeth these days. Nobody would speak badly of cluttermouths again. Thank goodness for those beautiful teeth, Neek thought.

Neek was sitting in his favorite swimming pond, the one from his youth, so near the opening where Whizzle had unwittingly sent Neek off on his grand adventure. The memory of that journey soon reminded Neek of his dear friend Mohmoh whom he so sorely missed. Neek brushed his claws against the tendrils around his ears and felt something like a beacon signal again, deep within his mind. Neek was sure it was pointing him in a particular direction. He would follow it and find out what it meant. As soon as the next established Wanderer arrived in response to Malika's request, Neek would go. It had been several days now. Neek was eager to leave.

As Neek dragged his tingling claws through the ground next to the pool, the tingling feeling intensified and Neek heard voices, many voices talking to him. "You must follow. Outside the caves. You must hurry." There were thousands of strange voices all speaking at the same time. And in that forest of noise, a soft, familiar voice rang out. It was Mohmoh!

"Don't be afraid, Neek," the voice told him. "A part of me is with you. The voices you hear are my ancestors." Neek's eyes were wide with shock. Somehow Mohmoh had shared his gift with Neek, the ability to communicate with the traces left by Pluffstack ancestors all over the world. "You must hurry though, Neek, I don't know how long I can survive separated like this." And for the first time, Neek felt he could hear fear in Mohmoh's voice. He shivered. He had never been so worried for his friend.

Neek bounded up out of the pool and back toward the caverns above. Despite the danger, Neek knew his friend was with him, at least a part of him, and Neek believed that together they would find some kind of solution. Neek would never give up on his friend.

As Neek finally returned to the yearling dormitory where he had been sleeping, he was surprised to see Malika and Chief MakMak standing next to a very strange but familiar Rockling with a large golden ring pierced through his nose. It was Reginald, the Wanderer. He was there!

Reginald was holding a large backpack and a bag of gear. "These are for you, my boy," he explained with a smile. "I was told you might be in a bit of a hurry. So, whenever you are ready, we shall go."

Neek quickly strapped on the pack and grabbed the bag from Reginald, thanking him. He hugged Malika warmly and thanked Chief MakMak for everything she had done. Neek said goodbye to all of his brothers and sisters, and his many teachers and friends. And then, off they went, little Neek, newest Wanderer of the Hardhands tribe, and Reginald Herringbone, possibly the most extravagantly dressed Rockling in the world. Two Wanderers on a mission.

Neek beamed with joy. For the first time in many days, he felt hopeful. The beacon in his mind rang out. I am coming, Mohmoh, he thought. And the young Rockling walked out the front entrance of the warren, leaving behind his home, his tribe, those familiar tunnels, his special world far beyond the sunlight.

AUTHOR'S NOTE

I wrote this book for my son, Oli. This is my attempt to put to paper the wonderful way he sees the world.

Of all the twists and turns in life, I have found being a father by far the most profoundly rewarding. I learn as much from my son as he does from me, at least.

Oli has always loved stories. He would demand them at bedtime, in the car, at meals, basically any time there was a pause in the action of early childhood life.

Oli loves telling stories as well. One of our favorite activities is to play tabletop role-playing games together, engaging in a kind of improv where we craft a story of adventure as a group.

For those of you that might not be familiar with role-playing games like Dungeons & Dragons or Rifts, the pre-written tales these games often present to you usually involve putting together a group of heroes who then go off to raid dungeons, fighting monsters and taking their treasure.

It became very clear, early on in our experiences together, that these kinds of stories would not work for Oli. He didn't want to hurt the "monsters". They didn't really seem like monsters to him. They were just interesting creatures. He wanted them to join the team. So our stories had to change to accommodate these unusual beasts, and find adventures we could all enjoy.

It was this unique and loving take on fantasy that I wanted to write out and put into the world.

My son's perspective reminded me to some extent of Grendel by John Gardner, a wonderful book which retells the epic legend of Beowulf from the monster's point of view. In writing this series, I followed a similar vein, taking the typical characters from a role-playing game but making a "low level monster" the hero. I also hoped to make all the characters, even the little ones like snakes and boars, into beings we could sympathize with or at least understand, even if they were making decisions we didn't like.

As he has grown into a fine young man, my son still shows this instinct, not just at the game table, but in life generally. He tries to find ways to cooperate with and befriend even people that are challenging to him. In a world where it often feels like people are always looking for a fight, Oli's way of handling conflict gives me hope for the future.

So, this book is my attempt to celebrate my son and his outlook on life, and to examine what a hero who was empathetic and loving like him would look like. I love you Oli, thank you for making my life more fun and interesting every day.

I'd also like to say a special thank you to my wonderful brother Sean for helping to inspire my love of the arts throughout my life, and for all his help with revision and motivation in getting this project done.

My parents were also a great source of support and encouragement. I know my mum feels abandoned since I decided to finish reading Watership Down on my own all those years ago, but hopefully she'll take solace in being the one to push the boat down the stream toward a brighter future.

Finally, a million thanks and kisses for my wife, the love of my life, who has always made me believe anything is possible.

CAVE SHADOW PRESS

Visit us online at CaveShadowPress.com to find more great books and connect with our authors. You can scan the QR code below to easily reach our website.

Printed in Great Britain
by Amazon